UNFORGETTABLE

UNFORGETTABLE

Elisabeth McNeill

This first world edition published in Great Britain 2001 by
SEVERN HOUSE PUBLISHERS LTD of
9–15 High Street, Sutton, Surrey SM1 1DF.
This first world edition published in the USA 2002 by
SEVERN HOUSE PUBLISHERS INC of
595 Madison Avenue, New York, N.Y. 10022.

British Library Cataloguing in Publication Data

McNeill, Elisabeth
   Unforgettable
   1. Widows – Fiction
   2. Woman journalists – India
   3. Journalists – India – Boml
   4. Bombay (India) – Fiction
   I. Title
   823.9'14 [F]

ISBN 0-7278-5761-4

Except where actual historical e
described for the storyline of this novel, all situations in this
publication are fictitious and any resemblance to living persons
is purely coincidental.

Typeset by Palimpsest Book Production Ltd.,
Polmont, Stirlingshire, Scotland.
Printed and bound in Great Britain by
MPG Books Ltd., Bodmin, Cornwall.

Dee Carmichael stood on the pavement of New Bond Street outside the office of the India Tourist Board and looked at the Air India ticket in her hand. Faint letters on the flimsy sheets inside the folder spelt out 'London/Bombay on January 5th' and 'Bombay/London on January 12th 1984'.

How generous! A week, expenses paid, and flying Club Class too, she thought. *But can I bear to go back?*

PART ONE

BOMBAY, 1984

Chapter One

A s she expected, Bombay ravished her heart, but ghosts were waiting for her there.

The smells of the city – throat-catching, sometimes seductive, often nauseating – were unchanged. Those smells, and the unique essence of the place, immediately took her back to the past. Coolies still pulled their burdens through car-choked streets, their raucous yells contrasting with hooting horns that were as loud and discordant as ever.

The Fort was almost submerged by high-rise buildings, but some imposing Victorian relics of the Raj still stood in shabby splendour in the centre. The sky was intense aquamarine blue, the nights deep velvet black, the stars diamond sharp as they had been since time began. The first Europeans to live on Bombay Island must have stared up at the same skies and been awed by their brilliance.

Notebook in hand, Dee did the rounds of familiar places, and it astonished her to see how many things had changed in less than twenty years.

Thomas and Raju, the chatty barmen who knew everyone and everything about the city, were gone from the Ritz bar. No one even remembered their names. The Ritz itself, once smart, now crouched in shabby insignificance with new hotel blocks towering all around it. The elegant stretch of Cuffe Parade – where Dee's friend Anne had lived in a ramshackle nineteenth-century bungalow – was gone, and a huge hotel stood in its place. Beautiful Back Bay, where dolphins used to play, had been refilled with rubbish and made into building land.

She looked up a few old friends but her hunt was restricted because Bombay's main telephone exchange burned out the week before she arrived and would not be operational again for another month.

The fire was a nuisance, but in a way it pleased and reassured her because it meant that the old, chaotic Bombay was pulsing subversively away beneath its sophisticated new persona. The city she remembered might be on its way to becoming another Manhattan, but its streak of anarchy was ineradicable.

It was not until her last morning that she steeled herself to make the trip she'd really come to undertake – the one she dreaded most of all, and the one where she was to meet up with the past in a strange and unsettling way.

When she got into the Tourist Board car at nine o'clock, her guide – a woman – sat smiling in the front seat. A heady scent from a twist of white jasmine flowers in her luxuriant black hair wafted through the air when she turned and asked sweetly, 'Where to today, Mrs Carmichael?'

'Let's go to Chembur,' said Dee. The deferred decision was made at last.

First they drove through Worli, where Ben's office was ruled over now by another man, who would not welcome a call from his predecessor's wife. The ice cream stall, where she used to buy tubs of *tooty prooty,* full of chunks of angelica peel and green pistachio nuts, had vanished. So had the slime-covered water tank, where lotuses flowered around the legs of little boys while they washed their buffaloes, perching on the animals' heads between the curving horns.

She looked out in anguish at what had been open country twenty years ago but was now covered with utilitarian-looking concrete blocks of flats and ugly houses standing in mosquito-ridden swamps where nothing grew. A miasma of stinking mist rose like a diaphanous curtain into the air.

In every vacant space, immigrants from the country had thrown up camps of waist-high huddled shacks made of

4

cardboard boxes and bashed-out Dalda cooking-oil cans. Naked children and scabby pi-dogs wandered along the verges of a potholed motorway. The poverty and over-crowding was even crueller than it used to be, and Dee wished she had not seen it.

Worse was to come, for Chembur village was unrecog-nisable. It had completely lost its old-world charm. With an indescribable pain in her heart, she stared around, vainly trying to recognise something – anything – that would agree with her memories.

Where was the little police station, with its bright blue verandah and the oil cans planted with marigolds lined up on the steps? Where was the open-air cinema surrounded by twenty-foot-high walls of fluttering canvas to prevent people seeing the films without paying? Where was Dr Bali's house, with his string bed sitting out in the front garden? It had stayed there throughout the seasons, rain or shine. Where was the grocery shop to which their villainous bearer Mohammed sold the stores he stole from the kitchen? Where was the wooden post office where the postman with the BA degree sorted through her letters before mounting his bike and taking them to her? They had vanished, all of them.

The only thing that was the same was Raj Kapoor's white-painted film studio. It looked as if it had been trans-planted from Los Angeles. A huge plywood cut-out of a mounted Rajput warrior brandishing his curved sword still stood alongside the arched front entrance.

'Where was your old house?' asked the guide, anxious that they did not get lost in this insalubrious suburb, and surprised that any British family had chosen to live in such a shabby place. Most expatriates preferred the blocks of luxury flats that were stacked up for twenty storeys, one jostling against the other, on Malabar Hill.

'It's not far now. Only a hundred yards or so along this road,' said Dee, sitting forward in her seat and staring out of the right-hand side window.

I hope I'm right. Everything's so different. Will I recognise the lane? she wondered, suddenly besieged by doubts. *Is our house still there, or has it gone too? Am I in the wrong place altogether?*

Her breath quickened and she could feel her heart thudding as if she'd been running. She was incredibly nervous.

Just then they passed a narrow opening between two concrete buildings that never used to stand at that spot. 'In there!' she shouted, pointing. The driver stepped on his brakes and reversed a few yards, making exasperated sounds when he realised how narrow the lane was. He just managed to squeeze the car in.

Suddenly time stopped for Dee Carmichael and she was back to the first time she ever drove up that lane.

Then – as now – tall, ferociously prickled cactus plants lined the sides of a rutted roadway; the same yellow and white trumpet flowers clambered over the cacti lobes; the surface of the lane was as dusty and deeply potholed as it had always been. At least here nothing had changed, thank God.

'This is the place?' asked the guide disbelievingly.

'Yes, our bungalow, the Gulmohurs, is up here. Not far. On the left there'll be a sharp corner with a wooden gate into Devnar Farm, and then it's only a short distance to the house. Raj Kapoor used to live on the right-hand side. He's probably still there,' Dee told the guide, who brightened and breathed the film star's name reverently, for Raj was hugely popular, and was revered like a god by his adoring fans.

The wooden gate to the fruit farm was closed. Dee's friend Shadiv and his family had long ago moved away. A crumbling stone wall still surrounded the well where the buffalo-camp women from higher up the hill filled their water cans morning and evening. Two peasant women stood by the well and stared at the passing car.

The garden hedge, planted by Ben and Guy, was straggling and overgrown. The trees from which Dee once strung her hammock had branched into impenetrable thickets, so it was impossible to see the bungalow where she and Ben had lived in blissful and impecunious happiness for the first two years of their marriage.

Their house had stood open and fearless then, but now it looked diminished, as if it was hiding fearfully, keeping out of the sight of predators. Some recent tenant had surrounded it with a hideous, ten-foot-high, chain link fence overgrown with climbing convolvulus. The arch of white and purple bougainvillaea that once festooned the gate, and the orange-flowered gulmohur tree that gave the house its name, had disappeared. The place looked hostile and desolate and there was not a sign of life.

'Stop!' cried Dee when the car reached the barred gate.

'Is this Raj Kapoor's house?' asked the star-struck guide in disappointed disbelief.

Dee shook her head. 'No, his is on the other side of the road, behind that wall.'

Raj's house looked unchanged. Its wooden gate was closed too, and a menacing Pathan with kohl-rimmed eyes was leaning on it, watching the strangers. He was much younger and more dangerous-looking than the old man with a red-dyed beard who had been watchman there in Dee's time.

'You are going to see Raj Kapoor?' persisted the guide, who was determined to get something worthwhile out of this tiring journey out of the city.

'Yes, I'd like to see him and his wife if they are at home,' said Dee.

The guide spoke to the driver who opened his door and shouted something to the Pathan, who shouted back in a guttural voice and then spat eloquently, sending a stream of red betel-nut spittle across the bonnet of their car.

'He is at home,' the guide told Dee, who was acutely conscious that everyone was staring at her, looking for action. Her reputation depended on this.

'Ask if I can call on him. Say it's one of his old neighbours from twenty years ago, the ones who used to play music all the time,' she said.

The message was passed to the Pathan, who sloped off nonchalantly as if he didn't give Dee much of a chance of getting through his gate. He was away for about five minutes, and when he came back he was looking slightly less disdainful. After much fumbling with bolts he swung back the gate and beckoned the driver to steer the Tourist Board car into his courtyard.

The interior of Raj's house was smart and very much upgraded, with a new wing built where the old telephone box and servants' rooms used to stand. Stepping through the pillared front entrance Dee found herself in a cool, elegantly decorated reception room. An air conditioning plant was humming discreetly away in the background.

Raj's wife Krishna – beautiful and dark-haired as if time had stood still for her – received the guest. She came forward smiling as Dee said, 'Do you remember me? I lived over there in the Gulmohurs with my husband Ben and our friend Guy. We played records all the time, and must have been a great annoyance to you.'

When Guy and Ben lived as bachelors in the Gulmohurs before Ben and Dee were married, they had rigged up a series of loudspeakers in the trees around the garden and belted out jazz classics. Benny Goodman, Louis Armstrong, Jack Teagarden, Art Van Damme, King Oliver and Sidney Bechet poured their music into velvety Indian nights. After Dee moved in, her favourites – Dave Brubeck, Billy Holliday, Fats Waller and Frank Sinatra – were added to the repertoire.

As she spoke to Krishna, she was filled with remorse when she thought how awful it must have been for their Indian neighbours to be deafened by Billy or Louis when their own taste ran to soft-sounding sitars and tablas.

Krishna laughed gaily. 'Of course I remember you. And your music. We liked it,' she said graciously, taking the guest's arm and leading her into the house where Raj – who had not been treated so well by time as his wife – lay in a darkened bedroom, wheezing from an asthma attack. They were shocked to hear about Ben as Dee told the story, fighting to stop her voice breaking when she spoke of it.

She stayed with them for over two hours, always conscious of the waiting guide and driver, and guiltily remembering how she used to leave her driver Jadhav waiting in the car for hours on end. During her few days in Bombay she'd tried to find him – as she'd also tried to locate her old bearer Babu and the second boy Prakash – but sadly without success in every case.

When she realised it was noon, she began making a move to leave. Raj obligingly agreed to meet the guide and sign autographs for her. While that was taking place, Krishna said to Dee, 'You can't go away without seeing your old home. It's empty but I have the key. Would you like to go over there?'

No, I can't, Dee thought in a panic. *Why don't I just leave now and not risk raising too many painful memories?*

Krishna stood up, draping the trailing end of her diaphanous sari over one arm, assuming that visiting the Gulmohurs was what her guest must want most of all. Realising there was no escape, Dee rose too.

'I'd love to see it again,' she lied politely. That was what she'd really come for, after all. It had to be done.

Across the lane, when she stepped through the gate, her original impression of disappointment at the change and desolation intensified. There used to be an enormous Swiss cheese climbing plant – with luxuriant leaves big enough to be used as umbrellas – covering the end gable wall, but it had been roughly torn down and the marks of its tendrils still remained on the stone.

She and Krishna walked round to the verandah steps. No deep cane chairs stood welcomingly there, no pots of flowers were lined along the top of the terrace wall. What was most distressing was the way the once beautiful garden had been

9

chopped in half, and fenced off from the nullah and lane by chain link fences. They made the enclosed empty space look like a prison exercise yard.

The luxuriant lawn, devotedly watered twice a day by their gardener Birbal, had completely disappeared and was now only a hard-packed square of earth. Dry clumps of yellowish grass were all that grew around its edges now. No canna lilies filled the flower beds – because there were no flower beds any longer. Sprays of white jasmine flowers, that once erotically scented the hot summer nights, no longer branched over the verandah rails.

As Dee stood surveying this devastation, she was acutely conscious of the jungle trees and bushes jostling together like a curious crowd, and imagined that they were whispering to each other, 'Look who's come back! What's she doing here? We've taken over now.'

Krishna climbed the verandah steps and unlocked the door into the house. Dee walked behind her, fearfully wishing she could close her eyes and not look. The sitting room was empty and seemed tiny. Was it always so small? How had they managed to fit in a dining table and six chairs, a sofa and a coffee table, two armchairs and a big book-case?

She turned slowly and stared at the space on the floor where the sofa once stood. Carole – Guy's Anglo-Indian mistress – used to lie there, sucking her thumb like a baby and driving Ben to raging fury by her indolence. A pang of sadness stabbed Dee's heart and she knew without doubt, though she had no reason for the belief, that hapless, luckless Carole was dead.

The bedrooms were empty and desolate. The bath, where they used to stack the beer bottles on ice when they held their riotous parties, was rusted and chipped. In the kitchen the stone worktops looked greasy, and Dee imagined she could hear the hideous rustle of cockroaches, angry at this intrusion into their insect kingdom.

'Will we go upstairs?' Krishna asked. Dee silently nodded. Having come so far, she could not stop now.

Though dusty and empty except for a couple of chairs, the upstairs room was still a magical place – long and narrow with windows around three sides and an enormous unglazed arch at the far end. Through that arch Dee had looked down into the nullah to see the first scarlet flowers of spring bursting out on the naked branches of the cotton tree, and through it too she'd heard the unnerving screech of the brain fever bird calling through the steamy nights before the monsoon broke. Ben told her its spine-chilling cries were credited with driving fraught Englishmen mad when they were stranded far from friends and home in hot up-country postings.

She and Ben had spent so many wonderful nights in the room, making love on cushions on the floor and listening to music. In her mind she heard the soft smooth voice of Nat King Cole – it still made her skin prickle with desire.

Unforgettable . . . that's what you are . . . Unforgettable . . . though near and far . . . Like a song of love that clings to me . . . how the thought of you does things to me . . . Never before, has someone been more . . . unforgettable in every way.

The words were so apposite for the way she was feeling, for the way she was ravished by memories, that it was difficult to fight against the tears pricking in her eyes. Unable to speak because of the strength of her emotions, she walked out on to the terrace. It seemed enormously wide, baking in the noonday sun.

Memories of dancing there with Ben came flooding back, almost too painful to bear. Shading her eyes, she went across to the wall and leaned shakily on it. *I shouldn't have come. I thought it would help me lay his ghost but I was wrong. It's agony remembering,* she thought.

Leaning her elbows on the hot concrete top of the wall to steady herself, she found she was staring down into the garden. As she looked, her heart gave an enormous jump of surprise.

The lawn was miraculously green again and tall spikes of orange, red and yellow cannas stood proudly in the oval beds. Somewhere in the distance she heard the *swish, swish, swish* of water sprinklers.

There were people down there too. A laughing young couple came walking hand in hand up the twisting path. They were obviously in love, hip bumping against hip, eyes fixed on each other. The girl was wearing a brightly patterned shirt over tight orange trousers. Dee remembered that shirt. She'd made it out of an old curtain.

The tanned and handsome man – blond-haired, broad-shouldered, barefoot and bare-chested – was dressed only in a tattered pair of old rugby shorts that he would never allow her to throw away. It was Ben.

She watched entranced as, happy in some other time and dimension, they came towards the house, blissfully unaware of the fact that they were ghosts from the past. *Was that what we looked like?* she thought and blinked. When she opened her eyes they had vanished.

Oh Ben, thought Dee in anguish, *don't go away again. What happened? Was our best time here? Is that why we are still wandering in this deserted garden?*

The plane took thirteen hours to reach London, and throughout the flight she sat back in her seat with her eyes closed, sometimes weeping silently, the tears snaking from the corners of her closed eyes and rolling down her cheeks. Though her mind was racing, she hung on to one idea. *I've got to remember everything from the beginning. I've got to clear my mind. I must sort it all out if I'm ever going to move on.*

Where to start?

It had to be the day when life changed completely – a bleak November Sunday in 1973. But remembering was painful and she'd been avoiding it for a long time . . .

PART TWO

LONDON, 1973

Chapter Two

'**B**en's dead!'
     The man sitting in the car seat beside her spoke in a hard voice. It was obvious he was finding it difficult to tell her in spite of his training in breaking bad news.

Hysterically, she almost laughed; the idea was so ridiculous. 'No, that's not possible,' she said firmly.

'Ben is dead,' he repeated.

Coming home from lunch with friends, Dee had been surprised to see one of the neighbours, an army captain called Chris Mayne, standing on her doorstep.

His arms were crossed over his chest and he looked very serious. Wondering what he was doing there, she smiled and waved through the windscreen. He did not wave back but jumped off the step and walked quickly towards the car.

Instead of opening her door as she'd expected, he got into the front passenger seat and turned to face her. The stark white glare of the street lights deepened the grim, solemn lines around his mouth as he said, 'Wait, Dee. Don't get out yet. I've something to tell you.'

A hot flush of fear washed over her and, in spite of what he said, she reached for the door handle. Her first thought was that something was wrong with one of her children. Chris put out a hand to stop her leaving. '*Wait*,' he said again urgently. 'Please listen.'

'The children . . .' she said in a stifled voice.

'No. They're all right. It's Ben.'

15

Her first feeling was relief that the children were safe, but that was quickly followed by puzzlement. Ben was inviolable as far as she was concerned. He sailed through every crisis, nothing could touch him.

He was due home from a business trip tomorrow and had probably sent a message to say he was delayed. That was all.

'What's the matter with him?' she asked, wondering why Chris was making such heavy weather of it.

He stared at her bleakly and she saw his throat move as he swallowed. Before he could speak, she asked, 'Is he ill?' Without giving him time to answer she then went rushing on, 'If he is ill, I'll book a ticket for Singapore and go out there at once. I'll phone Singapore Airlines now . . .'

Impatiently she shook off the hand he had put on her arm and tried to open the driver's door again – but again he stopped her.

'Ben's dead.'

She shook her head. 'But I spoke to him on the phone last night. He was perfectly all right then,' she said stupidly. It hadn't sunk in. She wouldn't let it.

Sitting in the car with Chris, she looked at her watch. Its hands stood at five o'clock. Soon it would be Monday morning in Singapore. Ben *was* there, waiting for his plane. He had to be. He had to be. This was all a terrible misunderstanding.

'There's some mistake,' she told Chris firmly, but he shook his head.

'Ben is dead. I'm sorry. There isn't any mistake. Two police officers came to your house when you were out and broke the news to your mother. She's asked me to tell you,' he said.

Why couldn't you tell me this terrible thing yourself? Why did you have to bring in a stranger to do it? It would have been an act of love to tell me, Dee silently accused her mother. But love was something she'd never had from Jean.

16

She shook her head, still in disbelief. 'The police came here? They must have made a mistake. You're sure they came to the right house?'

'Yes.' He was being incredibly patient.

She had a sudden idea. 'I know what's happened. Someone has stolen Ben's passport and that's the person who's died.' It was amazing how quickly her mind could fabricate possible solutions. Others started teeming into her brain.

Chris shook his head again, frustrated that she still refused to accept what he was telling her. 'I'm sorry, Dee, but Ben is dead,' he said emphatically.

'He can't be dead. I love him, you see,' she whispered brokenly.

'I know,' he said and watched as she gripped the steering wheel and laid her forehead on it.

Her moment of weakness soon passed, for she hated breaking down and showing weakness before a stranger. Suddenly she sat upright, opened the car door and jumped out, saying over her shoulder, 'I don't believe it. It's not true. I know what to do. I'll phone Raffles Hotel in Singapore where he's staying and they'll tell me this is all a mistake.'

She ran up the steps and into the hall. Jean, her mother, was standing by the kitchen door, nervously rubbing her thumb and forefinger together making a rough, rasping noise – an annoying habit she had recently adopted.

Dee ran past her without a word, secretly longing for her mother to reach out and hug her, to show some sympathy. What she needed most in the world at that moment was to be touched. Jean, however, did not move, but stood as if struck dumb, paralysed by her inability to express feelings.

Up the stairs her daughter went, two at a time, bursting into the main bedroom where a phone lay on the table beside a huge double bed. She kept a notepad there with the number for International Directory Enquiries written on it – Ben was away from home so much, she was always afraid that she'd have to track him down and alert him to some crisis with one of the children.

'Raffles Hotel, Singapore,' she said shortly to the disembodied voice at the end of the line. A detached part of her brain noted that such a legendary hotel was exactly the sort of place where Ben would want to die if he had a choice. He was spiritually at home in the east and should have been born a century and a half earlier, when he could have been the subaltern shooting a tiger beneath the hotel's billiard table.

After a short pause she was put through to an English-speaking desk clerk. 'I want to speak to Mr Ben Carmichael, who is a guest in your hotel,' she said, sharply conscious of her mother and Chris standing in the upstairs hall watching her.

There was a slight pause before the clerk said smoothly, 'Mr Carmichael is out.'

Oh thank God. He's not dead! I knew there was a mistake, she thought with a tremendous surge of relief that made her legs almost collapse beneath her.

'Who is speaking?' asked the clerk cautiously.

'It's his wife. When will he be back? Ask him to ring me,' she said.

'One minute, please. Hold on,' said the clerk, and there was a series of clicks on the line before a different voice – young, male and very Australian – spoke. 'Kevin Macartney speaking,' it said.

'Dee Carmichael,' she replied.

He went on rapidly, 'Mrs Carmichael, didn't you get the police message? I'm very sorry to have to tell you that Mr Carmichael died here today.'

'But your desk clerk just told me that he's out,' she whispered.

'That's our policy. We don't like—' He coughed as if he wished he could take the last words back. He was probably about to make an excuse for the desk clerk giving her wrong information, but Dee thought he was on the verge of saying hotels did not like guests dying on the premises.

'You're sure about this? You're sure it's Ben Carmichael who's died?' she insisted.

'Yes. I'm sure and I'm very, very sorry. He's been a regular guest with us for months. I knew him well and liked him a lot. It's true, I'm afraid. I'm so sorry.' He was obviously finding this conversation difficult, but she was not going to let him escape yet.

'What happened?' she asked, for in her stunned state she was avid to know every detail that might help her believe this awful thing.

Macartney sounded awkward and embarrassed. 'He had a swim in the morning. I saw him in the pool. Then he went back to his room. A short time after that he phoned the desk and asked for a doctor because he was feeling ill. I went up to see him. Like I said, we were friends. He was lying on the bathroom floor and he died before the doctor arrived.' Macartney's tone was very definite.

She held the phone away from her face and stared into the mouthpiece, trying to imagine the scene. It was obvious that the man at the other end of the line thought it indecorous to elaborate . . . but elaboration was what she craved. She wanted to know everything – what had Ben looked like, what was he wearing, what did he say? Most of all she wanted to know what he said.

'Were you with him till the . . . end?' she asked.

'Yes.' Only one word. He was not going to say any more.

'Did he speak? Did he say anything?' she was desperate.

'No. He said nothing,' was the bleak reply. Surely, she thought, Ben couldn't have died without calling for her.

'No. Sorry. He wasn't fully conscious when I found him and he died in a few minutes. They're doing an autopsy now, but they think it was a heart attack,' he said.

A detached part of Dee's mind noted that if she were

in Macartney's position, she'd have made up some final message, something to satisfy the woman left behind. But obviously this young man was not capable of such flights of fancy.

'Was he in pain?' she asked in anguish. She'd never seen anyone die and couldn't imagine it. She had to know every detail.

'No,' said Macartney in a tone that showed he thought she was overstepping the mark. She guessed he'd say that anyway, to spare the feelings of a grieving widow.

'Thank you,' she said and hung up. Then she stood with her clenched fists pressed into the mattress, staring at the rose-festooned wallpaper, thinking over and over again, *I should have been there. He wouldn't have died if I'd been there. I wouldn't have let him die.*

She walked towards the bedroom door where Chris and Jean were still lingering in obvious confusion. 'He says it's definitely Ben who's died,' she told them and they drew back without saying anything, as if she had become an untouchable figure of tragedy.

Turning to her mother she asked, 'Where are the children?'

'In the sitting room. They don't know. When the police left I told them their father was sick. Don't tell them what's happened . . .' said Jean, trying to hold her daughter back and prevent her rushing down the stairs. Dee swept her aside, speaking more roughly to her than she had ever done before.

'Get out of my way and don't be so *stupid*! Of course I'm going to tell them. Who else should do it but their mother? They love him too.'

She had to share her grief with the children, she had to comfort them and reassure them of her love. It was important to make them believe that their lives would not be ruined by this tragedy. She needed to feel their bodies pressed into hers, she needed the physical contact. She needed to weep with them.

Their four children – twelve-year-old Annie; ten-year-old Kate; Hugo, who was eight; and Poppy, the baby, only just over two – were huddled together like puppies on the big brown sofa downstairs. The television set was off and they had obviously been listening to everything that was going on outside the closed sitting room door. Normally they were not biddable children: it was a sign of their terror that none of them had tried to defy their grandmother and leave the sitting room.

With enormous scared eyes they looked up at their mother when she came in. Dee paused in the middle of the floor with her arms flung out, and cried in anguish, 'Oh my darlings, Daddy's dead!'

Even the youngest ones, who had no conception of the finality of death, knew that what had happened was something terrible indeed. Sobbing, they ran to Dee and she reached out, gathering them all towards her, drawing strength and consolation from the touch and feel of them.

'I'll take care of you,' she said and for the first time since the news was broken to her, she felt her hot tears flow.

That's how their new lives started.

Chapter Three

S he'd once read that soldiers who were mortally wounded on the battlefield could sometimes go on functioning for a long time before they finally dropped down dead. There was one horrific story about a man at Waterloo who continued running for quite a while after his head was cut off.

Like the headless soldier, Dee kept on going at full tilt that night while everyone tiptoed around, eyeing her with apprehension, waiting for total collapse.

The first thing she did after she broke the news to the children was to position herself at the end of the long kitchen table with an address book and start telephoning her friends and relations. They received the news with shocked disbelief, for Ben was young and apparently healthy.

Thankfully none of them cross-questioned her and it must have been the finality of her tone that told them it would be dangerous to probe too deeply. *Don't doubt me. Don't question me. Only accept what I am telling you,* was what she was saying.

Pat, her closest friend among the neighbours, heard the news from Chris's wife and turned up in tears. She burst into the kitchen and hugged Dee, who clung to her for a moment in despair, weakened by this demonstration of affection. She then pushed Pat away, for she dreaded breaking down again.

She feared it would be impossible to collect herself a second time and thought how awful it would be for the children if she started to keen like a madwoman. That was what she wanted to do, however – it would be a release and a comfort to tear her clothes, pull out her hair and cover herself with ashes.

Guy, who'd shared the Gulmohurs with Ben and Dee, drove up from Kent in response to her phone call and sat in the kitchen drinking whisky with her, wiping away tears and saying little. He undertook to register the death and deal with the formalities. Before he left, he sent for a local doctor.

'How can a man die in minutes, without any warning, just like that?' Dee asked the doctor when he arrived, snapping her fingers as she spoke.

It still didn't seem possible – Ben was always so vital, so much stronger than her. Throughout their marriage he had never been ill; surely he couldn't be extinguished like a burnt out match? And, she thought, what about his soul, that indefinable quality which Louis MacNeice called 'the white light at the back of the mind'? Where was his soul now?

What worried her most, however, was why she hadn't sensed that he was dying while she was out having lunch with her friends. *I should have known*, she thought.

The doctor frowned, unable to offer a theory about such an unexpected death, for Ben had never consulted him since the family came to Blackheath eighteen months ago. 'Was he a heavy smoker?' he asked.

'Yes, about sixty a day. And he drank. Quite a lot actually. Whisky usually.'

'Whisky wouldn't hurt him. In fact, if he died of a coronary, which is what it sounds like, it probably kept him alive longer than he would have lived without it,' the doctor said.

Dee was not consoled.

Before leaving, he gave her a bottle of sleeping pills, saying, 'They'll get you through the nights.' The bottle was a smoky brownish colour and as she held it up to the light, she estimated that there were at least fifteen pills inside. *Probably enough to kill me*, she thought.

'Don't you think it's risky to leave me with so many?' she asked.

He looked at her levelly and said, 'You're not going to overdose. I trust you because I can see you're a sensible woman.'

But I don't want to be sensible, she thought. *I want to be feeble, to scream and weep and throw a fit of hysterics. I want someone to see my need and let me be irresponsible. I want someone to take care of me.* But no one did, and, through pride and fear of becoming uncontrollable, she held herself in check.

Madeleine Blackwood – a tall, imposing woman in her early forties – picked up the telephone in her flat high up near the Castle in the Old Town of Edinburgh and said, 'Yes?'

She never gave her name or number to callers because, as a woman living on her own in a busy city, she didn't take chances. A crime reporter for twenty years, she was aware of all the dodges that malefactors use.

'Maddy?' said a strange voice.

Madeleine's own voice lost its hostile tone. 'Yes. Is that you, Dee? It doesn't sound like you. How are you?' Dee was one of Madeleine's oldest friends and their friendship dated back to the time when they started their journalistic careers together. Over the years they had stayed in contact, and eighteen months ago Madeleine had even gone down to London to stand as godmother for the Carmichaels' youngest child, Poppy.

Happily unmarried and not at all maternal, she'd already notched up six godchildren and esteemed them all in a dispassionate way.

'What's up, Dee?' she asked cheerfully.

There was silence at the other end of the line, and then it sounded as if her friend was choking.

'Are you all right?' Madeleine said again, more anxiously this time.

The voice that answered sounded cracked. 'Ben's dead, Maddy,' it said.

Madeleine shook her head and paused as if she suspected this was deception on a grand scale. Then she said, 'What? When?'

Dee's voice was totally flat now. 'Today. In Singapore. They think he had a heart attack or something. There's going to be an autopsy.'

'My God! I'll get the night sleeper. I'll be with you tomorrow morning.' Madeleine knew that this was not the time to try any cross-questioning. What her friend needed now was support.

She hung up, sat down and lit a cigarette – her twentieth of the day. She couldn't believe what she'd heard. Ben Carmichael was always full of life and energy, apparently indestructible.

After she finished the cigarette, she poured herself a stiff gin, ate some supper, put a few clothes in a travelling bag and walked down the Mound to Waverley Station, where she bought a first-class sleeper ticket to London. Madeleine always did things in style.

She arrived at the Blackheath house in a taxi at a quarter to eight next morning. The front door was unlocked, as if no one inside cared whether they were burgled or not. Dee, in a bathrobe, was sitting at the kitchen table with a cup of black coffee in front of her when Madeleine walked in and swung her travelling bag on to the table. 'Your door's not locked,' she said.

'Isn't it? It doesn't matter any more,' said Dee, getting up to pour coffee for her friend. She looked dreadful. Her hair was tousled and her eyes were red and swollen. As she held the pot she was shaking so much she was forced to use two hands to stop the coffee from slopping all over the table.

Madeleine walked across the floor, took the pot from her friend and hugged her tight. 'Have you any brandy to put in this?' she asked. Dee sat down gulping, and said, 'There's no brandy but I've a bottle of whisky in the cupboard.'

'That'll do. Where is it?' Following Dee's pointing finger, Madeleine found the whisky and poured two generous slugs into their coffees. *We're both going to need this*, she thought.

They drank silently and after a few moments Madeleine said, 'This is terrible. Tell me what happened. I'll do anything I can to help.'

'Thank God you're not telling me I'll be all right because I'm a strong and sensible woman,' said Dee in a broken voice.

'It's not that I don't think you're both those things but I reckon you're going to need a lot of help,' said Madeleine.

She sat smoking while Dee related everything she knew about Ben's death.

'You spoke to the man who was with him when he died?' Madeleine asked when the story ended.

'Yes. He's assistant manager at Raffles. Kevin Macartney's his name. He's Australian, judging by his accent.'

'And that's all he told you?'

'Yes. I could tell he was embarrassed. He obviously didn't know what to say.'

'And Ben hadn't been ill?' asked Madeleine.

'No. He's very fit. He does – did – forty press-ups every morning, has done for years. He had a health check-up through the Institute of Directors six months ago and passed it with flying colours. I can't understand it.'

'How old was he?'

'Forty-three, nearly forty-four. His birthday's next month.'

Madeleine frowned – she was forty-three herself, and felt at the peak of her powers. She'd have said Ben was too, when she last saw him at a party in Scotland two months ago.

Words poured out of Dee in an uncontrollable flow. 'I can't understand it. Why didn't I notice something was wrong? And I keep on thinking if I'd been with him, he'd not have given up and died like that. I wouldn't have let him! I'd have kept him alive somehow. I feel as if I've let him down because I wasn't there, and because I never had the least bit of apprehension until I was told he was dead. I was out having lunch with some friends. Why didn't I know he was in the throes of death? I should have known. Why didn't I *sense* it?' She stopped talking and put her blotched face into her cupped hands.

It was a relief to talk to Madeleine, to pour out her anguished thoughts. There was no one else who would understand her. All the others who'd tried to comfort her so far seemed to want to keep her off the subject. They were afraid that mentioning Ben would upset her or make her break down.

Madeleine silently drank her coffee and lit another ciga-rette. 'Where are the kids? Where's your mother?' she asked, looking around.

'Still in bed. They won't go to school today. I'll ring up and explain what's happened,' said Dee.

'No you won't. I'll do it. You go and have a bath and wash your hair. You look wrecked. I want to think about this for a bit and if the kids come down, I'll make them something to eat, though I'm not much good at breakfasts,' said Madeleine, who rarely got up before half past ten in the morning and then breakfasted on coffee. Daily newspapers, where she had always worked, do not impose early starts on their reporters.

Dee stood up and pulled her bathrobe tightly round herself. 'Thank you for coming, Maddy,' she said.

'You couldn't have kept me away,' said her friend. 'I've never told you this before but I've some idea of what you're going through. I wouldn't tell you now, except that it might help you a bit to know I understand how you're feeling. Three years ago a man I'd been in love with for years was killed in a car crash. He was married and his wife didn't know about us and neither did anybody else, so I couldn't mourn him openly. I cried on my own. I went to his funeral and sat at the back of the chapel. Everyone made a fuss of his widow, but *I* was the one who loved him, and he loved me. It's pretty tough but you get through it eventually. You really do, Dee.'

'Oh God, Maddy, I never knew anything about that. Who was it?' said Dee, shocked out of her own emotional agony for a moment.

'Tom Redshaw. You might not remember him,' said Madeleine.

'But I do. He was at some of your parties,' said Dee. She remembered the dashing Tom, a Fleet Street man who travelled abroad a lot on foreign stories.

'Yes. He came up to Edinburgh as often as he could. We were together for five years, but neither of us wanted to break up his family. He had two teenage sons that he loved very much,' said Madeleine.

'You'd have been so right together – the same sort of people,' said Dee sadly. She'd always known that her friend had love affairs from time to time, but these were usually ephemeral and uncomplicated, ending amicably with both parties remaining on good terms. It was chastening to realise that Madeleine had suffered a grievous blow and kept it to herself with such dignity. 'I never knew. I'm so sorry,' she said, going over to hug her friend.

They clung together for a moment in mutual grief till Madeleine said briskly, 'OK. Go and have a bath now. You smell of whisky.'

For the rest of the day she put herself out to talk to the stunned children and give them some reassurance that the disaster of losing their father was not going to ruin their lives or split their family.

'Your mother's a wonderful woman. She'll look after you all, but you must help her too,' she said as she grilled bacon and fried eggs for their breakfast.

Later she took the whole family out to a pub on the other side of the Heath for lunch, marching them across the grass while Dee reluctantly protested, 'I don't feel like walking. I don't feel like lunching.'

She looked miserable, clutching the tails of a voluminous cape she was wearing and leaning against the cutting wind. Madeleine, looking imposing in a long scarlet coat and a black astrakhan hat, paid no heed to her complaints. 'Exercise is good for you. You've got to eat and you've got to get out of that house,' she said.

When it was dark, after Jean and the children retired to bed, the two friends sat in the drawing room before a dying fire and drank red wine. 'I don't know how I'd get through this without alcohol,' said Dee, holding her glass up to the light.

'Yes, it helps a lot. I don't want to upset you but I've been thinking about Ben all day,' said Madeleine. 'I simply can't believe that he died of a heart attack. He wasn't the type. Has it occurred to you that he might have been murdered?'

Dee stared at her friend. 'The idea never crossed my mind. That Australian seemed to think it was a heart attack. He said Ben felt ill and asked the hotel to send for a doctor. Presumably the doctor who certified him dead would know if he'd been murdered?'

'Did he actually say it was a heart attack?' asked Madeleine.

'Not in so many words. He just said there's going to be an autopsy.'

Madeleine looked bleak. 'Heart attacks can be induced, and unless they're looking for something suspicious, doctors wouldn't know. A jab from a hypodermic loaded with the right stuff and that's it. No one would look for a puncture mark if they thought it was a heart attack, would they?'

'But why would anyone want to murder Ben?' asked Dee.

'He travelled a lot, didn't he? He met all kinds of people.' Madeleine had obviously been working on her suspicions, and it was almost a relief for Dee to go along with her in discussing them.

Instead of being upset, she seized on the murder idea almost gratefully. Ben was always very theatrical and extrovert so, if he had to be dead, murder was a less pedestrian end for him than heart failure. And in a way it absolved Dee from the guilt she felt for not spotting the signs of fatal illness in him. Yet in her heart she knew that it was an outlandish idea.

'He flew the equivalent of three times round the world last year, and that must have taken its toll on his heart. Maybe that's what killed him,' she told her friend.

In fact, it seemed that she'd spent the past few years of their marriage mostly on her own. A preparation for widowhood perhaps, she thought bitterly.

'What about his friends? Did he know any suspicious people?' asked Madeleine.

'He didn't have time for friends. There was always Guy, but they only met from time to time, and Guy certainly isn't involved in anything suspicious. He can't even get a job,' Dee replied.

In India, Guy had been employed by a firm run by friends of his father. When these friends died or retired, Guy was out. Since then he had worked as a sales representative for various firms but stayed with none of them for very long and was now unemployed. His public school accent made employers initially approve of him as a recruit, but they soon found out that he had no 'fire in his belly' as far as selling anything was concerned.

Madeleine knew Guy and agreed with Dee that he represented nothing sinister.

'Come on, Dee. Ben knew more people than him. You went out a lot, you entertained – who did you meet?' She was obviously taking the idea seriously, though to Dee it was really only a diversion from her main mental preoccupations.

Dee sipped her wine and said, 'We were invited to peculiar parties from time to time. Last month we went to one given by Cable and Wireless in the Travellers' Club. I wondered at the time why Ben was invited. He didn't seem to know anyone there.'

Madeleine nodded in encouragement. 'Go on. What about other things?'

'Most of the people he knew were business associates, men in the same company or the same line of work, but there's no oddities among them as far as I know. I can't really believe that anyone would want to kill him,' said Dee.

Madeleine looked disappointed and replied, 'It's just so unexpected, so hard to believe. If he'd died in an accident like my Tom, I wouldn't be so suspicious. It seems unfair somehow, so illogical, for Ben to drop dead without warning.'

'And you like things to be logical, I know,' said Dee wearily. 'Come on Maddy, we're making up a story as we go along. It's because we're journalists and always have to try to find the hidden agenda. It doesn't help anything this time though.'

Suddenly she was engulfed in misery. No matter what Madeleine said – no matter how she tried to divert her, no matter what sort of theories she conjured out of thin air – the fact remained that Ben was *dead*. Every time she allowed that thought to enter her mind a terrible bleakness overwhelmed her.

Chapter Four

M adeleine's departure two days later left Dee feeling defenceless and without anyone she could really talk to. Stranded in South London, she could not accept that her husband was lying dead in Singapore. Left on her own, she again began to fantasise that it was all a ghastly mistake.

Ben couldn't be dead. It wasn't possible. He hadn't suffered a heart attack. He certainly hadn't been murdered – even Madeleine didn't *really* believe that. After all, she hadn't brought up the murder theory again. She'd only floated the idea because it made Ben's death seem more plausible. He was still alive and trying to get back home to her.

As if to confirm her own doubts, she found herself trying out the idea of Ben's death on casual acquaintances, to see whether their reactions were as disbelieving as her own.

'My husband died on Sunday,' she heard herself saying, almost as an afterthought, while buying a bottle of gin from the middle-aged couple who ran the off-licence at the end of their road. Ben had patronised that shop often, and they knew him well.

Standing side by side behind the counter, they stared at her in frozen-faced horror, as if she'd uttered a terrible obscenity, and stammered, 'Oh dear, that's awful!'

In a peculiar way their confusion pleased her.

If acquaintances stopped her on the street and offered sympathy, she did not know how to accept it and heard her own voice saying, almost flippantly, 'These things happen!'

They must think I'm very casual, that I'm not really

bothered . . . when I'm anything but, she thought in anguish. But if she were to go into details, and start telling the awful story, she would certainly cry, and it went against the grain for her to weep before strangers. So she said the first thing that came into her head, desperate just to get away.

She was in a state of mental confusion. She did not know what she was thinking from one moment to the next, and wandered around in a kind of woolly haze as if she was cut off from the rest of the world by a layer of ectoplasm. She scrutinised people on the street and thought it peculiar to see ordinary life going on as if nothing had happened.

Her world had stopped, but their milkman still delivered bottles to doorsteps each morning. The simple-minded road sweeper in his black beret and big boots swept the pavement outside her line of semi-detached houses every day. She watched him from her kitchen window, and, on impulse, went out one afternoon to tell him Ben had died.

He looked at her with a furrowed frown between his eyebrows. 'I'm sorry to hear that,' he said gently, though it was unlikely he'd recognise Ben if he saw him. For most of the time that the Carmichaels lived there, Ben had been travelling abroad on business.

Days passed, nights dragged by. Had the sun disappeared forever? Dee wondered. Was the sky going to stay steel grey? A terrible depression settled on her and she spent a lot of time staring at the vast green expanse of Blackheath, half expecting to see her husband come swinging over the grass.

She rehearsed what she'd say when he arrived. 'A weird thing happened when you were away. They sent a message to say that you'd died!'

He'd laugh and with his wolfish grin tell her he was not so easy to lose.

Guy arranged for notices of Ben's death to appear in the newspapers, and immediately friends began telephoning or writing letters. The phone calls usually began with, 'I've just seen something awful in *The Times*. It can't be your Ben . . . can it?'

'Yes, it is,' said Dee bleakly every time. 'Ben's dead.'

Though she found it harrowing to tell and re-tell the story, she would not allow anyone else to answer the phone. In a strange way she still hoped that the voice at the other end of the line might be his.

She spent her days answering letters of condolence before carefully putting them into a red folder. *One day the children will read these letters and know what sort of man their father was*, she thought.

The most affecting letter came from Babu, their Bombay bearer, who had gone to one of the letter writers who sit on the pavement outside Bombay's main stations to transcribe his thoughts. Dee was not surprised to hear from him so soon – he must have heard the news of Ben's death through the infallible servants' information system.

Her driver Jadhav still worked for Ben's old company. Ben's successor would have either been telephoned the news or read it in the airmail edition of *The Daily Telegraph*, and as he talked about it, the news would sweep through the office and out into the city. Ben had been well known and very popular. She could imagine the shock of their Indian friends when they heard.

'I can't believe that my sahib is dead,' Babu's letter said over and over again. As Dee read it, she heard his voice and wept.

Many of her other correspondents wrote to say that Ben was too vivid and lively to make old bones. He'd packed at least ninety years of life into forty-three, they said. But that did little to console Dee, whose automatic response was, 'How am I to go on without him?'

Just as she pored over every word of the letters, she found herself listening intensely to, and analysing, everything her visitors said. Some of them annoyed her so much that they snapped her out of misery for a little while – especially the wife of the man who was to take over Ben's job in the company. She had looked over the drawing room with unconcealed satisfaction before saying, 'Of course, you'll be moving out of this big house and into something smaller. There's lots of nice little bungalows for sale in less expensive districts at the moment.'

Dee bridled and determined to sit tight.

Finally one morning a letter arrived with a line of colourful stamps on the envelope. It came from Singapore, and marked the end of her period of suspended belief. Inside the envelope was a thin sheet of paper printed with irregular-looking photocopied letters – an official death certificate.

At the bottom of the form was the name of the doctor who had examined Ben's body and a signature written in Biro pen. Benjamin Carmichael, aged forty-three, the doctor testified, had died as the result of cardiac arrest.

So that was it, short and to the point. Only a few words were enough to signify the end of a life.

This knocks Madeleine's murder theory on the head, Dee thought as she read the paper. Then she folded it up and put it away in the red folder that she thought of as Ben's file, the summation of his life.

The engineering company he worked for contacted her to suggest that it might be best to have the body cremated in Singapore. 'We'll fly you out there for the ceremony, of course,' she was told.

'No. I want his body brought back home. I want him to have a funeral here,' she said firmly. There was never any doubt in her mind that Ben must come home. It did not strike her that by so insisting, she was running the company into massive expense.

Nearly two weeks passed before he arrived in England. The night before the plane carrying his corpse was due to land at Heathrow, she had a dream in which she stood in a vast hangar watching the coffin being unloaded from the cargo deck. It was so vivid, and she was in such a state of confusion, that she was never absolutely sure she had *not* gone to the airport and seen his body arrive.

Once again, Guy swept into action and took over the arrangements for the funeral. He phoned Dee and said, 'I'll pick you up tomorrow afternoon so we can go to see the funeral director.'

Like someone on automatic pilot, she was waiting, dressed in suitably dark clothes, when he arrived. They drove to a discreet-looking establishment opposite the Brompton Oratory. The undertaker's rooms were hushed and respectfully chilling in spite of tastefully arranged bowls of flowers placed here and there on dark wood tables. It was the first time she had ever set foot in such a place and it repelled her, but the young man who met them looked like a rugby player, the sort of person with whom Ben would have felt comfortable.

He spoke in a low voice as they went through the details of the funeral. There was to be a service in the Scots Church at Pont Street, followed by cremation at Richmond and a reception for mourners in a central London hotel. Ben's ashes were to be interred in his family grave beside the church outside Edinburgh where he and Dee had been married fifteen years before.

The fact that these elaborate arrangements would be very expensive never occurred to Dee, who had blandly accepted the company's offer to foot the bill for everything. In fact, she hated Ben's employers. She thought they were to blame for working him so hard. It was their fault that he died so far away, she told herself.

She was thinking about this when the undertaker suddenly said, 'Do you feel able to select the urn today, Mrs Carmichael?'

'What urn?' she asked stupidly.

He coughed. 'For your husband's – er – ashes.'

Is it possible that all that is left of Ben will be put into an urn? she thought, but nodded and said, 'All right.'

She scrutinised a brochure showing funerary vases, all of

which looked chilling. 'It's like choosing a hat,' she said without thinking, but neither of the men smiled in sympathy, so she put her finger on the least offensive urn. 'I'll have that one,' she said.

The undertaker approved because she'd unwittingly chosen the most expensive in the brochure. It was made of bronze. Another three figures were added to the company's bill.

At last it looked as if her ordeal was coming to an end, but when she stood up, the young man gestured towards a discreet door at the side of the room and said, 'Yes, go in now, Mrs Carmichael.'

'Go in where?' she asked.

'To see the body. The lid of your husband's coffin is not screwed down yet. Just lift the corner and you'll be able to say goodbye to him.'

She reeled and shook her head. 'No. Oh no.' The idea of looking at Ben's corpse had never occurred to her. When she insisted that he be brought home, it was because she felt he deserved a proper funeral, one that could be attended by his family and friends – certainly not because she wanted to look at his corpse. There was nothing in the world she wanted to do less. In fact, she was terrified by the idea.

Guy and the undertaker were shocked by her refusal. 'But you should see him for the last time,' they said together, obviously considering this act of farewell to be her duty as a widow.

'No!' she almost shouted. 'Definitely not.' No amount of emotional blackmail would change her mind.

Guy stood up. 'I'll do it then,' he said and went through the side door. A few minutes later he came back, wiping his eyes. 'It's him all right,' he said. Dee knew that, like her, he'd been finding it difficult to believe that Ben was really dead.

The funeral service took place four days later. Wearing a black fur coat and a beret covered with black sequins that she had worn at her wedding, Dee drove through South London with her mother, Madeleine and the three oldest children. Poppy was left at home with a babysitter.

In an effort to lighten the tension in the car, Jean chattered inconsequentially about people she'd met years ago when she lived for a time in Lewisham. Finally, driven to distraction by her mother's voice, Dee snapped, 'For God's sake, shut up.' The rest of the journey was undertaken in total silence.

The church was packed when the family filed in. Muffled against emotion by tranquillisers and whisky, Dee almost forgot what she was doing there till she saw an immense coffin made of pale-coloured wood standing before the altar. On top of it was a huge wreath of red roses, from her to Ben.

Like a slap in the face, the full horror of the situation struck her, and she put her arm round Hugo, who was standing next to her, and clutched him close to her side. Throughout the service she held on to him, feeling his little body being racked with sobs.

Later that night, punch-drunk from the emotions of a church and crematorium service and anaesthetised by the champagne she had recklessly downed at the reception in the hotel, she rode home alone in the hired car along the Old Kent Road.

It was raining and the roadway was gleaming like silver. She'd always admired that road's kitschy ambience, especially a brightly painted shop that sold men's hats – toppers, bowlers, boaters and schoolboy caps – which looked as if it had been there since Dickens's time. She turned to the empty space by her side and said aloud, 'I love that shop, Ben.'

Then, for the first time, she fully realised that he wasn't there and would never be there again.

Chapter Five

A funeral marks the climax of grief. From then on a bereaved family is expected to get on with their lives, and they usually do.

Dee Carmichael, however, was still in shock – besieged by various anxieties and not able to concentrate on anything for long.

Her chief anxiety was about money.

A bumbling man in hairy tweeds – the company's personnel officer – arrived one afternoon to 'tidy things up', as he told her. Without realising it, he caused her much offence. First, he lit up a malodorous pipe without asking if she objected to its smell, and then said awkwardly, 'Don't you worry. You'll manage. You'll be all right. You're a strong, sensible Scottish lassie.'

A silent scream rose in her throat. *What is it about the Scots that makes everybody think they easily absorb all the blows that life deals out to them?* she thought. *I'm sick, sick, sick of people telling me I'm strong. They only say it to make themselves feel better and because they can't think of anything else to say.*

She wanted to yell at him, 'What the hell do you know about me? How do you know I'll be all right? How do you know I'm strong? How do you know I'm not going to overdose on a bottle of sleeping pills and do myself in? You know nothing about me.' She said none of this, however, and only glared at him. *What does he want?* she wondered.

He was too low in the company hierarchy to be able to

give her any reassurance about her financial future, and she felt it would be demeaning if she asked him directly whether the company intended to pay her a pension.

'What exactly have you come to say to me?' she enquired.

He looked flustered. 'To say how sorry we all are . . . and to make sure you're all right,' he told her.

But she thought he'd been sent out from Baker Street head office to stop her asking about money. 'I think you'd better leave now,' she said, rising to her feet and showing him the door.

When he left, she telephoned the office in high dudgeon and told them never to send him to her house again. She asked to speak to the managing director, thinking that because Ben had been employed in a senior position she should be dealing with men who were nearer his level. Instead, she was put through to the deputy MD, who sounded guarded. By this time the board were treating her like a primed bomb about to go off, and, unknowingly, she was living up to their worst expectations.

'I'm ringing to ask what financial arrangements will be made for me and my family,' she said bluntly.

'I presume your husband has left you with adequate provision,' he said.

Then you presume wrong, she thought. Though he was a high earner, Ben had died with an overdraft. He hadn't even left a will – but she was not going to reveal that to a stranger.

'That's not the point. He died on company business and I believe that it's usual to insure senior employees against such a thing happening. Did you insure my husband?' she asked, without knowing that she was adding to her bad reputation with the directors. With every move she made and every word she spoke, she was confirming her nuisance status.

'We might have,' he said coldly. 'But it is our insurance policy and it's up to us to decide what we do with it.'

A peal of alarm bells went off in her head. She was not only a widow – she was a poor widow. Her entire world had crashed around her.

Chapter Six

O nce more Madeleine's telephone rang and she heard her friend's broken voice on the other end of the line.

Without preamble Dee launched into an account of her telephone call to Ben's company. 'I don't know what to do. The only money I've got coming in for certain is the widow's pension and child allowance. I need to talk to someone about all this and you're the most sensible person I know . . . I'm sorry to be a pest, Maddy.'

'You're not a pest, but you'll have to pull yourself together. That house of yours is worth a bit of money and Ben had an endowment mortgage, didn't he? So it's yours now,' said Madeleine.

'Is it? He didn't leave a will, you know. Anyway I don't want to sell the house. Where else would we go?' Dee sounded desperate.

Madeleine sighed. 'Listen, I'm coming down to London next Saturday and we can talk this over then. The reason I'm coming is because some people I know are throwing a party. Why don't you come with me?' she said.

'Oh, I can't,' was Dee's first reaction. The idea of going to a party so soon after Ben's death filled her with horror.

'Don't be silly. It's exactly what you need. You have to start living again, you know. Come to the party. You don't have to stay long if you don't want to, but come at least,' said Madeleine briskly. She was afraid that Dee was on the verge of sinking beneath her problems. The thing to do was cheer her up somehow.

Dee stood with the telephone in her hand and stared at the claret-coloured William Morris wallpaper, which had a convoluted design of birds among pomegranates and ivy leaves. She'd selected it carefully two years ago. *Madeleine's right*, she thought. *I have to face up to this. She did it after Tom's death without anyone to help her. I mustn't be a wimp.*

'Are you still there?' Her friend's voice came from the other end of the line.

'Yes, I'm still here.'

'Will you come to the party? It's in Wimpole Street. You're not going into perpetual seclusion, are you?' Madeleine sounded brisk and made Dee ashamed of her own weakness and panic.

'OK. I'll come. I might not stay long though . . .'

'That doesn't matter, so long as you get yourself out of that house for a little while,' said Madeleine.

Who does she remind me of? thought Dee, and then remembered. It was Hughie, the groom, who had looked after Dee and her brother Colin when they were growing up. Hughie believed in building character, and his advice on being faced with a challenge was to treat it like a stiff fence on the hunting field and 'throw your heart over first'. Obviously Madeleine was another advocate of the 'heart over first' philosophy.

When Saturday evening arrived the thought of going to a party seemed appalling, but Madeleine had made it difficult to back out by arranging to be picked up at a specific place at a specific time and not leaving a contact number – deliberately, Dee guessed.

She dithered about wondering what she should wear. What was suitable for a widow going out for the first time after her husband's death? There were two dresses in her wardrobe that were good for party-going – a red crêpe with a flounced skirt, and a sleeveless black tube with a low neck and hobble skirt. The black was a suitable mourning colour but, in a mood of defiance, she chose the red.

Madeleine was waiting outside Victoria Station and climbed into the front seat of the car when it drew up.

'You've lost weight but it suits you. That dress is a nice colour,' she said approvingly.

As always, she herself was very well dressed, in a black dress with a multicoloured jacket that made her look spectacular.

'You're tremendously smart yourself. Who's giving this party?' Dee asked.

'Some journalists I know. One of them used to work on the *Express* when I was there. You'll be all right. They're our sort,' was the reassuring reply and it occurred to Dee that her friend had inveigled her into going to the party because she might meet useful contacts there. Madeleine was intent on solving her friend's financial problems by getting her back to work.

'If it gets too much for me, I'll just slip away. You won't mind, will you?' Dee said.

Madeleine shook her head. 'Of course I won't. I'm staying the night with the hostess and her husband. I'm glad you've got enough courage to come at all.'

'You've planned this. It's all part of the get-Dee-back-on-her-feet scheme, isn't it?' said Dee, but Madeleine only smiled. 'It'll be good for you,' she said.

The flat was on top of a red-brick house near the Portland Square end of Wimpole Street. It was quite small, with four rooms, a kitchen and a bathroom. People were packed in so tightly that the sight of them standing shoulder to shoulder and hip to hip, and the noise they made, cheered Dee up because it reminded her of riotous press parties she'd gone to in the past.

Nobody paid any attention to the new arrivals, till a woman with bright red hair and a tip-tilted nose that made her look like a cheeky doll rushed over to Madeleine and said, 'Darling, so glad you made it! Is this your friend? Grab a couple of glasses of wine and join the throng.'

In the kitchen Madeleine pressed a full glass into Dee's hand and said, 'Get in there now and mix. Nobody's going to talk about Ben or wills or funerals because they don't know anything about you. Forget your troubles for a bit.' With a firm hand on her friend's back she propelled her into the party.

The crowd opened up for them. People greeted Madeleine, laughing and exchanging gossip – she was obviously very popular. Dee, feeling anonymous and uninteresting, drifted from one group to another. She knew no one and was very conscious that she was out of touch.

Eventually she arrived at a window that stared over rooftops towards the BBC building in Portland Place. She was looking out at it when a voice behind her spoke.

'I met Madeleine over there and she said she'd brought an old friend with her,' it said.

I know that voice, she thought, and turned round to find herself staring at Adam – better known as Algy – Byron. He looked as laconic as ever, not a bit changed from the last time she'd seen him in Bombay more than five years ago, when he had almost literally tripped over her in Breach Candy swimming pool.

He grinned. There had always been a touch of *Just William* about him, and he'd probably look young and boyish till he was an old man. It was such a relief to see him, to be with someone who knew her, that she almost threw her arms round him – but held herself back.

'Algy! How amazing to see you. I'm always tripping over you in the most unexpected places. What are you doing here? You disappeared from Bombay in such a hurry we were vastly intrigued,' she exclaimed.

He shrugged. 'I left Bombay because I got an unexpected assignment. But, seriously, Madeleine's just told me about Ben. I'm very sorry. He was a good guy.' His words made tears spring into Dee's eyes – as they always did when Ben was mentioned – but she fought them back because she feared that if she wept in front of him he would reckon she was growing soft in her old age. She shook her head and managed to control herself as she replied, 'It's been a terrible shock.'

'Yeah,' he agreed. 'What happened?'

She wished he hadn't asked that question. 'He had a heart attack in Singapore.' Then she heard herself blurting out, 'Madeleine thinks he was murdered. Did she tell you that?'

He looked at her levelly and said, 'She mentioned it.'

'I don't think she's right. There's no reason why anyone would want to murder him. What do you think?' she said, eager now to talk about Ben's inexplicable death.

'I've no idea. Who told you he was dead?' he asked carefully.

'The hotel. He was staying at Raffles—'

'He'd appreciate that,' Algy broke in.

She nodded, 'Yes, wouldn't he? The hotel's assistant manager was with him when he died.'

'Chinese was he?'

'No, an Australian I think. He said his name was Kevin Macartney, but he didn't tell me much more . . . not as much as I wanted to know, at least,' she said.

'Probably trying to forget it,' said Algy, and she shivered.

This is as far as I can bear this subject to go, she thought, and asked him, 'Have you left the east? Are you living in London now?'

'Yes,' he said, but didn't say where. He never told anyone where he lived, she remembered. He was always a man of mystery and preferred to keep it that way. He'd vanished from the Bombay scene after her friend Lorna Wesley's lover, the gun runner Rawley Fitzgerald, was killed in a plane crash – one in which foul play was suspected but never proved. Rawley's mechanic had been killed too, and that murder was also unsolved. Suspicion had fallen on Algy, and his detractors were sure that if he was not the killer he was at least a spy of some sort.

46

Dee, however, had never really believed any of that and, looking at the boyish quiff of hair standing up at the front of his head and his broad, ingenuous grin, she reckoned the suspicions about him were definitely ludicrous.

'Where are you working now?' she asked.

'I'm running another news agency,' he told her, 'specialising in features. In fact, when Madeleine told me about Ben I wondered if you'd like to try your hand at writing some pieces for me. You were always good at features, but not so hot at news – as I remember from all that fuss about the gold smuggler.'

They'd both been working as journalists in Bombay when there was an outbreak of gold smuggling, and Dee had become involved in trying to get a story from an English smuggler for the *Sun* newspaper, for which she was the Bombay 'stringer'. Algy had consistently warned her to keep clear of the story, which he implied was trivial. He was probably right, she now thought, because the story came to nothing.

As he talked about his new job she remembered that he'd always been eager to help friends in trouble, but didn't want them to overwhelm him with thanks. He liked sorting out other people's lives, but preferred it if they didn't realise what he was doing.

The first time they ever met, nearly twenty years ago, he'd helped her get a story that ensured her being hired by the newspaper that was giving her a trial as a reporter. Now, by some miracle, he'd popped up to help her again – it was obvious that she'd have to earn money somehow.

'What sort of features are you in the market for?' she asked.

'Women's features as far as you're concerned. I've an office beside the office of *The Lady* magazine in Soho,' he said.

The association between Algy, the suspected spy, and *The Lady* made Dee smile. Algy seemed relieved to see a lightening of her expression. He reached into his pocket, took out a wallet and from it produced a business card, saying, 'Here's my card. Write me a piece, about five hundred words, and I'll let you know if it's any good.'

The card had his name on it and, in italics, *Corinth Features*, with a phone number and an address in Soho.

She took it, then gazed at him in consternation.

'But what will I write about?' she asked.

'You're a good journalist. You find the subject. Give me your card too,' he said briskly. She fished in her bag and produced one engraved with the names and address of Mr and Mrs Ben Carmichael. She'd not had the time – nor the inclination – to have a new one made. He took it without comment and, as if their transaction was finished, wandered off in search of another drink.

After he left, Dee didn't feel she could stay any longer at the party. All around her people were meeting their friends and she felt like the odd one out. Fighting her way through the throng she found Madeleine and said, 'I think I'll go home now.'

'That's OK,' said Madeleine. 'Have you met anybody interesting?'

'Only Adam Byron – Algy, remember? He said you told him about Ben.'

Madeleine frowned, 'Yes, I did. When he came in, he asked me about you. I haven't seen him for years. He's running some sort of an agency now, I believe.' She paused, gave Dee one of her searching stares and said, 'He's schizoid, of course.'

'Schizoid?' Dee stared at her friend in amazement. Madeleine was in the habit of giving utterance to startling ideas – like the murder theory – but this seemed strong even for her.

'Yes, at least if not actually schizoid, he's a bit nuts. I can tell by his hair.'

'His hair?' Except for his upstanding quiff, Dee had never noticed anything particularly odd about Algy's hair. It was mid-brown, slightly unruly, conventionally cut, and not yet greying.

'The way it grows up on his forehead. Like this . . .' Madeleine made a sweeping upward motion with her hand. 'That's typically schizoid. You take a look at it the next time you see him.'

There are times with Maddy, thought Dee, *when you're never sure if she's being serious or not.*

The car was in the Portland Square underground car park and as she drove home she thought about Algy's hair and it kept her mind occupied till she reached Southwark. For the rest of the drive, however, she was plunged back into depression – she realised that she'd just been to the first party she'd attended since Ben died, and in future she'd have to get used to going out alone.

Driving through the grim streets of Rotherhithe and Deptford, she wept, tears streaming down her cheeks. The nearer she got to Blackheath, the deeper her grief became. It seemed as if she was doomed to be always arriving home in tears.

Chapter Seven

The telephone was her lifeline. Every time it rang she ran towards it, anxious to be the person who lifted the receiver off the cradle. There was still a foolish little corner of her mind nurturing the hope she'd hear Ben's voice on the other end.

A few days after the party, she received a call from Lord Affleck, the business tycoon who had coaxed Ben away from India with the offer of a splendid job in England.

Ben worked for Affleck's organisation for three years before the engineering firm he'd been brought in to run was sold. Subsequently he found a new position with the company for which he'd been working when he died.

'Are you all right?' Lord Affleck asked Dee.

It was a comfort for her to realise that here was someone prepared to assume she might *not* be all right. At least he was not trotting out mollifying phrases about her being a 'strong Scots lassie', which always made her feel like a hairy-footed carthorse.

'No, I'm not all right, I'm afraid. I've only just realised that I've been left penniless and there's not a will. I don't even know if I own this house.' She told him about the director's chilling warning that the insurance money was the company's, not hers. She had enough respect for Affleck, and guessed he had for her, to know that he would not think she was asking him for money – which she was not. The idea of having to accept handouts from anyone made her cringe.

'I'm really worried,' she finally said, glad to have found

a detached listener who could be relied upon to give her an unbiased opinion.

'Have you a lawyer?' he asked.

'No. A local man did the conveyancing when we bought this house two years ago, but I wasn't impressed with him,' she said.

'You need a good lawyer. I'll speak to my company man and he'll get in touch with you. There'll be no charge,' he said and rang off, leaving her with an enormous sense of relief. She was lucky with her friends, and here was another one, who, like a *deus ex machina*, had swooped down from the clouds of despair and held out the hand of salvation to her.

Lord Affleck and his calming, competent lawyer exercised influence on Ben's ex-employers and a few days before Christmas, Dee was summoned to a meeting with the directors in the company head office in Baker Street.

She was good at putting on a front, and, though internally quivering with nerves, gave the appearance of calm when she was shown into the boardroom. The four hard-faced men waiting there looked anything but conciliatory – they were antagonised by what they saw as her intransigence, profligacy with their money and lack of co-operation.

Unfortunately the managing director had a pronounced stutter, and she was gripped by a fear that when she spoke, she would stutter too and he might think she was mocking him. It was such a struggle to keep her voice normal that she could hardly concentrate on what he was saying.

It turned out he was telling her that an insurance payment of £60,000 was to be put into trust for her children. She would only receive the interest and could not touch the capital, which would be administered by a bank – at considerable expense, as it turned out.

'Do you think I'm not capable of handling my own money?' she asked.

One of the men said coldly, 'It is not your money. It's

your children's. Your husband did not leave a will, I believe. Perhaps he had a reason for that.'

Such an accusation was impossible to counter, but the income from £60,000 sounded like a fortune to her in her new circumstances and her head swam with relief. It would provide basic security, and she fully intended to earn more for herself – especially now she had the offer of feature writing from Algy.

'Will you accept our offer?'

'Yes,' she said.

'In that case, you must sign a document saying that you will never ask this company for more money or make any claims on us,' she was told. It occurred to her that, judging by their behaviour, she might have grounds for a claim, but she was too punch-drunk with emotion to even consider such a course of action.

Glaring along the polished table towards the men at the other end she said haughtily, 'I assure you that I have no intention of ever asking you for anything.'

They relaxed and one of the men asked her if she wanted to buy Ben's company car.

She shook her head. It was large and expensive, which prejudiced garage mechanics against her when she took it in for repairs. It also seemed to bring out the worst in male drivers when she was behind the wheel.

'I don't want it,' she said.

'In that case, return it by the end of the month,' she was told.

The managing director then summoned a secretary and said, 'Will you please bring Mr Carmichael's briefcase from Mr Jellicoe's room.' Ben's place in the organisation had already been taken over, Dee noted. He used to think the business could not run without him, but the waters had closed over his head as if he'd never existed.

His battered black leather briefcase – which she knew so well and which he'd taken with him on his last trip to

Singapore – was borne in and emptied out on to the table. A passport, a leather blotting pad and pen box, a calendar and a few pens were revealed. The passport was the only item among them that he'd have taken to Singapore with him, she thought.

'Any papers he had in his briefcase have been retained by us because they related to company business,' the managing director told her.

'What's happened to his address book and personal papers? He had another passport as well,' she said. Ben always carried two passports because he sometimes had to travel between countries that were at loggerheads with each other.

The managing director shrugged and said dismissively, 'Only one passport was sent back.' Dee stared at him, remembering Madeleine's murder theory, but there was no point bringing that up now. Could Ben have been killed for a passport? She doubted it.

'Sign for his things, please,' she was told. She put her signature on the bottom of a sheet of paper without reading what it said.

What the hell, I don't care. I just want to be free of this and them, she thought.

While the secretary was showing her out, she suddenly turned towards Dee and said, 'I want to say that I'm very sorry for you. I'm a widow myself and I know what you're going through.'

This unexpected expression of sympathy almost undermined Dee. Her legs began to shake and her eyes filled with tears. The other woman, who was about ten years older than her, reached over and patted her hand. 'It'll get better, but you never forget,' she said.

A uniformed doorman showed her into the street. Five steps along the pavement stood a waste bin. Purposefully she pushed its lid open and shoved the briefcase and all its contents, except for the passport, inside.

Then, because it was December 23rd, she went to Harrods

and bought lavish Christmas presents for the children, recklessly using her account card. *The money can come out of the £60,000*, she thought.

She rode home to Blackheath on top of a number fifty-three bus, laden with Harrods bags. To the other passengers she must have looked like an ordinary mother who'd been doing last-minute Christmas shopping. As far as she was concerned, she was a burnt-out case, without feelings and without a future.

Chapter Eight

The consummate professional Madeleine came up with an idea suitable for Algy's Corinth Features.

'Do a piece about those new shops that people are opening to sell cast-off designer clothes. Most of the stock comes from celebrities who only wear their dresses once,' she said when Dee complained about not being able to find a good subject.

It was a huge distraction for Dee to be working again. Journalism is like show business – when working, journalists assume personalities often quite different from their real ones. They put on this other self – like a costume – and leave their own concerns, their joys and sorrows, in the wings.

In her newly acquired second-hand car, she forgot about everything except her story on the day she headed for Fulham to interview two women who had pioneered the upmarket used clothing idea. They provided good copy and gave her the names of other people who had followed their lead. The trail led on – as story trails do – to other boutiques scattered through Fulham and Chelsea with names like 'Second Time Around' and 'Glad Rags'.

One of these contacts sold fantastic evening dresses worn on stage by Danny La Rue, and another claimed that the pick of her stock – dresses and coats constructed like engineering projects out of slipper satin or slub silk – came from the wardrobe of Princess Margaret. She said the Princess's maid brought in the clothes for sale.

This surprised Dee. 'Don't you worry in case they've been stolen?' she asked. If there was any question of that she wouldn't be able to mention the Princess's clothes in her story.

The woman bridled. 'Of course not. I would never take them if I wasn't absolutely sure the Princess knew about the deal. The maid's only a go-between. I suppose Princess Margaret looks on it as recycling. All the society ladies do it – even the wives of multi-millionaires.'

Dee laughed. *Only people who are broke give things away to charity, I suppose,* she thought.

She sweated over that article and entitled it 'Second Hand Rose', in homage to the Barbara Streisand song. When she finished she realised that, for the first time since Ben died, she'd been totally absorbed in something other than grief. But she worried that her work would not be good enough, or that she had lost her touch – if she'd ever had one, which she currently doubted.

Eventually she was satisfied after several rewritings, and ran out to pop the envelope into the mouth of the red pillar box on the edge of the pavement opposite her house. Laying her hand on its domed top, she whispered, 'Be lucky,' and sent 'Second Hand Rose' on its way.

Luck *was* with her that week. Next evening, three girl students at Goldsmiths College, whose friend lived in a basement along the road, rang Dee's doorbell and asked if she would rent them rooms in her house.

The previous owners of the Carmichael house had converted the basement kitchen into a self-contained flat. It had been Ben's intention to turn it back into a kitchen and playroom for the children. However, after his death there was no money – or enthusiasm – for such a project, and it was used as a store for surplus furniture.

The students spotted the empty flat and were disarmingly friendly and charming when Dee showed them round. She liked them so much that she took them on as tenants and they agreed to pay her seven pounds a week – an unexpected and much-needed addition to her income.

Throughout the next week she anxiously waited for some reaction to her article from Algy, firmly resisting the urge to ring him up and ask if he liked it. On the eighth day, to her incredulous delight, she received a cheque for twenty pounds from Corinth Features. She looked at the cheque in disbelief. It was such a magnificent fee – especially since she knew that the normal going rate for five hundred words was between seven pounds fifty and ten pounds.

The cheque, she noticed, was drawn on an American bank – Chase Manhattan in New York. How glamorous! There was no covering note with it, however. Perhaps he'd made a mistake and sent her someone else's fee?

Next day she found her way to Soho Square. Only a modest plaque on a closed door marked the office of Corinth Features, which was on the top floor of a corner block overlooking a garden full of trees.

A bored-looking girl at a desk in the entrance hall casually directed Dee towards an unmarked door when she asked to see Mr Byron. Dee knocked on it and when a familiar voice called out, 'Come in,' she stuck her head round its edge and looked inside.

Algy was sitting in a tiny office at a desk facing a window with his back towards her. Without turning round, he said, 'Hi Dee.'

'How did you know it was me?' she asked from the doorway.

'The perfume. You've always worn the same one. What is it, by the way?'

'Guerlain's Mitsouko,' she said, disconcerted and feeling a little guilty – she knew she was sometimes too heavy-handed with her scent. She enjoyed the idea of leaving a trail behind her. For a moment she considered asking him if he liked Mitsouko, but rejected the idea because she suspected he'd say 'No.' Praise was what she craved at the moment, but knew that he, above all people, would not bother to butter her up.

Unlike the office Algy and his assistant Ernest Nilsen had occupied in Bombay, this cubby hole looked as if it belonged to a university don, for he sat surrounded by open books and piles of manuscripts. The only paper to be seen in his Bombay office was coils of tickertape that used to snake around him like long white worms.

'What did you think of my article?' she asked in what she hoped was a casual voice.

'It was OK,' he said. The mere fact that he'd accepted the piece should have been enough for her, apparently.

Then he looked up and added, 'You didn't put a covering letter in with it, but I knew it was yours because I could hear your voice when I read it.'

She flushed. 'How stupid of me!'

'Next time you send a piece out, put in your invoice or you might never get your money,' he advised. She was encouraged because that meant he thought her capable of selling more.

'Do you want me to send you something else?' she asked.

'If you find a good subject,' he said. He lifted a manuscript off his desk and said, 'I'm in the market for funny pieces and interviews with interesting people, but run the ideas past me first.'

'What sort of interesting people?' she asked.

'Famous people – writers, artists, sportsmen and women. And oddballs. You know as well as me,' he told her.

She laughed. 'I don't know anybody famous so I'll stick to the oddballs.'

Suddenly he became more solemn. 'What was the name of that Australian guy in Singapore you told me about? I've got friends in Singapore and one of them might be able to ask him more about Ben's death – that is, if you really want to know.'

Her heart gave a funny jump and she found herself frowning as she said, 'Kevin Macartney was his name.'

'I'll make enquiries,' he told her and she wondered if, like Madeleine, he thought there was something fishy about the way her husband had died. As if he could read her mind, he looked hard at her and said, 'It's all right. I like asking questions.'

She forced herself to smile. 'Anyway, thanks for the cheque. It was very generous,' she said.

'That's our rate,' he said casually and she thought, *I'm so glad I know you, schizoid hair or not.*

Encouraged by her first sale, she launched into a frenzy of activity, turning out articles about people who fell into the oddball category. They ranged from an old hatter, working in a grubby little shop in the backstreets of Peckham, who made the stetsons worn by Robert Redford and Paul Newman in *Butch Cassidy and the Sundance Kid*, to a taxidermist who sold realistic-looking, snarling, stuffed tiger cubs to business tycoons. He said that his customers tied the stuffed cubs to the legs of their office desks to scare their business rivals. His workshop in Clapham was so foul-smelling and sleazy that, after Dee finished the interview, she went outside and threw up on the pavement.

A more amusing interview was with a glamorous blonde – the only female boxing promoter in Britain – who lived above a pub in the Old Kent Road. She had a wardrobe of five hundred evening dresses and three hundred wigs, and proudly showed off her gowns, sliding back the doors of immense wall cupboards to display them on their padded hangers. The only possession of the friendly blonde that Dee coveted, however, was her lover – an inarticulate piece of male beefcake who stood around, arms folded over an impressive chest, following his mistress's movements with enraptured eyes.

Once a month she went into the Corinth Features office to talk her ideas over with Algy. There never seemed to be many people around – just the blank-faced girl on the desk and the odd figure flitting along a corridor – but he tantalised her with the names of well-known writers who, he said, contributed articles to the agency. It made her feel she was in good company.

He gave her confidence, and she set her sights on contributing to BBC Radio Four's *Woman's Hour*, a programme that she listened to with never-failing admiration.

Even before Ben died, she'd once or twice sent articles to the programme, but they were always promptly returned. When she picked her self-addressed envelopes off the doormat, her heart sank and she felt like a failure.

One day, however, she came across a story that she thought might be suitable for radio. Instead of sending it on its chancy way by post, she rang up the programme and asked to speak to a producer. Her luck was still running that day – the woman she spoke to was friendly.

'I'm not sure about your idea but I'll give you a voice test if you like,' said the *Woman's Hour* lady. 'Come to Portland Place next Friday at half past three and ask for Mary.'

Dee gasped. An invitation just to set foot in the Portland Place building, with its Eric Gill carvings above the main door, was a tremendous honour as far as she was concerned. She felt like an Egyptian peasant who'd been invited into the temple of Rameses.

This piece of luck was so amazing that she was afraid to tell anyone about it in case she jinxed her chance of success by boasting prematurely. Eventually, she could keep it to herself no longer and rang up Algy on the pretext of trying out another feature idea on him. 'By the way, I'm getting a voice test from *Woman's Hour* on Friday,' she said, dropping the news casually into the conversation.

He was unimpressed. 'Yeah? Good,' he said.

'I'm scared that I'm going to blow it,' she went on, for this was really what she wanted to say.

'You'll be all right if you have a drink before you go for the test,' he said.

'That might make me worse!' she protested.

'Not if you don't take too much. When's your appointment?'

'Half past three.'

'I'll meet you at Oxford Circus at a quarter to. You won't get too drunk between then and half past,' he said.

On Friday they sat in a dark pub near the tube station and she drank two gins before Algy headed her in the direction of Portland Place. He then wandered off into the crowded street without a backward glance.

Mary – plump, dark-haired and effervescent – liked the voice test. She also noticed the hectic glaze in Dee's eyes, and amusedly guessed the reason for it.

'I think we might be able to use you. Go home and write me something funny,' she said when they shook hands at the end of the interview.

By this time the effect of the gin had worn off. Dee climbed to the top deck of a number fifty-three bus and sat staring out of the window. Panic filled her. *I've done it this time. I've bitten off more than I can chew. I've said I'll write something funny! How can I do that when I cry myself to sleep every night?* she thought.

In fact, by some peculiar quirk, she was to discover that she found it easier to write funny material when she was feeling sad than when she was happy.

Her first contribution to *Woman's Hour* was about growing up under the tutelage of Hughie in her father's hotel in the Scottish Borders. Only when she began to write did she realise what a crazy childhood she'd had.

Mary accepted it by return and a quaking Dee was summoned to record it. When the piece was broadcast, the Carmichael family shut themselves up at home with the phone off the hook so they could listen and not be interrupted. After it was over, Dee sank her head in her hands and groaned, 'I'd no idea I've such a Scottish accent! I sound like Mrs McFlannel.' *The McFlannels* was a long-forgotten radio serial that always made Dee cringe.

When she said this to Mary, she only laughed and said, 'We've been looking for contributors with regional accents. You're lucky, you've come along at the right time. Write me something else.'

Chapter Nine

The family in the house next door to the Carmichaels consisted of a permanently tranquillised ex-model, an indifferent money-man husband and two designer-dressed children. From the beginning, they made it obvious that they wanted to maintain a gulf between themselves and their neighbours. 'The people before you were so nice. We never saw them, and we never spoke to them,' said the wife meaningfully to Dee.

Ben's funeral was long over before she stopped Dee in the street one morning to say, 'We heard about your husband. It's very sad. I think it must be bad for a while, like breaking up with a boyfriend, but you get over it, don't you?'

At least she's not telling me I'm a strong person, thought Dee.

The neighbour added, 'You're so lucky to have your mother to help you. Every time I pass your kitchen window I see her washing up at the sink.'

That rankled, how it rankled!

When Dee's father Archie died, Jean threw herself on to the mercy of her children. Archie had looked after her all his married life, and it was their turn now. Dee and Ben offered to buy her a cottage, but she would have none of it.

'Don't waste your money on me. I don't want to live on my own,' she said in a pathetic voice. She intended to divide her time between the families of Colin and Dee.

When Dee was having Poppy, Jean announced her intention of moving in with her daughter and son-in-law to 'help out'. Once installed, she was hard to shift and was still 'helping out' when Ben died.

Dee found that her mother's presence was just another irritant to add to her misery – and was growing more and more irritated. Jean seemed to think that she could justify her existence by hanging around the dining table, waiting to whip away plates the moment any member of the family stopped eating. Every time Dee stepped into the kitchen, she found Jean at the sink, wearing rubber gloves and wreathed in steam.

'For God's sake, sit down and relax,' Dee often snapped. She liked to take her time during the evening meal. It was the only chance she had to talk with her children, so they lingered over their plates and let discussions grow, but Jean's dishwashing paranoia was making that impossible.

'Your mother must be such a help to you,' repeated the neighbour.

'Oh yes, she's marvellous!' Dee lied.

It wasn't only the dishwashing that irked. Her mother's very presence in the house was a constant annoyance, for Jean lived her life by proxy. The moment Dee picked up the car keys, her mother ran to fetch her coat and hat, eager for an outing. It was impossible to go shopping or visit friends without taking her along as well. Jean had no friends of her own.

When callers came, she wouldn't leave them to talk in private but sat down and expounded at great length on how much she missed Ben, sobbing dramatically as she said, 'I loved him like a son.' From childhood Dee had admired her mother's theatrical ability to weep with effect.

It was impossible to believe that Jean had really forgotten how hysterically she'd behaved when Ben and Dee announced their intention to marry. Archie had opposed the marriage bitterly – not only did he dislike Ben, but, even more, he did not want to lose his best-loved child to India. His opposition to the marriage was fuelled by Jean, who seized on the opportunity – not out of genuine concern for Dee, but because she wanted to make trouble.

For a month Dee endured nightly rows and her mother's malice. 'He's only marrying you for your money. That's all he's after. He'd not look at you for any other reason,' she told her daughter. Jean justified these attacks by saying she was trying to stop Archie's heart from being broken. In fact, she was seizing the chance to break the bond between her husband and his daughter, a bond of which she had always been deeply resentful.

The result was exactly what she wanted. She drove Dee headlong into marriage.

Six weeks after they met, the young couple married with only two witnesses present. Sadly, the breach between Dee and her father was never really healed and the pain of their separation rankled with her forever – she had truly loved him. Now she was reluctantly living with the woman who stoked the fire of their conflict. The lack of sympathy between them oppressed her almost as much as her grieving.

As the days of her widowed sorrow became weeks and then months, Dee fretted at her own inability to be frank with her mother. 'I must tell her she's got to go back to live with Colin,' she said to Madeleine.

She was acutely conscious that her children were suffering, firstly through her fixation with her mother and secondly because of her absorption in work. It seemed that there was always at least one of the children in trouble or sad, and while she concentrated on that one, another was quietly going off the rails.

Whenever there was a crisis Jean was no help, but stood at the back muttering like a Greek chorus, 'I saw this coming.' She was always ready to provide more details of the child's perfidy or shortcomings.

One afternoon, Hugo came home in tears and at first refused to tell Dee what was wrong. 'Please tell me,' she pleaded. 'It doesn't matter what it is. I want to know.'

'I've been taking money out of your purse,' he sobbed.

'That doesn't surprise me,' interrupted Jean. She had never liked Hugo and made no secret of her feelings. Dee ignored her and said to her son, 'If you took money you must have had a reason. What did you spend it on?'

'I gave it to two big boys who wait for me on the Heath every morning. They told me that if I don't give them money they'll hit me.' Hugo was small and slight, not the fighting type, and certainly not the rugby hearty his father had wanted him to be.

'Have you told your teacher about it?' asked Dee.

'No, but I walk to school with a new boy called Donnie and they're taking money from him too. He's scared as well.'

'Is he stealing from his mother too?' Dee wanted to know.

'Yes,' said Hugo.

'Where does he live?' she asked.

'In a flat along the road. They moved in last month,' was the reply.

Hand in hand mother and son walked up the road to a house like their own which had been divided into flats. The door that led into the basement was painted bright yellow and had a chiming doorbell that played the first bars of *The Blue Danube*. When they knocked, it was opened by a small boy with a shock of curly blond hair and a pair of wire-rimmed spectacles perched on his stubby nose. The frame of the spectacles had been broken, and was repaired with dirty Elastoplast.

'Hi, Donnie,' Hugo blurted out without thinking. 'I've told my mum about the boys on the heath and she wants to speak to your mum about it.'

Donnie stared owlishly through his glasses and for a moment it seemed as if he was considering closing the door on them – presumably because he did not want his mother to know about his rifling through her purse – but a voice called out from behind him, 'Who is it? Bring them in, Donnie.' Reluctantly he did as he was told.

The front door opened into a damp-smelling passage that led to a sitting room facing out into a grassy bank and an overgrown garden. The room was very untidy, with pots and crockery piled in a sink beneath the window. Plates covered with congealing food were pushed to the side of the table. Clothes were heaped on a long couch covered with brown corduroy.

A woman about the same age as Dee, with orange-hennaed hair and a heavily made-up face, was sitting at a table sticking pins into what looked like a misshapen wax doll. It had long flowing yellow tresses and two blue beads were stuck in its face to represent eyes. Long dressmaker pins were sticking out all over its shoulders and belly.

The doll abuser looked up and grinned, obviously delighted to have a visitor. Her skin was papery white and she had a peculiarly flat profile that looked as if it had been cut out of a sheet of paper, like a silhouette. There was no depth to it, only sharp angles – a jutting narrow nose, a sticking-out chin and sunken eyelids underscored by dark purplish-looking bags.

'Hello. Hold on a minute till I finish this. I've seen you going around in a little white car. You live along the road, don't you?' she said in a friendly tone to Dee before adding, 'I'd offer you a drink but there's nothing in the house. You can have tea though.'

Looking at the dirty dishes, Dee declined the offer and introduced herself. 'I'm Dee Carmichael. This is my son, and I've come to ask you what we ought to do about those boys who are terrorising our sons,' she said, eyeing the doll figure that was still being viciously stabbed with pins. It had well-developed breasts and looked like a transvestite version of St Sebastian being martyred.

The orange-haired woman held it up and squinted at it. 'I'm not much good as a sculptor, am I? That's the best I can do though. It's a voodoo doll.'

Dee asked, 'What do you want it for?'

'It's meant to be my husband's mistress and I'm putting

a spell on her. She's got long yellow hair and blue eyes – ugh, I hate that kind. I tried it once before and it worked a treat. The very next day they had a flood in their flat. When he tried to phone for help the receiver gave him an electric shock. Serves him right, the rat!' She laughed and nodded towards Donnie as she spoke. 'It's his father I mean. He knew it was me who'd done it. He rang me up next morning and said, 'Lay off or I'll break your legs!''

She laughed and Dee laughed too, hoping she was joking.

'Yeah, it's funny isn't it? He thought he could trade me in for a newer model, but he's not seen the last of me yet,' she said, stabbing the doll through the belly with another long pin. Dee flinched.

The doll was laid down on the table at last and Donnie's mother stood up, wiping her hands on a blue and white dishcloth before she stuck one in Dee's direction and said, 'I'm Josie Styles. Donnie and I moved in here last month. A terrible tip, isn't it?'

Dee couldn't take her eyes off the doll. 'What are you going to do with that now?' she asked curiously.

'I'll put it on top of the bathroom cupboard and wait. Something'll happen to her. You'll see. It always does,' was the baleful reply. Picking up the doll by the hair, Josie walked towards the door. 'Back in a jif, going for a leak,' she said over her shoulder. Now that she was on her feet it was possible to see that she was tall and very thin, dressed in a sprigged Laura Ashley dress with flounces round the hem and long dangling earrings. The boys and Dee stared after her, all of them looking stunned.

'Sure you don't want tea?' she said when she came back.

'Quite sure. I think we ought to phone the police about those boys on the heath,' said Dee. 'They're terrorising Hugo and Donnie.'

Josie seemed to be incapable of conducting a normal conversation or keeping to the point. She said, 'Hugo, that's a nice name. Is it in your family? I like fancy names but

his father insisted on Donnie, short for Donal – that's Irish.
I've a boyfriend called Clive and he's a real gentleman –
public school too. He went to Harrow. I met him at the
Grab-a-Granny club. Are you on your own?' she asked.

'What are we going to do about those boys?' Dee persisted
doggedly.

'What boys?' asked Josie. She seemed utterly indifferent
to any reason Dee might originally have had for calling on
her.

'The boys who are taking money from Donnie and Hugo
every morning. Do you think we should phone the police?'
said Dee.

How her son got hold of his ransom money did not seem
to concern Josie one bit. 'Oh yes, let's call the police. I like
policemen. Men in uniforms always turn me on,' she said.
Then at last she turned to Donnie and said, 'What's this all
about anyway?'

He told his story, which was the same as Hugo's. For the
past fortnight they'd been waylaid in the morning by two boys
who at first took only their dinner money but then started
forcing them to produce more out of their mothers' purses.

Josie smote her brow with a beringed hand. 'And me on
the dole!' she exclaimed.

'Let's report it to the police. They can set a trap and catch
them,' persisted Dee.

'A sting!' exclaimed Josie, 'That's a good idea.'

'Where's the phone?' asked Dee looking around. An
ivory-coloured instrument sat on the floor beside a sagging
settee. As she walked towards it, Josie said, 'Don't bother. It
only takes incoming calls. The bill's overdue, you see. Can't
we use your phone?'

They all walked back to Dee's house, where Josie prowled
the downstairs rooms commenting on the furniture and pictures. 'Very arty,' she said approvingly.

Jean watched balefully from the kitchen, like a cat watching
another cat that might turn into a tiger. Once they'd made the

69

call, Dee, amused by her new acquaintance, opened a bottle of wine and Josie sipped it appreciatively.

'What is it?' she asked lifting the bottle to read the label. 'Chat – ew What?'

'Château nothing. It's ordinary Chablis.'

'Chab – lis,' said Josie pronouncing each letter and laughing. 'I'm not much good at the *français* stuff.'

Within half an hour two constables arrived from Greenwich Police Station. The older of the two – a solemn, greying man – took statements from the boys while the younger constable, who had curly black hair, attempted to question the mothers. After Dee had said her piece, he went on to Josie, who soon had him pinned against the wall, one long bare arm alongside his head, while she regaled him with the details of her divorce.

'Cashed me in for a younger model, didn't he, but I can tell you there's many a good tune played on an older fiddle,' Dee heard her saying to the bemused-looking man whose uniform cap was slipping down over his eyes as she pressed into him.

It was dark before Josie decided to take her son home. When they left, Jean said in prophetic tones, 'Watch out for that one! You shouldn't have given her wine. She'll be round here all the time looking for more.'

Next morning the police roped in two tough-looking lads who were waiting for Hugo and Donnie. As they closed in on the smaller boys, and started to punch them because they had refused to hand over any more money, a plainclothes policewoman pounced. The bullies were carted off, kicking and cursing with remarkable fluency for lads of their age.

Later Josie came rushing along the road to discuss the incident. She told Dee, 'I'm going to ask my mother-in-law to look after Donnie from now on. It's dangerous for him to live in this place, but it's all I can afford on the money her son's paying me.' She blandly ignored the fact that her flat was in one of the smartest parts of Blackheath.

'Won't you miss him?' asked Dee, who could not contem-plate giving up any one of her children.

'*Of course!*' was the vehement reply. 'But it's for his own good. I'll sacrifice myself for that. Besides, if he goes to stay with his granny, I'll be able to get a job and I won't have to find a babysitter when I go out. A woman needs to go out sometimes, doesn't she?'

'What sort of job will you be looking for?' Dee asked, eyeing Josie's flower-child get-up doubtfully. Today she was wearing a battered-looking wreath of artificial flowers in her hair.

She frowned and bit her lip. 'I'm a trained nurse . . . well, almost trained . . . but I don't want to go back to bedpans. I fancy trying something else now that I'm free again.'

'Like what?' asked Dee curiously.

'I might be an artist's model . . . or a child minder,' was the reply.

'But you'll only just have got rid of your own child,' said Dee.

'It's different when you're minding them. I'll put an advertisement in the paper shop in the village and offer to go to people's houses. I can save a fortune that way because they'll have to feed me. It's not hard work. You pop the kid in front of the telly and have a bath, or read their magazines. People like that always have the classiest magazines. *Vogue* and *Harper's Bazaar*, stuff like that. I won't have to spend money heating up my own water tank either and the stuff they put in their baths is lovely. They usually buy it from places like Harrods – and you know what that costs,' said Josie.

Dee laughed. 'You'll be out on your ear inside a week. Maybe it would be safer to stick to modelling,' she said.

When Josie left, Jean went into the attack again. 'You shouldn't be associating with a woman like that,' she said. 'You know what people say – birds of a feather flock together. They'll think you're as bad as she is.'

71

'I don't think she's bad. She's just dizzy and funny. She makes me laugh,' said Dee unrepentantly.

It was true. Josie was funny. Everything that happened to her was turned into an anecdote and from then on, hardly a day went by without her rushing in, bubbling over with some ridiculous story. Most of her tales concerned men she'd picked up and she seemed to have a genius for gathering in a bizarre collection of eccentrics.

Jean was barely able to maintain icy politeness towards Josie. 'She'll end up murdered in that flat of hers. Mark my words,' she said unfeelingly. Dee shuddered, remembering that Jean could always be relied on to pinpoint flaws in other people's characters and predict the worst for them. The mention of murder brought Ben's death back into her mind. She suddenly realised that when Josie was around, she was able to forget about it for a while.

Chapter Ten

The phone calls started to come after Dee had been widowed for a year. At first she did not realise what was going on, but when she told Josie about them, she laughed and said, 'You are green, aren't you? They're after a bit on the side.'

'But I know their wives,' said Dee.

'That won't stop them,' replied Josie.

'And anyway, I don't fancy any of them,' said Dee.

Josie looked levelly at her. 'There's something wrong with you. It's essential for your health to have plenty of sex. Don't you miss it?'

'Of course I do.' Dee missed it more than she was prepared to admit. 'But missing it doesn't make me ready to jump into bed with just anybody. I have to fancy the man first,' she said.

Josie shook her head in despair. 'You're too old-fashioned. You're never going to find another man at your rate. Give me your hand and I'll tell your fortune.'

Dee's first instinct was to refuse – she always had a great fear of fortune-telling – but she could not summon up enough belief in Josie's clairvoyant powers to be afraid of anything she might say. She stuck out her hand and the bright red head bent over it.

'Yeah, there's tragedy in your middle age. I see a break in your love line. That's your husband dying. You were forty then, weren't you?' said Josie in a portentous tone, as if she was discovering all this for the first time. Dee laughed.

Elisabeth McNeill

One of Josie's advantages as a friend was that she'd never seen Ben and so there was no need for him to be brought up in conversation any more than was absolutely necessary. There was none of the 'I remember when Ben said this, or did that' which cropped up when talking with older friends.

'Is that all you see?' she asked sarcastically.

'You have a fairly long life line. Four children. But you know that already. No remarriage though.' Josie dropped the hand as if anything apart from that was unimportant.

In spite of herself Dee was disappointed. It would be consoling to think that one day she'd meet someone who she wanted to marry – in spite of what she told Josie, she was painfully lonely. But realistically – and statistically – she knew that her chance of marrying again was unlikely.

'So that means I've got to reconcile myself to being propositioned by other people's husbands?' she asked.

'Looks like it,' said Josie indifferently.

'Can you read your own fortune?' Dee asked.

'I've tried it but it doesn't work. At least I hope it didn't, because I didn't like what I found out,' Josie said.

'Are you going to marry again?' Dee asked. If husbands were to be found by persistence, Josie would definitely be able to pull it off. She belonged to at least three singles clubs, had signed on with practically every dating agency in London and answered lonely hearts advertisements in magazines. Hardly a week went by without her dragging another new man back to the basement flat. Most of them stayed one night and then vanished.

'Maybe.' Josie was being uncharacteristically reticent on the subject.

'You sound as if you don't have any faith in your own predictions.'

'I thought my life line showed I'm going to die young – but I had my hand read by a woman at the fair on the Heath last year and she said I'll live to be ninety,' was the short

74

reply. It sounded as if Josie did not want to be convinced by her own clairvoyant powers.

Dee shivered. Her old terror of fortune-telling returned. 'I don't believe in all that stuff anyway,' she said, getting up to make the supper, thinking that Jean was right: it was amazing how frequently Josie turned up in time for meals, or when a corkscrew was taken out of the kitchen drawer.

'Seriously,' said Josie from her seat at the kitchen table. 'It's bad for your health to be celibate at your age. I've been reading all about it in *Nova* magazine. You should do something about it.'

Dee turned from the cooker to face her and said with desperate seriousness, 'Maybe I should, but I don't know what to do. Anyway, I can't stop thinking about Ben. I can't get him out of my mind. I'm stuck with him somehow. I'm still very much married to him.'

A friend of hers, a kind widower, had told her that his depression and sense of loss began to lighten after the first anniversary of his wife's death. Dee waited eagerly for the end of her first year of widowhood, hoping for an easing of her state of mind, but, far from lessening, her feelings of grief and desolation were growing worse. The only respite she had from sorrow was when she was working – which she did compulsively – or when she was listening to Josie's nonsense.

'I don't think I'm ever going to be free of this heartache,' she said sadly.

'What you need is a man,' said Josie firmly. 'I'm going to a Divorced and Separated Club meeting at a pub at Charing Cross on Saturday night. I'll take you with me if you like.'

'I couldn't do that!' Dee was horrified at the idea.

'Why not? It's a laugh. Most of the men aren't divorced or separated – they're just on the hunt. But as long as you realise that, it's a good night out. We have a few drinks and we dance. I've met all sorts of people there. That's where I found Clive and Harry.'

Clive, the ex-Harrovian, was a frequent visitor to Josie's flat. Always dressed in conventional city gent-type clothes, he was very short and fat and had an unnerving way of giggling while he spoke. His cold eyes belied this jollity, however, and he gave Dee the creeps.

She'd never seen Harry, but he frequently figured in Josie's anecdotes and from time to time she disappeared for a few days and came back saying she'd been staying with him in his luxurious flat in Putney.

'I don't think I'd fit in at your club,' said Dee. As a girl, she had always felt agonised at dances when lining up waiting to be asked on to the floor.

'Give it a try. Come with me. If you don't like it you can always leave. The pub's just beside the station. You can be back on the train to Blackheath in five minutes if you chicken out. It's a laugh. You don't have to take it seriously,' said Josie, who took very little seriously.

Dee, shamed by the suggestion that she was sexually abnormal, allowed herself to be persuaded, and on Saturday night her friend turned up to supervise the choosing of an outfit.

'Haven't you anything low cut?' Josie asked, rattling the hangers in Dee's wardrobe.

'If I did I wouldn't be wearing it tonight,' said Dee firmly, pulling out a silk blouse and a grey Jaeger suit with a tight skirt and a close-fitting jacket.

'At least don't button the blouse all the way up,' said Josie, but Dee ignored her and secured the shirt buttons firmly.

It was raining when they set out for the station and Dee carried her precious new red umbrella that Madeleine had given her as a birthday present. It had a curved ivory handle and ruffles round the edge of the frame. Josie's brolly – a discarded black one of Clive's – had a broken spoke.

The Divorced and Separated Club met in a big room on the first floor of a busy pub down a dark alley. Before they went upstairs Dee and Josie left their coats and umbrellas in a cloakroom that smelt of beer. Then they bought double gin and tonics to give them Dutch courage.

The moment the reception room door was pushed open, a row of men – all ages and sizes – immediately turned to stare at the newcomers. Dee's heart sank. Their calculating eyes made them look like farmers at a market sizing up the beasts for sale.

One or two of them already knew Josie and she waved to them, carolling their names. In seconds she was off into the middle of the throng, leaving Dee on a chair in the corner, cursing herself for agreeing to come.

'I'm too much of a snob for this,' she thought as she looked at the gathering. Wherever she went, she compared the men she saw to Ben – and none of this lot measured up. He was handsomer, sexier and better dressed. His suits were made in Savile Row. These men were wearing cheap clothes in man-made fibres, and none of them looked as if they could talk about anything except football or what was on the television.

The women were just as bad – mostly in their fifties or older, they were dressed in shiny lurex plunging-necked blouses, were heavily made up and sat sipping brightly coloured drinks from long-stemmed glasses. Every now and then one among them would shriek with laughter, but the underlying atmosphere throbbed with tense desperation – from men as well as women.

A thin man with slicked-down black hair detached himself from the crowd and came over to sit beside her. 'New here, aren't you?' he asked. His accent reminded her of Ronnie, the gold smuggler she'd known in Bombay.

My God, imagine if I met him here! she thought in horror and shrank back in her seat as she told him, 'Yes. I came with my friend Josie. She's over there.'

He brightened up when he heard that. 'So you're a friend of Josie's. Quite a girl she is. Live near her, do you?'

'Yes, a couple of houses away.'

'Nice district that.' He must have been fished up in one of Josie's trawls.

'Yes, it is.'

'Own your own place too, do you?' he asked, trying to appear casual.

She sipped at her gin and tonic and shook her head. 'No, I don't. I rent a flat and live with my six children. It's a bit of a squash because there's only two bedrooms but we manage—'

He got up quickly. 'Nice speaking to you,' he said and disappeared.

After a while another man came sloping over. He wore a worried expression and couldn't look her in the eyes, but embarked on what was obviously the well-worn introductory gambit, 'New here, are you?'

'Yes.' This time all that was required of her was to listen. He launched into a sad tale about how his wife had run off with the man next door and left him with the kids. All he wanted to do was talk about the ruination of his world. She couldn't wait to get away from him before his bitterness and desolation transferred itself to her.

'Excuse me,' she said at last and rose to her feet. On the landing she found a secondary flight of stairs that led down to a back door, which she pushed open and found herself in another alley that opened into the Strand. She didn't stop running till she was on the train. It was only when she got off at Blackheath and started to walk across the heath in the rain that she remembered she'd left her raincoat and umbrella in the pub.

There was no way she was ever going back to retrieve them though – not now or in the future.

Chapter Eleven

M adeleine came to London several times over the next couple of years. Each time she took Dee out for lunch so they could sit for hours talking without Jean hovering over them. Dee saved up her problems and frustrations to share with her friend, who was always extremely sensible – except on one subject. Madeleine persisted in her theory that Ben had been murdered.

'I've been making enquiries about ways it could have been done,' she said one winter day as they sat in their favourite French restaurant in Elizabeth Street.

'Oh no! Not that again. Ben had a heart attack. I've got the death certificate and I'm only now coming to terms with that,' Dee replied. She did not want to continue pursuing the murder here.

Madeleine ignored her. 'Apparently it's quite possible to make a death look like a heart attack. Even doctors can be deceived. There's a drug called methamphetamine that'll do it, and insulin injected in sufficient quantities can induce a heart attack too. There's no trace afterwards,' she said.

'But why should anyone want to kill Ben?' asked Dee.

'He could have been collecting information for some agency or other. He might have known too much. He might have found out something inconvenient. You said he was drunk the last time you talked to him – he could have been speaking out of turn to somebody else as well as you,' said Madeleine.

Dee twirled her wine glass. 'You've been reading too

many novels, Maddy. Things like that don't happen to people like us.'

'I don't want to upset you, but it seems to me that Ben was *exactly* the sort of person to get mixed up in espionage of some sort. It would appeal to the swashbuckling side of his nature,' said Madeleine.

'I suspect that most spies don't look like swashbucklers. That would be too obvious. They all probably look like bank clerks,' replied Dee. In spite of herself she was getting drawn into this.

'But the bank clerks need other people to divert attention from them. Ben could have been a decoy,' said Madeleine.

'That's not very flattering for him. You've really gone into this, haven't you?' said Dee.

'Yes, I have. It's just so unlikely that he would die from a heart attack like that. He didn't look the type. He didn't fit the profile.' A first-class journalist like Madeleine was difficult to divert once she got her teeth into a subject.

Dee groaned. 'Even if you're right, what good will believing it do now? Ben's dead, Maddy. He's been cremated and his death's been certified as natural. We'd never be able to find out anything more.' She said nothing about Algy's offer to make enquiries in Singapore – she'd heard no more from him about it and, besides, she knew how Madeleine felt about him.

'Maybe one day you could go to Singapore and look at the police files or something,' said Madeleine.

Dee shivered. If she was offered a ticket to Singapore tomorrow she wouldn't go.

'No way. I never want to go there. Anyway, it's been three years since he died and nobody there'll remember anything about it now.'

'It'll be on record and I bet that hotel manager remembers,' said Madeleine.

'Please let's stop talking about this,' said Dee with such vehemence that Madeleine did as she asked.

Madeleine's words stayed with her, however, popping into her mind every now and again over the next few weeks. *If I could speak to the Australian again, perhaps he'd tell me more about how Ben died,* she thought. It was not the murder theory that spurred her on as much as her unsatisfied longing to be told all the details of Ben's death, no matter how upsetting. She really wanted to know as much as possible in the hope that having all the information would alleviate some of the darker imaginings that still plagued her mind.

She suffered from sleeplessness, and during the early hours of the morning confused thoughts went round and round in her mind as she lay staring up at the ornate cornice of flowers and fruit on the bedroom ceiling. Over and over again she challenged Ben. *You believed in life after death. You said that if you died first you'd come back and prove it to me. Come on then, prove it now! Give me a sign.*

Nothing ever happened – except that she noticed how the plaster cornice of fruit and flowers on the bedroom ceiling only extended round two sides of the room. The other two walls were unadorned. *Why? Did the workmen get fed up with moulding grapes and pomegranates before they finished the job?* she idly wondered as she lay looking upwards in a fruitless search for a sign from Ben.

Eventually, early one morning, after a night of debating Madeleine's theories, she gave in and lifted the telephone to ask for the number of Raffles Hotel. This time, when she asked for the manager, she was put through to a man who spoke with an Italian accent.

'I want to speak to an Australian gentleman called Macartney who was assistant manager in your hotel three years ago,' she told him.

'You must mean Kevin. I'm sorry madam, but he has returned to Australia,' she was told.

'Oh that's a pity,' she said.

'Can I help you?' said the Italian. His voice was so pleasant and sympathetic that she poured out her story – though not the bit about the murder suspicions.

'You see, I was never told the exact details of my husband's last hours, and I would really like to know as much as possible. I hope you don't think I'm being morbid but it's really important to me . . .' she said lamely.

'I understand completely,' he said with genuine warmth. 'But Mr Macartney left here about a year after the date you say your husband died. Kevin was ill and I have no address for him on hand immediately, but I'll look through our records and see what I can find out either about him or about your husband's death. If I discover anything, I'll get in touch with you.'

She gave him her telephone number and said, 'Thank you very much. It's sad that Mr Macartney became ill. He sounded young when I spoke to him. I hope he's all right now.'

'Yes, he was young, only in his early thirties, I think. But he had diabetes and had been neglecting his medication. That's why he had to go home,' said the Italian.

After she hung up the phone, she sat thinking about what she'd been told.

So Macartney had diabetes. Madeleine said heart attacks could be induced by an insulin injection . . . Don't be silly. Pull yourself together. You're as bad as Maddy at making up stories, she scolded herself.

Chapter Twelve

In the months that followed, troubles piled up. The chief cause of them was Annie. Her father had died at the stage in her life when she was beginning to be besotted by him and, at fifteen, she was out of control. Disobedient, insolent and disruptive at school, she was well aware that she was running wild and secretly panicked, but couldn't stop herself.

For a long time, the prestigious establishment for the education of young ladies which she attended – paid for now by the trust fund – treated her unruliness with tolerance. Eventually, however, a letter was sent to her mother protesting that Annie was a bad influence on the other girls. If her behaviour did not improve, there would be no alternative but to expel her.

Before her father's death, said the letter, Annie had been an excellent pupil, but since he died, both her interest in work and her behaviour had deteriorated dramatically. Perhaps Mrs Carmichael would make an appointment to discuss her daughter with the headmistress.

When Dee read this she exploded with rage, especially because the previous week Annie had come home with a plastic bag full of tawdry goods – cheap tights, a plastic hairbrush and garish make-up. When asked where she'd got the money to buy them, she defiantly boasted that she'd shoplifted them from Woolworth's in Lewisham. Though Dee ordered her to go back and replace the stolen things on the store's counters, she had no confidence that Annie actually did so.

'You can't say a civil word to anyone in this house, and now it seems you're in trouble in school as well,' she shouted at her daughter. 'For God's sake, sort yourself out or you're going to end up in the juvenile court.'

Annie whirled around in the kitchen door, long-legged, white-faced, pubescent and miserable. 'I know what's wrong with you. You're jealous of me. All my friends say it's because you haven't got a man,' she snapped.

Dee felt as if she'd been punched. *Would it help my relationship with my daughter if I found a lover?* she wondered. It was doubtful, but Annie's accusation rankled nonetheless.

Maybe Josie's right, maybe I am unnatural, she thought. *But I like men, and I used to like sex a lot. If I'm as normal as I always thought, why haven't I found someone to fancy by now?* She felt deeply unattractive and asexual, a complete failure.

Though many of the people who she and Ben had known as a couple had dropped her since his death, she was lucky that a nucleus of friends continued to invite her out. Whenever she went out to where she would meet new people, she secretly nurtured a hope that the man of her dreams would be there. But it never happened, and little by little, like a plant shrivelling, her hopes of romance died. As the months passed, her loneliness and insecurity grew and overwhelmed her.

Josie didn't help. By now she was spending almost as much time in the Carmichael house as she did at home, and she shook her head at Dee's lack of enterprise in the mating game.

'Buy some make-up,' she advised critically. 'Do yourself up a bit. I can't understand you.'

Her continual presence irritated Jean, who viciously criticised her and repeated her doleful warnings that Josie was well on the way to becoming a murder victim. 'She brought a different man back again last night. I saw them getting out of a car in the lane. I don't know how you can associate with a woman like her. You weren't brought up like that,' she scolded.

Her rebukes fell on stony ground, however, for Josie was the only bright spot in Dee's life.

While the private family row was raging among the Carmichaels about the note from Annie's school, Josie came rushing up the front steps and hammered at the door, frantically shouting through the letter box, 'Let me in, let me in.'

'Pretend we're not here,' said Jean, but Dee got up to let her friend in.

In the hall Josie gabbled, 'Call the police! Clive's just tried to kill me. He was going to stab me with his umbrella.'

Clive was rarely seen without a furled brolly and normally Dee would have considered the idea of him using one to kill Josie as ludicrous, but her laughter died when she saw that her friend really was terrified.

'What did he do?' she asked.

'I've been away for a couple of days at Harry's. When I came home he was waiting in the hall and ran at me with that old umbrella of his out like a lance. I side-stepped – I'd have got it full in the chest if I hadn't. He really meant to do me in,' gasped Josie, her kohl-rimmed eyes rolling.

'Where is he now?' Dee asked.

'Still in the flat as far as I know. He won't be going any place in a hurry because I kicked him in the goolies. Call the police.'

Jean, who was standing behind Dee, said sharply, 'But if you're not hurt it's only your word against his. If you call the police he could charge *you* with assault. Anyway, you probably provoked him.'

Though she said nothing, Dee agreed with her mother. Josie looked at her and asked, 'Whose side is she on? Phone the police. I want him arrested. That'll scare his fancy parents. They think I'm not good enough for him.

They phone him up in my place and tell him to go home at once. They call me "that awful woman". Bloody nerve.'

Because Dee doubted Josie's account and was reluctant to involve herself in a police investigation, she tried to calm the situation by saying, 'Come into the kitchen and I'll give you a drink. You look as if you need one.'

The offer was accepted. With a glass of wine in her hand, Josie calmed down and Jean climbed the stairs to her bedroom, not to be seen again for the rest of the night.

As she sipped her drink, Josie said, 'Your mother hates me, you know.'

'Does she?' said Dee cautiously, though she knew that what Josie said was true.

'It's because I know about the drinking,' said Josie.

'Whose drinking?' asked Dee, pouring herself a glass of wine.

'Hers of course. She tells you she's hard up, but she buys a half-bottle of gin from the supermarket in the Standard every morning and another one from the off-licence most evenings. They've told me. And she drinks anything you have in the house. It's a miracle you had any wine to give me right now. Haven't you noticed how it all disappears?'

Accustomed to liberal entertaining in India, Dee dispensed drinks with a generous hand, never measuring it out, so she hardly noticed how rapidly the levels in the bottles went down.

'Come to think of it, I have been getting through the alcohol rather fast recently,' she agreed, and then realised that her mother was acting strangely these days, sometimes appearing distracted and at other times skittish. She'd started taking a malevolent delight in teasing Kate and Hugo – the two children she liked least – shrieking with laughter if she upset them.

Once, Hugo complained that his grandmother had shut him up in the dark cupboard under the stairs and left him inside, crying and terrified, for three hours while Dee was out of the house. When Dee asked Jean if this was true, she denied it, and Dee did not persist.

Josie now fixed her with a fierce eye and said, 'You shouldn't let her take Poppy out, you know. I saw her dodging across the main road and nearly getting hit by a lorry the other day. She was blotto.'

Dee felt as if a cold hand touched her heart and was squeezing it tight. Her mother *did* take Poppy out on shopping expeditions to Blackheath village, crossing the busy A2 on the way. There was no pedestrian crossing near them, and Josie was right – Jean had a kamikaze-like attitude to crossing the road. *If anything happened to Poppy I'd never forgive myself or her. That would be the last straw,* she thought. The shopping expeditions, which Jean and Poppy both enjoyed, must stop.

The next day Dee, in her most conservative clothes, went to see Annie's headmistress, who, in spite of an intimidating appearance, actually had a kind heart and felt pity for the distraught-looking woman on the other side of her desk.

Dee was alone because Annie had refused to get out of bed that morning.

'We've made every allowance for your daughter because of her losing her father so suddenly, but she seems intent on driving the situation to a climax. All my warnings have been ignored and every teacher who has anything to do with her complains about the way she behaves. She flaunts all authority, and it can't be allowed to go on because it sets a very bad example for the other girls,' the headmistress said.

Dee nodded and said, 'I understand, but I don't think she's a bad girl really. She's just terribly unhappy. She won't talk to me about it, but I feel she's trying to drive me to some sort of extreme reaction. Quite frankly I find it difficult to know what to do to help her.'

'Do you work?' asked the headmistress.

'Yes. I'm a freelance journalist.'

'You work full time?'

'No, I work when I choose, but I'm very busy.' The list of buyers for Dee's articles was steadily growing and she was making her name. As well as selling work to Algy's Corinth Features and the BBC's *Woman's Hour*, she was regularly contributing articles to women's magazines and daily newspapers. Often she stayed up till the early hours of the morning to write her pieces.

Juggling her commitments and domestic life was a constant worry, but there was no way she was prepared to abandon her career after having broken through at last. Fiercely ambitious, she felt that the only positive thing to come out of Ben's death was the opportunity to make a name for herself. She took a fierce pride in knowing that when she spent money, she had earned it herself. Ben had not been generous with his money and she always felt guilty spending it.

'Like you, I used to feel that Annie was basically a good girl, but I'm afraid something has happened that's made me question that judgement now,' said the headmistress sadly, leaning forward.

Dee stared wordlessly at her as she continued, 'Information has been given to me by a senior pupil – a prefect, a girl who is trusted by the staff – that Annie has been selling cannabis resin to the other girls.'

The breath came out of Dee's lungs in a sudden gasp. 'Cannabis?' she repeated.

The headmistress nodded as if she was explaining something to a child. 'It's a drug. Selling it is a serious offence, Mrs Carmichael. I wanted to talk to you about it first. You see, we are reluctant to call in the police at this stage because of the recent tragedy in your family.'

'What do you want me to do?' asked Dee.

'I want you to withdraw your daughter from the school. If you don't, I'll have to expel her and give the reason in my report, which will follow her wherever she goes.'

Dee shook her head. 'I don't believe she's been selling cannabis. Where would she get it? Where would she get the money to buy it? What would she do with the money she made from it? She never has any money . . .' Her voice trailed off.

'She was seen in a corner of the exercise yard giving a group of her friends small lumps of black material. The girl who told us watched her handing it out. She managed to procure some herself but was so horrified at being in possession of such a thing that she flushed it down a lavatory. Perhaps Annie was not selling it but only giving it away. Even then, it is a police matter,' the headmistress told her.

'Have you questioned Annie about this?' Dee asked.

'She denies it, of course.'

'Have you questioned her friends?'

'They deny it too. Obviously they don't want the matter to be taken up with their parents.'

'I'd like to speak to the girl who reported the matter,' said Dee.

'I don't think that can be allowed. She is a sixth-year girl from a good family, very well behaved – a prefect, as I mentioned,' the headmistress said.

Dee stood up to go. 'I'll have to think about this and I must talk to Annie before I make any decisions. I'll get in touch with you tomorrow and tell you what I've decided.'

The headmistress saw her to the main door of the school and said very earnestly, 'I'm genuinely sorry, but I can't allow things like this to go on. I hope you see that I'm trying to make it as easy for Annie as possible.'

On her walk home across the heath, Dee wrestled with this new problem. If Annie was to be expelled with a bad character, she would probably be set on the downward path forever. If she was removed from school and sent to the local comprehensive – which was very rough – she would almost certainly gravitate towards bigger villains than herself.

In spite of the headmistress's certainty, however, Dee could not believe her daughter was guilty of drug dealing. Annie was behaving badly at the moment, but her crimes were much less organised than drug dealing – they were more like mute lashings out against authority.

It rankled with Dee that the girl who was her accuser had been described as coming from 'a good family'. There was much written in the newspapers about the problems of single-parent families; and when delinquent children appeared in court they were often described as being from 'broken homes'. If Annie was hauled up before a court, she too would be described as the product of a one-parent home and a working mother. The tag would be stuck on her to explain why she went wrong.

How unfair! thought Dee.

She let herself in the front door very quietly and climbed the stairs to the top floor where Annie slept. The girl was lying in bed with her face pressed into the pillow and did not move when her mother spoke to her.

'Did you sell or give cannabis to girls in your school?' asked Dee quietly, sitting down on the tumbled covers.

Annie turned round. 'So she told you that! I wondered if she would. It's a lie. I was handing out Pontefract cakes to my friends and that sneak Ursula Candless saw me. It wasn't pot.'

'Pontefract cakes?' *Small lumps of black material*, thought Dee. She knew that Annie was inordinately fond of the liquorice confection, but she could hardly believe that it could be confused with cannabis.

'Did you tell the headmistress you were passing round sweets?' she asked.

'Of course I did, but Ursula Candless said she got some and it was cannabis.'

'And could she produce it to prove what she said?'

'She told the teachers that she flushed it down one of the loos. And they believed her. I suppose you'll believe her too. You never believe anything I say.' Annie's face was red and flushed.

'To be honest I don't believe her, but I want you to swear that you've never had any cannabis,' said Dee.

Her daughter lunged towards her and flung herself into her mother's arms. 'I have had some in the past – but only just enough for a reefer. Most of my friends have tried it too. I swear I was not passing it out or selling it. Ursula Candless is a bitch and she hates me because I took her boyfriend off her. She said she'd get me for it but the teachers believe every word she says because she pretends to be such a goody-goody.'

'I've got to be sure you're telling me the truth if I'm going to do anything about this,' persisted Dee.

'I *am* telling the truth,' said Annie vehemently. 'I swear it. Please believe me.'

'OK, I'll think about it,' said Dee and went back downstairs.

Jean, who knew something serious was going on, was waiting in the kitchen.

'What's that girl done now?' she asked.

'Her school is talking about expelling her for bad behaviour,' said Dee shortly. She was not ready to go into the details.

'That doesn't surprise me. She's got bad traits. They must come from the other side of the family,' said Jean, treacherous in spite of the fact that she always claimed to love Annie best of all the children.

Dee said nothing and her mother pressed on. 'She drinks, you know.'

This time Dee did speak. 'Drinks what?'

'The stuff in your cupboard. Your gin and your whisky,' said Jean. 'You're keeping track of it now but she's the one who's been drinking it.'

After Josie accused Jean of drinking, Dee had taken to checking the bottles – and made sure her mother knew what she was doing.

'I just didn't like to tell you. She was in here the other night with two of her friends when you were out and they drank all your gin.'

Instead of being angry at Annie, red rage now rose in Dee against her mother. She knew without a shadow of doubt that it was Jean who'd taken the gin and was now grasping the chance of blaming it on Annie. Memories of occasions in the past when Dee herself had been unfairly accused of various misdemeanours, and the way her mother manipulated her father to believe the charges, came flooding back to her.

You're a wicked woman, she thought as she turned and walked away, grabbing the car keys as she went.

'Where are you going?' Jean called after her.

'Out. I'll be back in an hour,' she said.

Not caring if she got a parking ticket, she parked the car in a resident's space in Soho Square and walked to the Corinth Features office. Algy was reading *The Times* when she walked into his office. He looked up at her with raised eyebrows and said, 'You look as if you've been in a fight.'

She sat down and said, 'Just listen and tell me what you think.' Then she launched into the tale of Annie's misdemeanours and the school's accusation.

Algy sat in silence till she finished and then asked, 'Do you believe the kid?'

'Yes. But maybe only because she's my daughter and I love her.'

'You're not a dope. You can tell a liar from someone who's telling the truth. You should insist that the school conduct a proper investigation of these charges, because they're really serious. That bit about the other girl throwing away the evidence is a bit suspicious, I think, but

your Annie could be put on probation if the police are
called in.'

'I know and it worries me. I don't want the police to be
involved. Even if she's innocent, she could end up with a
record or something,' said Dee.

'I bet the school governors don't want the police to be
involved either. That wouldn't do their reputation any good
with the snooty parents who pay big fees for their daughters
to attend that establishment, would it? You could force the
issue by threatening to hire a lawyer and bring a case for
false accusation, you know,' he said.

She stood up and said, 'Thank you very much. I didn't
know who to ask for advice, but you've cleared my mind
for me.'

'That's OK,' he said, lifting the newspaper again. 'Just be
sure that she's telling you the truth before you do anything
though.'

'I believe her,' she said and went back downstairs to the
waiting car, which was still ticketless. She took that to be
a good omen.

From Soho she went back to the school, arriving just
before the end of the afternoon session. In a cold, controlled
voice she told the headmistress that she insisted on a proper
investigation of the charges against Annie because she had
reason to believe that the girl who informed against her had
acted out of malice.

'If necessary I'll hire a lawyer to conduct the questioning
for me,' she said.

'Let's keep the matter among ourselves at this stage,' said
the headmistress hurriedly. 'I assure you that I will leave no
stone unturned to get to the bottom of it.'

Next morning Dee received a telephone call from the
school and was told that Ursula Candless had broken down
under questioning, admitting that she'd told lies hoping to
get Annie Carmichael into trouble. They had fallen out
over a boy.

'And what are you going to do about Ursula? Will *she* be expelled?' asked Dee.

'Oh no, she's about to sit her Oxford Entrance. She has a good career in front of her,' was the reply.

'In that case I want a written apology for my daughter and I want it read out at school assembly,' said Dee. 'If I don't get that, I'll be taking the matter further.'

She knew what the headmistress was thinking – She's a journalist! I don't want the press brought into this! The apology arrived by first post on the following morning, which was a Saturday.

When Dee read it, she took it up to Annie's room and laid it on the bed. 'You can get up and go back to school on Monday. And don't be late because Ursula Candless will be reading out her apology at assembly. In future, for God's sake try to stay out of trouble and don't eat any more Pontefract cakes,' she said.

There was something else she knew she must do. Her brother Colin was at home when she telephoned and said, 'I want you to take our mother back to live with you. She's been with me for over six years and I can't stand much more of her.'

Colin, who had always been Jean's favourite child, sounded apologetic and anxious to placate his sister. 'Certainly. She can stay here as long as she likes. How will you get her up to us? Will you drive her?'

'No. I'll buy her a train ticket. She'll be with you the day after tomorrow.'

Though she would prefer to stay in London where she had a room to herself in a spacious house, Jean knew her time had run out and made no protest when Dee told her that she was to go back to Scotland.

On Monday morning, Jean and three large suitcases boarded the Carlisle train. She waved cheerfully from the train window, like someone going off on holiday.

Back in Blackheath, Dee telephoned an advertisement to

the local newspaper asking for a reliable woman to act as a mother's help, and then went upstairs to clean out her mother's room. When she opened the large walk-in cupboard, a cascade of empty gin bottles came tumbling out and piled up round her feet. She collapsed on to the bed and started to laugh hysterically, in huge gulping guffaws that hurt her chest. Then she fell backwards against the pillows and the tears began to flow.

Chapter Thirteen

Carrying a bundle of women's magazines, which she was returning to Josie, Dee ran along the pavement to her friend's flat. In spite of the fact that Josie always complained about poverty, she spent lavishly on glossy magazines, which she then passed on to Dee.

Josie was sitting slumped on the brown corduroy sofa with her head on her fists. 'This place is a tip. What can I do to cheer it up?' she said when Dee entered.

Dee looked round. The walls of the sitting room were shabby and stained, and the patterned wallpaper with drawings of wineglasses on it was peeling off in one corner because of the damp. Water stains sprawled across the ceiling from the time a washing machine upstairs had flooded.

'You could paint the whole place white,' she suggested.

'What's the point?' said Josie. 'Maybe I should just sell up and rent another flat somewhere cheaper. Then I'd have money to spend.'

She sighed deeply. For weeks she'd been sinking into depression and the prospect of plunging to the depths terrified her, for she'd been there before. Something had to be done to fend off total collapse.

Suddenly she sat up straight as an idea occurred to her. 'I know what I'll do. I'll bring Donnie back. He's as stubborn as his father but at least he's company and we could paint this place together. I could do with a bit of company.' From where she was lying on the sofa, she dropped a hand to the floor, groped about till she found the telephone among

96

thrown-off shoes and old magazines, and started to dial a number.

'What are you doing?' asked Dee, but Josie ignored her and when the phone was answered she trilled in the high, cheerful voice that she could assume at will, 'Hi Marie. How's Donnie?'

From where she stood by the sofa Dee could hear the other woman's reply. 'Donnie's very well. His school work has improved tremendously. He's very happy.'

The disembodied voice, Dee realised, belonged to Marie Styles, Josie's long-suffering mother-in-law who had taken Donnie in over a year ago.

'I thought I'd pop over to Beckenham today and collect him. What time does he get back from school?' said Josie brightly.

'But it's only Tuesday. He has to go to school tomorrow,' Marie replied in a shrill tone.

'He can go back to his old school here. I'll take him over tomorrow morning,' said Josie.

There was a note of panic in Marie's voice now and Dee sympathised with her when she said, 'But you can't do that, Josie. He's been here with us for over a year and you've only paid him five visits in all that time. He's got friends and he's settled down well. You can't take him away. His father won't permit it.'

'His father's got nothing to do with it,' snapped Josie. 'The court gave *me* custody. His father's only got visiting rights and he's married again anyway to that fancy woman of his. I want my son back.' Colour was rising in her white cheeks as she spoke.

'Josie, Josie, please be reasonable. The boy is happy here. He's like a different child since we've had him with us. He doesn't wet the bed any more. He's eating properly. He's reading and writing well. You'll ruin his life if you take him away.' Marie's self-control was cracking and she sounded as if she was on the verge of tears.

Something snapped in Josie and, forgetting Dee's presence, she abandoned caution as she shouted, 'You're a bitch! You never liked me, did you? I wasn't good enough. You can't have my boy. He's all I've got since my marriage to your poxy son finished. I'm coming over tonight to fetch Donnie. Have his things packed or I'll go to a lawyer and get him back through the courts and then you'll never see him again.'

When Josie had started the telephone call she'd merely been following an impulse, but now Dee could see that she was deadly serious. Her husband James and his parents wanted Donnie but she was going to get him back – even if it was only to spite them.

'Please think of what's best. Come by all means, but let's ask Donnie what he wants—' Marie never got to finish her sentence before the phone was hung up.

Josie sat back on the sofa breathing heavily. 'That bitch,' she said. 'She'll be all dressed up in a crimplene frock with gold buttons, and black court shoes. Her hair'll be blue and set like the Queen's in one of those styles that look as if a force ten gale can't ruffle it. And her house! It's a semi with matching curtains and duvet covers from Marks and Spencer in the bedrooms, and two big china greyhounds on each side of the fireplace. Everything's spotless. She hates me because she thinks I'm a slut.'

As if she'd forgotten about Dee, she rose from the sofa and went across to the sink to find a glass, which she rinsed under the tap. From a cupboard beside the cooker, she took out a bottle of cider and filled the glass. She went into the bathroom where she found a bottle of tranquillisers, shook five into the palm of her hand and swilled them down with the cider. Then she filled the glass again and went back to lie on the sofa. 'Have a drink,' she said to Dee, nodding towards the cider bottle.

Dee shook her head. 'No thanks, but listen Josie, maybe it's not a good idea for you to bring Donnie back here . . .'

Josie closed her eyes. 'Don't lecture me. I'll do what I want. Go away.'

Dee left.

Next morning there was sharp rapping on Dee's front door and when she answered it, thinking the caller was the postman, a huge bunch of narcissi was stuck into her arms and Josie cried out, 'Happy birthday!'

Holding the flowers, which were dripping water from their severed stems, Dee said in confusion, 'Thanks, but it's not my birthday, not till next month.'

'Happy birthday in advance then,' said Josie. She looked strangely euphoric, Dee thought, as if she'd gone through some sort of transcendental experience.

'It doesn't matter. Happy anything,' she went on. 'What time is it? All my clocks have stopped.'

'It's only half past eight. I thought you were the woman who's coming for an interview for my mother's help job. She's due at nine,' said Dee, still looking doubtfully at the flowers in her arms.

Josie was surprised. 'Is that all? I've only just wakened up. Are you really looking for a mother's help? I'll do it.'

'No thanks. I've heard your theories on child minding, and anyway I couldn't afford to keep you in bath salts. Where did you get those lovely flowers? You didn't grow them in your garden, did you?' said Dee.

'Of course not. They're a present because I was rotten to you yesterday. Bye-ee,' cried Josie and hurried away.

The mother's help arrived half an hour later and turned out to be a motherly, middle-aged woman with the lovely name of Mercy. She and Dee took to each other and it was arranged that she was to start work the following week.

When she was showing Mercy out, Dee saw a knot of her neighbours standing in one of the nearby gardens, discussing and gesticulating. Curious, she went along to join in and one of them, a mild-mannered accountant who worked from home, turned to her and asked angrily, 'Have your flowers gone too?'

'My flowers?' she asked in confusion.

'Have you any flowers left in your garden?' he snapped. She shook her head. 'I don't know. I didn't notice.'

'Then go and look,' he told her.

Most of Dee's front garden was given over to a red-gravelled parking lot, but there was a long side bed where she grew shrubs and flowers. Last night there had been clumps of pale pink tulips there. Today there was nothing. Every flower had gone. The back garden, which was fenced off from the lane by a wall and a locked gate, was untouched.

When she returned to report to the neighbours, they chorused, 'It was vandals! We've lost all our flowers from the front as well.' Some of them looked to be on the verge of tears because they took great pride in their flower displays.

'I've lost all my prize narcissi. I bought the bulbs at last year's Chelsea Flower Show and they were lovely. I'm going to phone the police,' moaned the accountant.

Dee backed away with a terrible thought forming in her head. After the neighbours dispersed, she sneaked out of her house and ran along to Josie's. The door was locked but Josie answered it when she knocked. Dee stepped into the sitting room and saw that the entire floor space was covered with jars, vases and plastic buckets full of spring flowers.

'Oh my God!' she exclaimed, pausing in the doorway. The smell of flowers was headily overwhelming.

Josie looked pleased. 'Yes, it's like living in bleeding Kew Gardens, isn't it?'

'Close your curtains, lock the door. The neighbours are phoning the police,' said Dee. Without waiting for Josie to do as she was told, she rushed across to the window and pulled the flimsy curtains closed. Then she turned and asked, '*Why?*'

'My husband came over last night. He said he wouldn't let Donnie come back here because I live in squalor,' Josie said as she looked around the sitting room. 'So I thought, 'What can I do to make this place look better?' Then I decided I needed flowers. They cheer everything up, don't they?'

Dee walked round the brimming buckets. It was late spring and only yesterday the gardens of her neighbours along the road had been burgeoning with tulips, hyacinths and daffodils. Now the amputated, multicoloured heads were all in Josie's flat – hundreds of them.

'It must have taken you ages to do this,' Dee said.

'Yeah, it did. I waited till it was really late, then I got a pair of scissors and went out. It took eight trips. When I woke up this morning I got a big surprise, because I'd forgotten what I'd done, you see.' Padding barefoot across to a bucket full of yellow tulips, she picked out one with gently frilled petals that would have excited the cupidity of a seventeenth-century Dutch collector and sniffed at its open cup in delight.

'The neighbours are furious. They're blaming vandals. I hope the police will be too busy to come. They've got more important things to worry about. What on earth possessed you?' Dee was genuinely concerned.

Josie started to make coffee, apparently unconcerned. 'It was my husband's fault,' she said.

'How was it his fault? He didn't pick them, did he?' Dee asked.

'No, but he came here hammering at the door because I want Donnie. When I let him in he said this place was a pigsty and he wouldn't let Donnie live here. I told him I only live like this because he pissed off and left me without any money. He said if I don't give up my claim to Donnie, he'll stop paying my mortgage.'

'What did you say to that?' asked Dee, more gently this time.

'What could I say? He's not a tough man but he has tough friends. He said if I don't do what he wants I might have an accident and you know what that means.' Josie's hand was shaking as she stirred sugar into her cup.

101

'So you gave up Donnie?' asked Dee.

'Yeah. Then I had a few more pills and some cider. It seemed a good idea to steal the flowers . . .' Her voice broke and she burst into tears. 'Donnie's all I have. I'm lonely. I want his company. He's my son.'

Dee stared at her friend in despair. 'Oh God, Josie! Stealing flowers won't help you.'

Josie shrugged. 'They're only flowers. They'll die anyway. I've saved the neighbours the trouble of cutting them down. The people round here are all middle-class snobs, like James. They have nice clean houses and nice clean cars and nice tidy gardens where the flowers all grow in rows. I liberated their tulips. It's lovely in here, isn't it? Like being at a wedding. I had roses in my wedding bouquet. What did you have in yours?' Her voice had become dreamy.

'One orchid, that's all,' snapped Dee. 'Keep your curtains closed. Someone passing by might see into your sitting room and spot the floral display. God knows what they'd do to you. Probably have you locked up.'

Josie laughed. 'Locked up? That's not a bad idea. It'd get me away from all my problems if I was.' Then she lay down on the settee and breathed in the heady scents. She liked the way the room looked with the curtains closed – the darkness covered up the dirt and the damp marks.

So she never opened the curtains again.

Chapter Fourteen

The most persistent of Dee's telephone suitors was Calum, an old boyfriend from her reporting days when she lived in Edinburgh. For more than three years after Ben's death he rang up – usually late at night when she was in bed – and entertained her with rambling conversations which reminded her of Ben.

Ben had also been a great talker. She missed their late-night bedtime discussions almost as much as she missed making love with him. They lay in the dark with Ben smoking – the glowing red tip of his cigarette the only light in the room – and debated all manner of things, from the state of the Conservative party, which he supported and she did not, to the vexed problem of life after death. Their conversations usually ended mid-sentence, when one or the other drifted off into sleep.

Calum had hung around the press crowd some years ago, but later became what he described as a 'property developer'. He'd been married twice and during his calls he told Dee that his second wife had left him and they were getting a divorce.

'I want to come and see you,' he told her. 'You've always been the love of my life.'

She stalled for months because, though she was desperately lonely and wanted to believe what he said, she was reluctant to embark on any sort of relationship with him. As a young man he'd been a heavy drinker and a philanderer, and when for a while she'd fancied herself in love with him, he'd come close

103

to breaking her heart. After she married, they had remained intermittently in touch but every time he and Ben met, the two men vied like fighting bulls.

He would probably never have overcome her reservations if it hadn't been for what he said to her late one night.

'You're fooling yourself about Ben. You needn't go on making him into a saint. He played the field in a big way,' he told her spitefully when she said that she was not ready for a new relationship because she was still in love with her dead husband.

'He did not!' she protested. By this time Ben had achieved the status of sainthood in her eyes.

'Come on, you know he did. He once told me he had women all over the place,' said Calum.

'He told you that?' she gasped.

'Yes. He boasted about it.'

'I don't believe you,' she said and hung up.

Ben wouldn't betray me like that, especially to Calum, she told herself. *If what he said was true – which she doubted – Ben could only have been boasting, taunting Calum in some sort of primitive man-to-man way.*

The allegation stayed in her mind and rankled, however.

One of the ways Dee earned money in her widowhood was to teach a creative writing class once a week in a Woolwich adult education college. There were usually about fifteen people on her roll and the same students came back every year – which meant that she was forced into changing her curriculum in order to keep them interested.

Most of the students were retired women with time on their hands and no intention of ever writing anything. Only a handful produced any work, but those who did were very keen. One was a young woman who was halfway through her first novel, and the other was John – a glamorous, bearded young man with black curly hair, a beard and gold earrings – who wrote good poetry. His talent was as exuberant as his personality and Dee was much drawn to him.

The night after her unsettling conversation with Calum, she was discussing the work of Tom Wolfe with her class, specifically *The Electric Kool-Aid Acid Test* and *The Kandy-Kolored Tangerine-Flake Streamline Baby*. She'd chosen these books as a challenge to her students, though she knew that only two of them would really appreciate her selection.

And she was right. From the faces round the long table that stretched down the middle of the room, she could tell that, apart from the man with the beard and the embryo novelist, no one had any idea what the author was talking about. The disaffected majority shuffled their papers and tried not to catch the tutor's eye – they much preferred it when Dee told them to write about memories of their childhood.

'Hasn't anyone read Tom Wolfe since I spoke about him last week?' she asked, addressing the body of the meeting and passing over her favourite students.

The most vociferous member of the class – though the least keen in writing anything – was a grey-haired widow called Nellie Hallam, who shook her head and said, 'Oh dear me no. I tried, but it's not my sort of thing really. Why don't you ask us to read someone nice like Catherine Cookson? I got a book of hers out of the library last week and the way she talked about how the heroine felt when her hubby died really made me cry. I felt exactly the same way when my Gilbert passed on . . .'

Dee felt rather than heard the collective sigh that swept the class at yet another mention of the blessed Gilbert Hallam – who his widow talked about at every opportunity.

'Catherine Cookson is a very good writer,' she said swiftly. 'But in a class like this we have to explore all kinds of writing.'

'Yes, dear,' said Nellie kindly. 'And you do. But it's just where *emotion* is concerned that Catherine Cookson is so good. She knows how a woman feels when she loses the perfect man . . .' And off she went into another eulogy about Gilbert that was only ended by a suggestion from one of the others that it was time for the coffee break.

Gathering up her papers at the end of the session, Dee looked up and saw that one member of the class was still with her. It was a woman called Mrs Jarvis, a strong-minded, witty Cockney, whose comments, though few, were always pithy and apposite.

'I hope you're not bothered by Nellie Hallam,' she said. 'Don't worry about her. We all know she's living in a fool's paradise.'

'How do you mean?' asked Dee, and Mrs Jarvis laughed. 'When her Gilbert was alive she was terrified of him. He was the meanest man in Plumstead, and one of the nastiest. She came to life when he died because when he was alive she wasn't allowed to say a word or spend a penny. It makes her feel better now to talk about him as if he was a saint because she was so pleased when he popped off.'

Dee laughed. 'I'll not feel so angry with her in the future then,' she said.

'That's fine, but don't be too kind to her either, or one of the rest of us'll probably attack her – especially somebody who knows the truth. She's one of those head-in-the-sand widows, you see,' said Mrs Jarvis.

A head-in-the-sand widow, thought Dee as she drove home. *Is that what I am too? Have I been deceiving myself about Ben, just as Nellie is conning herself about Gilbert? Is that why I was so angry when Calum said Ben had other women? Of course not. I'm not so stupid as to con myself like Nellie . . .*

But it was as if a rent had appeared in the curtain in which she'd shrouded herself since Ben died. Though she tried, she could not rid her mind of Calum's claim. The next time he telephoned, she agreed that he could come down to visit her in London. 'Let's see how it goes,' she said cautiously.

Because she was doubtful about what she was doing, she telephoned Madeleine and casually mentioned that she and Calum were back in touch and planning to meet.

'I remember him. Don't do anything silly. And don't lend him money. I've heard he's in financial trouble and drinking heavily,' warned her friend.

Madeleine's always so careful, thought Dee.

Josie was more enthusiastic when she heard that a man was coming to stay. 'Great. A man's what you need. I was beginning to wonder about your sexuality. I've always said you should find yourself a man, haven't I?'

She had taken to reading women's magazines that stressed the importance of the orgasm and talked about it incessantly. Her interest in Calum seemed uncharacteristically half-hearted and she'd been very distracted since the night she stole the flowers. It was as if her mind was away on some other tack entirely.

Calum arrived on a Tuesday. In the old days he had been handsome and dashing, but the man who got off the train at King's Cross station looked shabby, flush-faced and unreliable. His clothes were crumpled, his tie askew.

The moment Dee laid eyes on him she thought, *Oh God, I've made an awful mistake.* But she forced herself to smile.

He was introduced to the children as an old friend who had come to spend a short holiday with them. For the next three weeks Dee abandoned common sense, as if she'd gone mad. Starved of sex, all she wanted to do was go to bed with Calum. She didn't want to go out with him, she didn't even want to talk to him. As soon as the children left for school, she hauled him into bed. As far as she was concerned, he was there for sex only.

He was unaware of this, however, and seemed determined to move in on her life. He began by trying to ingratiate himself with the children, but met with stolid resistance. Making no headway with them, he began trying to charm Josie, who regarded him with an uncharacteristically sceptical eye. He quickly turned against her.

'That woman's a nut case and a scrounger. Don't have her in the house,' he said to Dee, who ignored him and continued to feed her friend whenever she turned up. She was not prepared to let him organise her life – already she knew that he was only a bird of passage. While he was in residence, however, it was no longer possible to enjoy long conversations with Josie because he was always there, frowning and disapproving.

She deliberately avoided introducing him to her friends, and when they went out as a couple it was to obscure pubs in Greenwich where it was unlikely she would meet anyone she knew. After those nights out she felt ill all next day because she always drank more than was good for her in order to stop herself from thinking.

I hate myself. I want rid of him, but I can't bring myself to tell him to leave, she thought over and over again. She wished he would go away on his own, but of course he didn't. The atmosphere in the house became more and more tense and one evening, when Dee was upstairs, she heard him and Josie shouting at each other.

'You're sponging on her,' Josie yelled.

'You should know all about that! You're the champion sponger. You turn up every time you're hungry. She knows what you're like. She's told me,' he retorted.

Like a coward Dee stayed out of sight till she heard the front door bang and knew that Josie had left. When she went downstairs she found Katie sitting at the kitchen table eating a sandwich. 'Did you hear all that? When's he leaving, Mum?' she asked.

'Soon, he's going soon,' said Dee.

As if he knew his time was running out, Calum attempted to bring matters to a head that evening.

'Will you marry me?' he asked Dee.

She did not have to hesitate for one minute, but looked him in the eye and said, 'No. I think you should go back to your wife,' she said.

By now she accepted that her original motive in taking him as a lover had been to drive out Ben's memory – in a strange way, to revenge herself on her husband. His boasting to Calum about affairs with other women had burned a hole in her heart and if she could have confronted him, she would have been violent. The affair with Calum was really a fight against Ben. She was getting her own back by taking Calum into her bed – but had achieved nothing by it. Calum grated on her sensibilities and during the time that he was in her house, she could do no work, which worried her.

He said nothing when she refused his proposal, but the following night, after they'd spent an evening avoiding each other and as if the matter had never been mentioned between them, he announced, 'I hope you don't mind but I'm going back to my wife.'

She felt laughter bubbling up inside and the relief that filled her was immense. 'I've been telling you to do that for ages,' she said.

He pretended she hadn't spoken. Crassly, as if he was the one who was letting her down, he said, 'I've been speaking to her on the phone and we're going to try again, you see. Do you want me to leave now?'

It obviously suited him to behave as if he was letting her down lightly and she realised that by going along with it, she would get rid of him quicker. If she protested, he'd probably stay. She looked at her watch. 'It's after midnight. All the buses and trains have stopped running. How are you going to get to King's Cross?'

'Will you lend me the money for a taxi?' he asked.

She laughed outright this time. 'No way. I'll drop you off tomorrow on my way to the BBC, if you like.'

That night they slept in separate beds. She had had her fill of him. When she let him out of the car at the station next morning she wept – but not from sorrow at the parting. Her tears were caused by chagrin at having got herself into an impossible and shaming situation in the first place. *Josie can say what she likes about needing a man in my life. Never again, never again,* she swore to herself as she drove away.

When she returned home in the afternoon, she longed to talk with someone about what had happened. Madeleine would only say that she should have known better, and it was not something she cared to bring up with Algy. Only Josie would understand and could be relied upon to see the funny side of the situation. Anyway, it was time to make up the breach between them.

Pulling on her raincoat, she ran down the road to Josie's flat and was disappointed to find all the curtains tightly drawn and the door firmly locked. She stood there for a long time but there was no reply to repeated rings on the bell. Remembering Jean's predictions about Josie's untimely end, she then went from window to window, peering through the glass in a hopeless attempt to find a gap between the curtains, but could not see inside.

Over two days she kept returning to the deserted flat but failed to raise any response, and finally, in desperation, she consulted the phone book and rang the Beckenham number of Josie's mother-in-law.

'I'm sorry to bother you, but I'm one of your daughter-in-law Josie Styles's neighbours and I'm worried about her. She seems to have disappeared,' she explained.

The senior Mrs Styles was a kindly woman and, in spite of Josie's considerable capacity for making trouble, she still felt pity for her.

'Don't worry dear, she's not gone far,' she said. 'She's only up the road.'

'Up the road? Where?' asked Dee, confused.

'Well, it's rather difficult. She's in the mental hospital, you see. She committed herself two weeks ago. She's been in before, you know.'

'I'd no idea. Is it possible to visit her?' Dee felt terribly guilty. Surely the row with Calum had not driven Josie over the edge?

'No. She didn't want visitors, not even Donnie, which is just as well because James wouldn't have let him go anyway. She's had treatment and is so much better that she's being discharged tomorrow. You'll be able to see her then.'

Early next evening, a thin pencil of light could be seen shining faintly between the edges of the curtains of Josie's sitting room. When Dee knocked on the door, her friend's voice called out, 'Come in. It's not locked.' To her relief Josie sounded cheerful.

The hall was almost blocked by an empty cardboard box and for some strange reason smelt of cats, though Josie kept no pets. Dee negotiated a way past the rubbish and pushed open the sitting room door to find Josie – in the familiar cheesecloth dress and long earrings – lying on the sofa with what looked like two pink plastic pancakes clamped to her temples.

She waved a hand in the direction of a chair and said, 'Hi, Dee. Sit down. I've almost finished my session.' Without saying anything Dee perched on a seat and watched with fascination as Josie closed her eyes and began a low murmuring chant. 'Um, um, uuum, uuuum . . .'

After about five minutes of this, Josie disentangled herself from the pancakes, which turned out to be electrodes of some sort and were plugged into an electrical socket by the television. Sitting up she said, 'You've no idea how much better that makes me feel. They gave me electric shock treatment in the hospital, you see, and it worked so well on me that I thought I'd keep it up at home as well.'

'For God's sake, you could kill yourself. What on earth are you using?' asked Dee.

'It's slimming pads. I've just bought them. They're the things you put on the fatty bits of your thighs and hips.

111

They're meant to throb away and break down the fat. I'm letting them throb away on my brain,' said Josie.

Dee was bemused. 'Are you sure it's safe?' she asked.

'Of course. People who get slim with them are OK, aren't they? And that electric shock treatment really works. I'm a different woman now. The only bad thing was that it blackened my teeth. Look.' Josie gave a broad grin which showed that her front teeth were badly stained. They were streaked with brown and looked as if they'd been burned.

'Oh God, Josie,' said Dee going over to hug her. 'I don't think you should be messing about with things like that.'

Josie shook her head. 'But you don't understand. Anything that brings me out of depression is welcome. In the hospital they told me that my personality might change after the treatment, but that wouldn't be a bad thing, would it?' said Josie who was obviously trying to be brave.

'Don't change. I like you the way you are,' said Dee vehemently. 'Oh Josie, I hope that row you had with Calum didn't have anything to do with you cracking up. He's gone, by the way. I got rid of him three days ago.'

'No, of course not. I felt myself going down for weeks before he turned up, but it's good you've got rid of him. He was a rat. But I don't suppose I should call anyone a rat, should I? All the men I know fit into that category. Ratsville, that's London.'

This was more like the old Josie so Dee grinned and said, 'Come on, get up and comb your hair. It's a lovely evening – though you can't see it through those closed curtains. Let's take the kids down to the pub by the river in Greenwich and have a pint of lager.'

As the sun sank, they sat on wooden benches on a sunny terrace at their favourite pub and drank beer as they watched the tourist boats go up and down the river. Though they joked, laughed and waved to the tourists, Dee noticed that Josie seemed to have sobered up since her sojourn in hospital.

Her jokes sounded strained and when her face was in repose, she looked spectral. The electric shock treatment had indeed changed her. It was only to be hoped that the change was not permanent.

Chapter Fifteen

A week after Calum's departure, Algy telephoned and invited Dee to dinner. He'd never done anything like that before.

Hiding her surprise she said, 'I'd love to come. Where will we meet?'

'At my place. You'll meet Isabel. She lives with me – or at least I live with her.'

Gosh, thought Dee, *this is a big breakthrough. He's actually introducing me to his lady friend.* He had never referred to any women in his life before – she didn't even know the names of any of his three wives. He had always been notorious for keeping his personal arrangements secret. She wondered why he had decided to come out of hiding now.

The address he gave her was in Fulham. She was told to be there on Saturday night at half past seven.

The flat turned out to be on the ground floor of a pleasant block not far from a line of imposing studio houses where many famous painters used to live. Three steps with iron railings led up to a front door that was answered by a beaming Algy dressed in a sporty-looking sweatshirt and jogging pants. His leisure gear surprised Dee, who had never thought of him as an action-man type.

Behind him stood a tall, formidably elegant woman in her fifties wearing tight black trousers and a green silk blouse with big pearl buttons that screamed *expensive*. She was leaning on an ivory-handled walking stick and when she moved she walked with a pronounced limp.

Unforgettable

Her name, Dee was told, was Isabel Woodhouse, and she was obviously a well-bred American WASP. She demonstrated an almost motherly condescending air towards Algy, calling him 'Adam-honey'. In spite of the fact that she was at least ten years his senior, they seemed to be on very familiar footing. Dee was invited by Isabel to leave her overcoat on 'our' bed. Then Algy was given bossy, wife-style instructions about serving the drinks and decanting the wine.

Amusedly watching him as he sliced lemons for gin and tonics, Dee wondered how he'd become entangled in such domesticity, for there didn't seem to be much common ground between the couple. As far as she knew, Algy never went anywhere except to his office and the pub. In all their years of acquaintance she'd never heard him mention going to the theatre or even to the cinema, but Isabel talked knowledgeably about opera-going and visiting art galleries in various European centres of culture. The pictures that adorned the flat walls were hers and she referred to them as 'my Edward Burra, my Francis Bacon and my John Nash'. Until that night Dee would have doubted if Algy knew the difference between the works of Edward Burra and Mabel Lucie Atwell.

When she asked Isabel which part of the United States she came from, the reply was, 'New York, but I wouldn't want to live there now.'

New York was like Mecca for Dee, who had never been there but longed to go. 'I've heard such wonderful things about it. Isn't it a thrilling city with marvellous art galleries?' she asked.

'Oh sure, the Met and the Guggenheim are good but nothing like as imposing as galleries in Madrid or Paris. For culture, give me Paris every time. It's my favourite place and I want to live there when I'm an old lady,' replied Isabel.

'Is Paris your favourite place too? Is that where you'll go when you retire?' Dee mischievously asked Algy, who'd taken no part in the cultural discussion.

115

He frowned as he said, 'I used to think that if I had to pick a place where I'd like to spend my old age I'd go to Kyrenia in Cyprus. It has sunshine, lemon trees, a little port, good cafés and a beach . . . paradise. I had a place there once but it was wrecked in the Turkish invasion and I can't go back now, unfortunately.' He sounded truly devastated and Dee sympathised with him. Imagine working for years to buy your ideal home and then having it snatched away from you by war.

She was about to commiserate when Isabel interrupted to say, 'You should always have known that Cyprus wouldn't last. Didn't you get advice? Anybody could have told you that the Greeks and the Turks have been at each others' throats for years. I lived there for a bit in the sixties and I was always aware that it was going to erupt very soon.'

Algy said nothing, just went on slicing lemons.

Dee felt it was necessary to keep the conversation going by asking another question. 'Did you meet each other in Cyprus?' She could not imagine a situation that would throw together Isabel, the aesthete, and Algy, the hack.

Isabel smiled. 'Oh no, we met here in London. He answered my advertisement,' she said.

Dee looked askance at her old friend, unable to hide her astonishment. Surely he didn't go trawling for love in the classified section like the miserable specimens she'd met with Josie? Her hosts saw her surprise and Algy hurriedly explained, 'I was looking for a place to live at the same time as Isabel advertised in *The Times* for someone to share this flat.'

Dee nodded and said, 'I see.' She remembered how he moved from place to place when he lived in Bombay, never staying anywhere for long and never telling anyone where he was going next. His secrecy had seemed paranoid then but it was later explained by the suspicion – never confirmed – that he was linked with the American secret service.

'So how long have you been living here then?' she asked,

determined to keep on finding out as much as she could while
he was in an expansive mood.

'About six months. I was in Soho for a bit but that lease
ran out and I was very lucky to find such a good flat – and
such a wonderful landlady,' he said, grinning at Isabel who
sent a meaningful smile back.

'It was lucky for me too,' she added. 'The rent here is high
and I've shared with women before but I prefer to have a man
as a tenant – for security, you know. A woman on her own
– or even two women – can be *so* vulnerable. None of my
previous tenants have been as compatible, or as easy to get
along with, as Adam.'

'Easy to get along with' was not the description that Dee
would have applied to her old friend – in her experience
he was erratic and unpredictable in mood. She wondered
how much Isabel really knew about Algy. *And how about
his schizoid hair?* she thought as she looked at his coiffeur
and saw with surprise that the characteristic quiff was sleeked
neatly down as if it had been barbered by Trumper's. He really
must be a changed man.

Surprising herself, Dee suddenly felt pique that some other
woman had achieved this transformation, but then she saw
the funny side of the situation and had difficulty concealing
her amusement. Domesticating him would be like training a
man-eating lion to be a mouser, she thought, and she wished
Isabel the best of luck.

At that moment he looked up, caught her eye, and something like complicity flashed between them. Then, more
chillingly, as she saw him complacently sipping his glass
of wine, she realised that this was not a joke after all. She
really was watching a wild animal playing at domesticity and
wondered why she'd been invited along to see it happening.

Chapter Sixteen

The evening with Isabel and Adam-honey was a diversion in another black period for Dee because, after Calum's departure, her misery about Ben deepened again. Her dreams, always vivid and colourful, began to play tricks on her – almost every night she dreamed that Ben had come back to life. He told her he'd been kidnapped, or hijacked, and once he even said he'd been in prison. She accepted the excuses every time, and woke filled with happy elation, which soon dissipated when she slid her hand across to his side of the bed and found it empty. Then she stared up at the unfinished bedroom ceiling in bleak despair.

She could not come to terms with why she was finding it so difficult to reconcile herself to his death. *There's something wrong with me. Why can't I shake myself out of this terrible bleakness?* she asked herself.

She developed worrying physical symptoms too. The skin under her wedding ring developed a red, swollen rash and itched unbearably. No application of over-the-counter medicines succeeded in soothing it. Eventually she consulted her doctor, who prescribed a stronger ointment – but that did no good either.

'I'm afraid you'll have to take off your wedding ring till it clears up,' he told her when she went back for a second time. It seemed like disloyalty to do that, but the finger was so red and swollen that there was a risk of it becoming poisoned. The area of irritation had spread round the lower segment of the finger like a red bandage and it was

118

difficult to dislodge the ring, which she had worn since her wedding day.

Next morning, however, the itch began to disappear, and in two days, so had the rash. On the fourth day she tried replacing the ring. Within twenty-four hours, the itching started again. Three times more she tried to put the ring back on, three times she failed.

I'm rejecting my wedding ring. Why? she asked herself, but did not ask her doctor. If there was an explanation, she did not want to hear it.

One miserable night, while fog drifted over the heath, swirling round the tops of the tall concrete lamp standards that shone down on the cars and lorries swishing along the A2, she looked out of her kitchen window and saw Ben emerge from the darkness.

He walked into view with his habitual, splay-footed stride and paused at the other side of the road, waiting to cross. He was wearing his grey business suit, and the black leather briefcase that she'd stuffed into the Baker Street rubbish bin hung from his right hand. Her first feeling on seeing him was terror. 'Don't haunt me. Go away,' she cried out.

When she blinked, he was gone. Desperate to catch him, anguished in case she'd driven him away by her cry of rejection, she ran out of the house, across the road and on to the spongy, wet grass – but the heath was deserted.

That night she thought hard about her situation. *I can't sort this out in my head. I wish I could talk to someone about it,* she thought.

There was no one, however. Josie had retreated into a state of detached conformity – a sad difference from her previous lifestyle – and there were too many private issues for Dee to discuss them with casual friends. Madeleine wouldn't be much help because she was a pragmatist, and Dee was more in need of spiritual and emotional advice.

Little by little, without being aware of the extent of her degeneration, she slipped deeper into depression. One morning, in the supermarket near her house, she felt her heart starting to beat fast very suddenly. Terrified that she was going to faint in the check-out queue, she abandoned a full trolley and ran to her car, where she sat trembling till she felt strong enough to drive home. After that she sent the children shopping because she dreaded the indignity of fainting in public.

She was mortally afraid of dying and leaving her children to be unloved orphans. A secret little voice in her head taunted, 'What if you drop dead like Ben? What would happen to the children then?' She knew it was all too easy to die. Ben had done it in ten minutes.

Worry twisted her mind. She lay in bed at night listening to her heartbeat thudding erratically in her ears. *I could have a serious heart condition and know nothing about it till it kills me,* she thought.

At last she consulted her doctor again, complaining about high blood pressure but unable to bring herself to tell him about the strange behaviour of her heart. He jollied her along as he took her blood pressure. 'There's nothing wrong with you. I wish my blood-pressure reading was as good as yours,' he said, rolling up the sphygmomanometer.

She was not reassured – Ben, too, had been given a clean bill of health just before he died. Her fears – and the symptoms that terrified her – grew worse, but she kept on working like a maniac. The only time she was not worrying was when she was busy.

The students in the basement, who were always ready to look after the children when Dee was out, and Mercy, the new mother's help, proved to be towers of strength. Mercy in particular brought previously unknown order to the household. She was kind to the children and even kinder to Dee, who she treated as if she was also a child in need of nurturing. Almost every week she turned up with packets of soap powder, tins of Vim or bundles of yellow dusters. When Dee asked how she came by so many household supplies, she only laughed and said, 'Fell off the back of a lorry, didn't they?'

One day when the electricity bill was so large that it made Dee gasp, Mercy offered to bring her husband along to connect the power meter to the pavement lamppost outside. 'Then you won't have to pay for any electricity,' she explained.

'Oh God, no,' gasped Dee. 'With my luck I'd be found out and sent to jail!'

Mercy thought it was stupid to be so law-abiding and cautious, but Dee refused to allow the electricity meter to be tampered with, and went on paying the bills.

In the middle of her period of deepest depression, Algy telephoned again. This time his tone was different – sharp, urgent and peremptory.

'Don't send any more features to Corinth Features. We're closing,' he snapped. He sounded out of breath, as if he'd been running.

This was a terrible blow and she felt sick when she realised that one of her principal sources of income was disappearing. 'Closing? For good, you mean?' she asked. There had been no suggestion that such a thing was likely to happen.

'Yeah, immediately. And I want to ask you a favour. Can I leave some stuff with you?' he said.

'What sort of stuff?' Something about his tone warned her to be cautious.

'My papers and a couple of bags of clothes.'

'No papers. I can't take anything dangerous, Algy. I've got kids in the house,' she told him.

'All right, just take the clothes then,' he said, accepting her reservations without argument.

'You're sure it's safe?' she said reluctantly, wondering what she was letting herself in for and why.

'Positive. Can you pick the bags up today? Now in fact,' he said urgently.

'Where from?' She was still reluctant.

'Isabel's place. I'm leaving tonight.' He was good at

dramatic disappearances. When he left Bombay, he was around one moment and away the next. This sudden desire to fly the coop was true to type.

Intrigued in spite of herself, she drove to Fulham. Algy answered the door, looking unusually flustered, and with the hair standing up on end again. Two canvas holdalls and a large suitcase were waiting in the hall and, as he started to lift them up, Dee saw Isabel's face staring balefully from the window. As soon as she saw Dee watching her, she drew back out of sight.

'Just a minute. You're absolutely sure there's nothing in those bags that could get me into trouble or attract unwanted attention?' she asked as he toted the bags down the steps. She was more worried for her children than for herself.

'Nothing. I swear to you. It's only my clothes. I've got rid of the papers elsewhere,' he said over his shoulder as he hefted them into the car.

'Why don't you leave them with Isabel?' Dee asked.

'She's pretty fed up with me and she's told me to get my stuff out,' he replied, slamming down the boot lid on his three bags.

She was still unsure that she ought to be accepting his stuff. If Isabel didn't want to give it house room, why should she?

'Listen,' he said. 'It's just my clothes. I'll come back and get them as soon as I can but I won't tell you where I'm going because it's best you don't know.' His urgency convinced her. She jumped into her car and drove away, still conscious of Isabel's face at the window.

At home she did not unload the car boot till darkness came, and then she carried in the bags one by one, stowing them on top of the spare room wardrobe. With an effort of will she fought the temptation to look inside them. For her own peace of mind she had to take his word for what they contained. She was far from sure that she'd ever see him again and wondered if she'd have charge of his bags for the rest of her life. Madeleine was right. He was trouble.

The explanation for his sudden decamping was not long in coming, however, and when it came it took everyone by surprise.

Annie, who had left school on her sixteenth birthday and found a job in Harrods, went out with some of her friends one night and at about eleven o'clock phoned her mother from a central London phone box.

'Mum,' she said breathlessly. 'What's the name of that agency you wrote all those features for?'

'Corinth Features. Why?' said Dee, puzzled at being asked the question.

'Oh God, Mum, you've been working for the CIA,' said her daughter with a laugh. 'I've just been to a lecture given by a man called Philip Agee who's a defector from the CIA. He said that Corinth Features was a news disseminating service for the agency. He said it was run by hardcore agents! Are you an agent, Mum?'

'Of course not!' snapped Dee before she hung up the phone and went to sit at the end of the kitchen table with her head in her hands.

I should have known, of course, she thought. *In fact, I did know. I just chose not to acknowledge it. He more or less told me several times. And those cheques came from an American bank. How could I have been so stupid? Oh God, I've got his stuff upstairs! What if my name's on some sort of a list? It must be. What if they come looking for me?*

Who *they* would be, she had no idea – but she was in the state of mind to believe anything about anybody.

She got up to make a cup of black coffee – she was living more or less on strong coffee these days, which did not help her erratic heartbeat. While she stood waiting for the kettle to boil, a laugh unexpectedly bubbled up inside her. She bent over and guffawed. How ludicrous that the CIA had been financing her in her widowhood! What on earth did they think they were doing, buying articles about an old man who made hats for cowboy films and a woman who had five hundred evening dresses? How could anyone in their right mind believe that articles like hers were going to undermine the Communist system? Algy must have been running a benefits agency for his old pals.

Chapter Seventeen

A demented-looking woman turned up three or four times a week to scatter bread for the pigeons on the stretch of heath opposite Dee's house. Her arrival was eagerly awaited by the birds, who perched, beady-eyed, along the pediments of the houses.

Such lavish scattering of food enabled a pigeon population explosion, and grossly plump birds started pecking holes in the wooden eaves to make nests where they raised hundreds of little pigeons that cooed and clucked by day and night. Before very long they had drilled their way into the roof cavity of the house, and the bolder spirits among them began to roost at night in the upstairs lavatory. Annie, who already had a bird phobia, erupted into screaming hysterics one night when an overfed pigeon succumbed to a heart attack and fell on top of her head while she was sitting on the toilet.

Next morning the bird lover was back, scattering her bread as usual. An exasperated Dee rushed out to tackle her.

'Please don't feed those pigeons,' she said when she went across the road.

'Why not?' The pigeon lover looked like a bag lady, and was obviously more on the side of birds than people.

'Because they're pecking holes in my roof and they're disease-ridden pests. They've all got syphilis and TB,' said Dee.

The woman recoiled. 'What a terrible thing to say! Poor birds. You're only worried about your property. That's all you care about. They're God's creatures and you can't stop me feeding them,' was her defiant reply and a crust of wholemeal bread went whizzing past Dee's ear.

From then on the pigeon-feeding was stepped up to every day except Sunday. Word must have got round among the pigeons – even more of them arrived to peck bigger and better holes in Dee's roof.

The bearded poet in her creative writing class – who had become a friend, and almost even more – offered to climb on to the roof and seal the pigeons' holes, an offer which was accepted gratefully. He skimmed over the slates with catlike dexterity and when Dee complimented him on his skill, he laughed and said, 'Between you and me, I'm a cat burglar. And I've put the word out among my mates to tell them to give your house a miss. You'll never be burgled.'

She was unsure whether to believe him or not, but began to notice the frequency of break-ins among her neighbours, while her house was never touched. She realised that if she wasn't careful, the friendship between herself and the poet might get out of hand.

Though the pigeons were temporarily repulsed thanks to the poet's handiwork, other parts of the roof started to leak in a spectacular fashion. When it rained, Mercy ran about putting buckets on the stairs to catch the drips. In spite of her efforts, however, the fitted stair carpet shrank and soon looked as if it had been designed in a scallop pattern.

Then the car broke down and cost a tidy sum to repair. It was only back in the parking bay for one day when Katie came running in to say, 'Mum, a tree has just fallen on your car.'

Is it April the first? Dee wondered, but when she went to the kitchen window to look out, sure enough a massive branch off their acacia tree had fallen across her car, almost flattening it. 'Oh God, what's going to happen next?' she groaned.

She didn't have to wait long to find out. The friendly girls in the basement, who for three years had babysat, gardened and generally cheered her up, suddenly gave notice. They had all graduated and were either getting married or going abroad to find work.

At least she still had Josie, who was again showing sporadic flashes of her old wit and was dating again – though none of her swains stayed around for longer than twenty-four hours.

'I'm fed up with men. I'm thinking of becoming a nun,' she told Dee one day. 'I was brought up a Catholic, you see.'

'Have you a vocation then?' asked Dee.

'Yeah, my vocation is I want to keep on eating.'

'You'd be better to get a job,' Dee suggested.

'I've tried that. The only jobs that'll take me, I don't want. They all think I should get up early in the morning and wear frumpy clothes.'

'Nun's clothes are pretty frumpy,' said Dee.

'Yeah, kinky! I'd pull the men dressed like that, wouldn't I?' Josie was trying to be funny, but her fooling around seemed more forced nowadays. There was a darkness beneath the joking.

When Josie heard that the girls in the basement were leaving and Dee complained that she'd never find such good tenants again, she said, 'Don't worry. I'll ask around and find you another tenant.' It didn't take her long to produce one. When she brought him around to see the flat she whispered, 'He's a friend of Harry's and his marriage has just broken up. He works for BBC Radio Four, in the sports department. That'll suit you down to the ground, shouldn't it?'

The sports reporter had a lounge lizard look that Dee instinctively distrusted, but she agreed to let the flat to him and his girlfriend, a pinched-looking French interpreter who he'd met when covering the Olympics for the BBC. They moved in, but by the time their second rent payment was due the cheque bounced.

At one time Dee would have been able to see the funny side of her problems, but this time, as one piled on top of another, her sense of humour deserted her. She went downstairs to harangue the tenants and then telephoned Madeleine to let off some steam. 'The car's wrecked, Algy's agency has wrapped up, the girls in the basement have left and the new tenants are crooks!' she spluttered.

'Troubles never come singly,' said Madeleine briskly. 'But you mustn't let them get you down. It seems that money's your biggest problem. If you've lost the Corinth Features connection, get another outlet. Acquire a speciality!'

It sounded like a slogan, but it was good advice. As always when faced with a challenge, Dee's first thought was, *I can't do it*, but then she remembered Hughie's slogan of 'heart over first', and set about looking for an area that was not worked to death by other freelance journalists.

A small paragraph in the *Financial Times* alerted her to the fact that Bonhams, one of London's biggest auction houses, was offering a stuffed mermaid for sale. She went to the viewing and saw a hideous-looking thing – a faked-up amalgam of a stuffed fish's tail and the body and head of a monkey – but she wrote an article about it that attracted a lot of interest when it appeared in a London evening newspaper. Bonhams' press officer was so pleased with the publicity that she started telephoning Dee with exclusive stories and her antiques trade connection began.

The anxiety attacks that had plagued Dee for so long were no better and, because of her terror of waiting in check-out queues, she'd given up going to supermarkets. Instead she bought food from small local arcades of shops where she could park the car at the pavement edge and retreat quickly back to it if she felt unwell.

An old woman, with a face as brown and wrinkled as a walnut, served in a small vegetable and fruit shop in the line of shops called the Standard behind the Carmichaels' house. This woman was obviously intrigued by her customer's peculiar behaviour, for Dee would literally leap out of her car at about half past five in the evening, grab whatever she wanted and bolt back to it again.

'You all right, dear?' the old woman asked one day while weighing out an order of potatoes.

'Yes, fine thank you,' said Dee automatically. She never admitted to weakness, no matter how bad she felt.

'You don't look all right.'

'Don't I?' It terrified her to be told that.

'You look a bit tired.'

'I suppose I am. I don't sleep very well,' Dee said wearily.

'Where do you live?'

Dee gestured. 'Over there. On the A2.'

'The traffic must be keeping you awake. Which house do you live in?' asked the old woman curiously.

'Number fifteen.'

'Is that the one on the corner of the little lane?' The greengrocer's assistant had lived in the district all her life and knew each house well.

'Yes, it's the one with the modern extension at the side.' The kitchen of Dee's house was out of character with the rest of the house, the main part of which dated from around 1840. The kitchen, however, had a huge plate-glass window overlooking the heath and was built in the brutalist style of the 1950s.

'Oh yes, that's the one the flying bomb dropped on,' said the old woman, tipping the potatoes into Dee's shopping bag.

'A flying bomb!' Dee was shocked. The thought flashed through her mind, *So that's why we only have cornices on half of the ceilings.*

The greengrocer's assistant said, 'Yes, dear, didn't you know? In 1944, I think. One of those buzz bombs it was. Just dropped out of the sky and killed the family living there. He was a clergyman of some sort and he was hiding in a cupboard under the stairs with his wife and children. The bomb hit them full on. They were blown to bits,' she said with relish.

The house was empty when Dee went home, for Annie

129

was working and the other children were at school or nursery. With terror in her heart, she opened the door of the hall cupboard where Jean had once incarcerated Hugo, and was overwhelmed by the feeling of total malevolence that seemed to gush out of it. In a panic, she slammed the door shut again but the spirits she'd released did not go away.

This house hates us. It's evil, and it hates everyone who's ever lived in it since the bomb fell, she thought with sudden certainty. She was beyond reason, beyond logic. The house hated her, she was sure. It was the house that was at the root of all her problems.

She reviewed its recent history. She and Ben had bought it from a couple who were in the middle of a bitter divorce. They told her themselves that their marriage had begun to deteriorate within months of moving in. They'd only lived in it for two years.

Dee was on good terms with the wife from that marriage, and rang her up to ask, 'I'm sorry to bother you, Miriam, but have you any idea what happened to the people who sold this house to you?'

'Yes. It was sad. We bought it from a widow who developed a wasting disease of some sort and had to go into permanent care. She moved to Devonshire and died there, I believe,' was the reply.

'And do you know anything about the people before her?' Dee asked.

'Sorry, I'm not certain about them, but I think they left because their son went to prison for something,' was the reply.

Dee hung up the phone and thought, *Four owners, four tragedies – incurable illness, divorce, despair and death.* Surely that was enough to confirm the malevolence of the house. Cold, primitive fear gripped her heart. *What's going to happen next?* she wondered.

She told no one about these thoughts because she feared ridicule. How could a house manipulate the lives of the people inside its walls? She prided herself on being a logical, radical thinker. She used to scoff at ghost stories too – but now she was terrified in case malevolent spirits were manipulating her own life. *Don't be so stupid!* she scolded herself, and for a while the fears were quietened. They did not disappear entirely, however, and she went on worrying in secret.

At ten o'clock a few mornings later, Josie was lying with the slimming pads clamped to her head when the telephone rang and Dee said in a strange voice, 'Could you come along for a minute, please, Josie?'

'Sure. Why?'

'Just come, please.'

The tone was urgent and Josie knew she had to go at once. When she arrived, the front door was unlocked and Dee was sitting on a chair in the sitting room with the hoover lying on its side beside her. She looked up when her friend entered and said, 'I think I'm terribly ill.' It was the first time she'd admitted the terrors about her health to anyone.

Josie knelt down beside her and took hold of her hand to check the pulse. 'You look awful. You're cyanosed,' she said, dredging the word from her memory of once-studied medical textbooks.

'What does that mean?' gasped Dee.

'It means your lips have gone blue,' was the reply.

Dee got up and staggered across to a mirror above the fireplace. The face that stared back at her was ghastly white with a circle of purple round her lips.

'I knew it. I'm dying. The house has won,' she said and started to cry. Though she was shivering with cold, beads of sweat were erupting like pearls on the backs of her hands. She had never felt so ill in her life.

Behind her she heard Josie talking on the telephone. 'Send a doctor immediately. It's an emergency.' For once she sounded remarkably sensible, obviously stimulated by the excitement.

'I don't want a doctor,' protested Dee.

'It doesn't matter what you want. Lie down,' ordered Josie, and without protest Dee did what she was told.

The emergency doctor who arrived was a kind and efficient woman. In spite of the patient's protests, she called an ambulance to take Dee to the Brook Hospital for tests.

'Come on love, do what you're told,' said the ambulance men as they wrapped the struggling woman in a blanket and bore her out to their waiting vehicle.

'But the children . . . what about my children?' she wailed.

'I'll stay here and look after them,' said Josie.

That didn't make Dee feel any better. 'Oh my God,' she wailed.

In Brook Hospital she refused to be admitted, insisting that she had to go home. They let her go, but told her to see her GP the next day.

Fortunately, her own doctor, who always refused to admit that Dee might be really ill, was on holiday. His locum took a more serious view of her situation. 'I'll refer you to a specialist in Greenwich Hospital for heart tests,' he told her.

It was a confirmation of everything that she most dreaded and she was sure that she was about to be given a death sentence.

A week later, when she went down into Greenwich Hospital for the dreaded tests, the rain was pouring down, the streets shone like silver and the normally attractive buildings alongside Greenwich Park looked grim and bleak. The nurses in the cardiac department weighed her, asked for a urine sample, prodded her all over, stuck tags on her chest and recorded her heartbeat, made her run on a treadmill and took phial after phial of blood for testing.

But no one asked if she had any worries. 'Come back in a week for the results,' she was told before being sent home with her heart thudding worse than ever.

Weepy and trembling she returned to the hospital for the

verdict on the appointed day. *They're going to say, sorry, but you're dying. What's going to happen to my children?* she thought as she walked across the road from the car parking space to the hospital's front entrance.

The consultant who saw her looked uncannily like Jack Payne, the 1940s band leader. He was small and dapper with plastered-down black hair that was like a cap of patent leather stuck on his head. In a perfunctory manner he flipped through the report on his desk and said, 'Um yes. You'll have to take pills to control your heartbeat and blood pressure.'

'For how long?' she asked shakily.

He did not even look up as he said, 'For ever.'

She stared at him with her heart thudding and words boiling up in her mind. *What's wrong with me?* she wanted to know. *What's my illness called?* But he was so disdainful and unfriendly that she was afraid to ask. She took the prescription he scribbled out for her and managed to say, 'Is there anything else I ought to do?'

'Yes. Change your way of life,' was the snapped reply.

Her legs were wobbling like jelly as she walked back to the car. The rain was still teeming down. A car park attendant in a yellow oilskin coat stood watching from the door of his hut as she walked across to her car and laid her head down on its roof.

Change your way of life, she thought. She wondered what sort of life the doctor imagined her to be leading. *What the hell does he know about me or my way of life? Does he think I'm an alcoholic or a drug addict? The only personal question they asked me in the hospital was whether or not I smoke – and I don't. That doctor doesn't know anything about me and he doesn't care, because he probably thinks I'm a self-indulgent neurotic, which I may be. I don't know.*

Words were banked up inside her like a wall of water. *If I could only talk this through with someone, I'm sure I could find things out about myself that would help enormously*, she thought. But who was there to listen to her? No one.

About one thing, however, she was determined. *Heart over first.* She was not going to sink.

Chapter Eighteen

H er visit to the hospital convinced Dee that she must leave her house. Abandoning logic and disbelief, she was now convinced that the house was evil and, once that idea took root in her mind, there was nothing to do but escape from it before it caused any more harm to her or her children.

She was terrified of it, so terrified that if she woke in the night she was too scared to get up in case she met the lurking spirits of the unhappy family who had been annihilated by the flying bomb, for she was sure the evil started with their deaths. Somewhere she'd read that ghosts were the manifestations of angry people whose lives had been abruptly cut off before they were ready to die.

Once the agonising was over and the decision to go was made, Dee, a typical Taurean, swept all before her and put the house on the books of three estate agents at once. Though she did not share her fears about the house's evil with the children, she'd asked their opinion about leaving and, to her relief, everyone was in favour of a move. It was as if they too were anxious to put the miserable past behind them.

Everyone took great pleasure in discussing where they should go next, for Dee had given very little thought to that. All she wanted was to get away.

Making a decision was not urgent, however, because the first people who came to view the house recoiled from the state of the roof and the incursions of the pigeons, but every time another prospective buyer turned up, hope filled the Carmichaels. They spent the next few nights round the kitchen table with an atlas open in front of them, debating possible destinations.

Annie missed these discussions because she had left home, having gone to Dundee on a journalist training scheme, but London still pulled her and she phoned home to record her opinion that the family should look for a house in Chelsea. Annie always aimed high.

On Sundays Dee and the other children drove round West London, looking out for agents' boards and fantasising about the properties for sale, but they were only indulging themselves on Annie's behalf – they knew Chelsea prices were beyond them.

'What about Canada?' asked Hugo one night, putting his finger on a brown line on the map that marked the Rocky Mountains.

'My father was there before the First World War,' said Dee. 'He fought in the trenches in the Canadian Army and when it was over, he was given a stretch of land on Vancouver Island.'

'Do you still have it?' asked Hugo hopefully, but she shook her head. 'He never took up the claim. He didn't go back to Canada, though I think he missed it a lot. Anyway, what would we do, stuck in the middle of a strange country?'

'We could build a log cabin and shoot things,' said Hugo.

Dee smiled. 'Those days are finished, I'm afraid. We'd probably be living in a suburb in a house like the ones round here.'

'Where would *you* like to go, Mum?' asked Kate.

Dee turned the pages of the atlas till she found India. 'There,' she said, pointing to Bombay. 'That's where I was very happy. But it's impossible to go back because people like us can't live in India unless they're contributing something, and I've nothing to give any more. What about you, Kate? Where do you want to go?'

'Ireland would be nice. We could buy a place like Flurry

Knox's and keep lots of horses,' said Kate, who was reading Somerville and Ross's book about the Irish RM.

Dee laughed. 'I fancy that too, but what would we live on in Ireland?'

'We could keep hens and goats and grow things. Like *The Good Life* on the telly,' suggested Hugo.

This idea appealed to them all and the possibility of self-sufficient living took root. They spent hours talking about going back to nature while London throbbed around them and nose-to-tail traffic on the A2 roared past their windows.

Enthused by her children's dreams, Dee bought a selection of country life books that gave instructions on how to grow vegetables and make your own wine. Richard Mabey's *Food For Free* and the writings of John Seymour especially appealed to her. Even Poppy, who was the least keen on leaving Blackheath, agreed it would be satisfying to harvest fruit from the hedgerows. She was a very practical child.

One evening while they were poring over their maps, the phone rang. 'Hi,' said a man's voice when Dee answered.

It was a long time since she lifted the phone expecting Ben to be on the other end of the line, but now her scalp prickled because the speaker's Edinburgh accent was very like his. So she said nothing, only swallowed and shook.

The voice said 'Hi?' again, with a questioning note this time. *It's all right. It's only Algy*, she realised in a rush of relief that made the backs of her hands prickle.

'Where are you?' she asked. He could be in Moscow or Shanghai – you never knew with him.

'I'm in London.' As usual, he wasn't specific.

'Oh,' she said, and added, 'I saw all the stuff about Philip Agee and the CIA after you went away.'

'Did you? That was a while ago now and it's all blown over. I'm back and I was wondering if I could come along and pick up my stuff.'

'Of course,' she said. 'Are you sure you're all right and nobody's tailing you or anything?'

He laughed. 'I'm fine,' he said, as casually as if he'd just been out for a pint of milk. Naturally, she thought, espionage would have appealed to him tremendously. In spite of his phlegmatic manner, there was nothing he enjoyed more than living in a continuous drama.

Her mind was wandering and she'd been silent for a few seconds so he said, 'Come on, Dee, don't mess about. When can I come for my stuff? I've nothing warm to wear in this weather.' It was bleak outside and the rain was falling.

'Tomorrow's Saturday. Come to lunch and meet my children,' she said.

After he hung up she realised she hadn't told him how to find her house and began to wonder if he'd turn up. He did, of course. He knew exactly where she lived because she'd once given him her card and he never lost things like that.

Dee took care not to tell Josie he was coming because she didn't want her dropping in to scrutinise him as a possible successor to Calum – though since his departure she had stopped urging Dee to find herself a man.

Algy arrived promptly at noon, dressed in faded jeans, loafers and a washed-out-looking checked shirt under a thin jacket. The skin of his face was so tanned that his eyes, which Dee had never particularly noticed before, looked as blue as aquamarines.

She'd made lamb koftas, surprising herself by taking a lot of trouble with the menu, chopping up red onions with tomatoes for a dip, and making cucumber and yoghurt sauce to accompany the curry. The pudding was the children's favourite – a chocolate mousse that they always asked for at their birthday parties. They all sat round the kitchen table eating, drinking beer, talking and laughing.

'Where have you been for the last six months?' she asked him.

He shrugged. 'In Spain. For a while I lived in the hills

above Granada and then, when things calmed down a bit, I went on to the coast to a village near Algeciras. It's great. There's an ancient ruined Roman town there and you can see Africa across the Strait of Gibraltar. The nearest town is called Tarifa and it's the farthest south in Europe. A ferry runs from it to Morocco.'

'Did you go to Morocco?' asked Hugo, who was fascinated by foreign places.

'Yeah, a couple of times. It's popular with Germans. I lived with a German girl there for a bit but she got fed up with me and moved on. I'm not all that keen on Germans really – I prefer the Spanish people,' he said. His eyes were alight with enthusiasm, which surprised Dee for he was usually very reticent.

'Can you speak Spanish – and German?' she asked.

'I speak good Spanish now. My German's not so hot – though I learned all the swear words,' he said and laughed as if his relationship with the German girl had been a fiery one.

'Why did you come back to London?' Dee asked. She guessed that Algy in Spain was a different man to Algy in Soho Square.

'My money ran out and the panic was over,' he replied in something more like his usual laconic delivery.

'You must like travelling,' sighed Hugo, who kept the *Reader's Digest World Atlas* under his pillow so he could read it before he went to sleep at night.

'Yes, I do, but not as much as I used to,' said Algy.

'We're going travelling soon,' said Hugo. 'Mum says when we sell this house we'll go someplace exciting.'

Algy raised his eyebrows at Dee and asked, 'You're leaving? This is a nice house.'

I can't tell him how much this house scares me. He'd think I'm crazy, she thought, so she said, 'We all want to try somewhere else. And this place is expensive to keep up . . .' Her voice trailed off but he nodded as if he understood.

'Don't go any place without leaving me your address,' he said.

'I will – provided I know where you are at the time,' laughed Dee and he laughed back.

'That's always a problem,' he agreed.

At half past four he hefted his bags, called a taxi and left without telling her where he was going or suggesting they meet again. When his cab drove off, Katie, who was watching from the kitchen window, clasped her hands together and said to her mother, 'Isn't he glamorous!'

Dee laughed. 'Glamorous! Did you think so? Oh no – he's just Algy.'

When she was told that the Carmichaels were thinking of moving, Josie had begun growing odd and distracted again. As if she was making the break before it happened, she stopped coming around so much and spent a lot of time with a new friend called Celia, who she had met in the mental hospital. Like Josie, Celia had needed treatment for depression. Through her kitchen window Dee often saw Celia drive up in a white mini to collect Josie. The two of them then went off together on mysterious expeditions, sometimes with Josie behind the wheel of the car.

Though Dee was happy that Josie was making new friends, she felt slightly abandoned and missed her friend's constant presence.

One afternoon Josie came home alone and parked the mini in the lane. Seeing Dee and Mercy looking out of the kitchen window at her, she waved and came running in through the back door. Giggling and almost like her old self, she asked without preamble, 'Do you fancy a new umbrella?'

Dee laughed and shook her head. 'No thanks. I bought another one after I left my red one in that singles' club pub.'

'Come with me and see what I've got,' said Josie, pulling at Dee's arm. Mercy followed them outside, and when Josie threw open the front door of the car, they saw a blanket-covered heap of something filling the back seat. Like a conjurer, Josie whipped off the blanket and revealed dozens of umbrellas, all piled up higgledy-piggledy. There were brollies of every size, shape and colour, striped golfing umbrellas, long elegant ladies' fashion accessories, city gentlemen's brollies and children's umbrellas with jokey heads in the shape of horses or flowers. Some had price tags dangling from their handles. There must have been at least eighty of them packed into the back of the car.

'Where on earth did you get all these?' asked Dee in amazement.

Josie, who was unusually exhilarated, threw back her head and laughed. 'You know my friend Celia? She pinched them.'

'How do you mean?' asked Mercy suspiciously, lifting a price tag and reading aloud. 'Eight pounds fifty . . . what a price!'

'She shoplifted them. From all the best shops too – Harrods, Harvey Nichols, Libertys, and Simpsons in Piccadilly. I drove the car and she went into the shops. It took us all day.'

'Why umbrellas – and why so many?' asked Dee, shaking her head in amazement. This was worse than the flower robbery.

Josie shrugged. 'Why not? Celia fancied a new umbrella and she got carried away.'

'What are you going to do with them?' asked Mercy.

'I don't know. Take one.'

Mercy drew back, dropping the price tag as if it were red hot. 'No way. Things are bad enough in my place with the stuff my old man and the boys bring in, and I don't want the coppers feeling my collar for this lot. If I was you I'd take them to the river after dark and dump the lot.'

'That'd be a pity. There's some very nice ones in there,' said Josie, closing and locking the car door.

'For God's sake, at least cover them up!' protested Dee, making Josie unlock the door and do as she was told.

Back in the house, Mercy made a pot of tea and said sternly to Dee, 'That woman's trouble. Don't get too involved with her and don't take one of them umbrellas.'

Dee laughed. 'You sound like my mother. She says Josie'll end up murdered.'

'I wouldn't be a bit surprised,' sniffed Mercy.

'But she cheers me up. She's funny – or at least she used to be – and you never know what she's going to do next,' said Dee.

'There's funny ha-ha and funny peculiar. Now she's just funny peculiar. Don't you get involved,' warned Mercy like a parent admonishing a foolish child.

Chapter Nineteen

A fter three months of raised hopes followed by disappointments, the house was still unsold and life was unvaryingly dull. Dee continued turning out articles for a variety of outlets, but her work no longer stimulated her as much as it used to. It seemed as if she was never going to escape the clutches of the house, which, as the weeks passed, seemed to grow more shabby and threatening.

The only interesting thing that happened was when Josie came storming in one day and sobbed to Dee, 'You'll never believe this! Clive's just told me that he and Celia are getting married. How can they do this to me? He was my man and I was the one who introduced them!'

Dee thought this development a lucky escape for her friend – Clive had a violent streak that he often showed – but Josie was devastated by his loss. As the days passed, she became more and more morose and spent most of her time lying on the sofa with the slimming pads on her head. Nothing Dee said could rouse her out of her torpor. The only thing that cheered her slightly was when Celia came round to tell her the engagement with Clive had been called off. It had only lasted a month.

Then everything changed. One morning Dee's phone rang and a man's voice said, 'My wife and I were wondering if you'd accept an offer of eight thousand less than the asking price for your house.'

Dee knew who was speaking. He was Lionel Green, a local Conservative party activist who she'd met at functions with

Ben. He was young, and recently married. Moreover, he had political ambitions – his dream was to stand for the local seat – so an impressive-looking house would be a good showcase for him.

Dee liked him and Beth, his pretty new wife, so her first reaction was to say, 'Are you sure you want to buy this house, Lionel?' For a moment she considered warning him off it.

'I'm absolutely set on buying it, Mrs Carmichael,' he said eagerly. 'It's a lovely house, perfect for raising a family. Beth has just discovered she's pregnant, you see. If it helps, we could go up another three thousand . . . but that's as much as we can raise.'

A drop of five thousand pounds was a disappointment, but at least it was a firm offer. 'Let me think about it,' she said carefully. 'I'll get back to you.'

All that night she wondered what she ought to do. The problem was not the price – Lionel's offer was acceptable. What she had not envisaged was being struck by conscience about selling her house. If she hadn't known the Greens it would not have bothered her so much, but smiling, pleasant Beth was pregnant . . . Was it fair to deliver these innocents up to the malice of the spirits inside the house?

She told herself, *You're being fanciful. Why should you prejudice the chance of a sale because of your fevered imaginings?*

She got up early and walked through the rooms, noting the ravages of time and heavy use by children. The pigeons were playing havoc with the roof again, but her burglar friend was not available to seal up their holes because he was in prison. The police had caught him on the roof of a factory, helping himself to lead.

Dee was desperate to sell. Why not to the Greens who were young, obviously in love, and both with good careers? The house's animus against its owners – if it did harbour such a thing – had probably worked itself out by getting rid of Ben so dramatically. It might have no evil left to direct towards any new owners.

As soon as she guessed Lionel would be in his office, she telephoned him to say, 'Yes, I'll sell the house to you for five thousand less than the asking price, provided it's a private deal and we don't go through an agent.'

He was delighted. 'Done. I didn't hear about it from an agent anyway. My mother has had her eye on it for ages. She thought you might sell after your husband died and she suggested I approach you. We've a flat in Greenwich to sell first, but it should go quickly. Will you wait till it does?'

'I'll wait,' promised Dee, feeling that the die was cast for all of them.

The family debate about where to go next grew more intense. At half-term they piled into the car and went on a tour of the West Country looking for a suitable *Good Life* property but, on their third day, Dee stopped the car in the main street of a Wiltshire village and said, 'Sorry, kids, I just don't feel right in this sort of country.'

'Why?' asked Kate, who was seduced by pretty gardens and thatched roofs.

'It's too soft. It's not my sort of place. I'd feel better in harder, more basic countryside. Some place with more open spaces and more sky. It's difficult to explain,' said Dee.

The children accepted this objection and on the way home Hugo said, 'If it's open spaces you're after, why don't we go to Australia? That's pretty basic.'

'Maybe *too* basic,' said Dee with a laugh. The idea of the Australian outback terrified her.

When they returned to London she found that Josie had disappeared again and her flat was closed up. Remembering how oddly she'd behaved before the last time she went into hospital, and how strange she'd been recently, Dee wondered if she had gone for more treatment. She decided to wait a few days before trying to find her.

While Dee was wrestling with her relocation problems, Algy phoned to let her know that he was working in central London. He invited her to call and see him next time she was in town.

'Where are you exactly?' she asked.

'In an office in Northumberland Avenue, near the Embankment end. I've something to tell you. We could go out and have a coffee or something,' he said.

Driven by curiosity about what he wanted to tell her, she went into central London a couple of days later and sought him out.

Algy's new office was in an imposing building with no address plates on the walls. A moustached and uniformed doorman said it was necessary to check that Mr Byron knew her before she could go any farther than the front door. Eventually she was shown into a starkly furnished ground floor room overlooking the street. There she found Algy sitting at a broad desk facing a dark-haired, condescending-looking man who was introduced as Major Hugh Bullivant.

She was surprised to see that, for the first time in their acquaintance, Algy was dressed like a city gent, in a dark navy pinstriped suit, a pink shirt and a boiled white collar. Bullivant was wearing similar clothes. On him they looked right. On Algy they looked ridiculous.

The desk that separated the two men was completely bare except for a device on a tripod that looked as if was used for reading microdot messages. There was nothing else of interest to be seen – not a book, photograph or picture, not even a sheet of paper or a ballpoint pen. Their office was like a waiting room in which they were simply passing time.

Bullivant was in his late thirties and very pukka – typical army officer material – but there was something unpleasant about him, and Dee thought he was probably not to be trusted with women, men, or, as Hughie would have said, with horses.

'So you're a journalist too,' he said affably to Dee as Algy explained their connection.

'Yes, I am,' she agreed.

'Why don't you go into television? I could give you a course on how to present yourself before the camera. I've done it for several people including . . .' He named a couple of women who were making their names on the box already.

'I'm quite happy doing what I do,' she said cautiously, for she did not like the condescending Bullivant and had no wish to become involved with him.

Algy suddenly stood up and said to Dee, 'Let's go out and have some coffee.'

Without speaking they walked a short distance to a tourist café near Trafalgar Square and sat at a rickety table while Algy ordered two cups of what turned out to be a vile brown brew. She knew he had something to tell her and waited for it to come out.

At first he only seemed to want to chat idly about old friends and his sojourn in Spain. She asked about Bullivant, but he told her nothing other than that he was a good enough chap. After a while, when the coffee was finished, he looked at his watch and said, 'I'd better be getting back now.'

She nodded. 'But you said you'd something to tell me?'

His manner changed as he leaned forward and said earnestly, 'What was the name of the Australian guy in Singapore who was with Ben when he died?'

'Kevin Macartney,' she said, feeling herself go cold.

'That's what I thought.' He reached into his inside pocket and brought out a small newspaper cutting that was folded down the middle. 'This'll interest you,' he said handing it to her.

She took it from him and read it swiftly. In the margin was a date and the name of a Sydney newspaper. The story consisted of only three paragraphs describing the death of a man called Kevin Macartney, aged forty-two, who had plunged to his death from the top of a parking block in the city. Mr Macartney, said the report, was employed as a hotel manager in the Sydney area and had previously worked in Singapore. The date, written in the margin in ballpoint ink, was two weeks ago.

She read the story again and then stared across the table at Algy. His face was impassive.

'Where did you get this?' she asked.

'I told you I've got friends out there. I put the word out long ago that I wanted to hear about Macartney, and one of them sent that cutting to me last week.'

'What does it mean?' she asked.

'That he jumped or was pushed. We'll never be sure either way.'

She shook her head. 'I don't know what to think,' she whispered.

He fixed his eyes on her face and said quietly, 'I'll tell you what to think. Think it's over. No matter what happened, it's over. Your Ben wasn't involved in anything undercover. I've asked about that too – he wasn't the type. If that guy Macartney had anything to do with his death, it was personal and he's paid the price.'

Dee felt as if he'd lifted a burden off her shoulders. She folded the newspaper cutting and put it in the pocket of her handbag.

Algy stood up to go, saying, 'Keep in touch, Dee.'

She nodded. 'I will. Thank you very much for doing this for me.' Her legs were shaking and she couldn't get up from her chair yet – she didn't trust herself not to faint.

As was his habit, he only grinned and went off without a backward glance.

Dee waited in the café for a little while before walking across Trafalgar Square to a number fifty-three bus stop. On the way home her mind raced around between the Macartney story and speculation about Algy's new situation. What was he up to now? Playing big boy games with Bullivant could be dangerous – perhaps too dangerous even for him, she feared.

Next morning Mercy came into the house looking unusually serious.

'It's sad about that mate of yours,' she said to Dee as the coffee pot was boiling.

'Which mate?' asked Dee, brows furrowed.

'The one that nicked the umbrellas.'

'Josie? What's happened to her?' Dee felt a terrible shiver of apprehension as she spoke. She had seen no trace of Josie for ten days, though she often went to her flat looking for signs of life.

'She did herself in, didn't she? In the hospital,' said Mercy.

The room swayed and Dee clutched the table edge in an effort to keep standing. 'Oh no. No. She can't have.' Tears filled her eyes and she started to cry. 'Poor Josie, poor, funny, sad Josie!' she sobbed.

Mercy was surprised by the force of Dee's reaction and said, 'Oh, I'm sorry for springing it on you like that but I thought you'd have heard. One of my neighbours knows her mother and she told me.'

'Her mother? You mean her mother-in-law?' asked Dee, wiping her eyes with the back of her hand.

'No, her mother. She lives beside the gasworks in Greenwich. And there's two sisters living in one of those big tower blocks in Woolwich.'

Josie had never talked about having any family nearby. In fact, she'd led Dee to believe she was an orphan without any close relatives at all.

'What happened to her? How did she do it?' she asked.

Mercy had all the details. 'She was a voluntary patient in the nuthouse, like I said. She'd been in for more of that electric shock stuff. They thought she was getting better and said she could go home. On the morning she was due to leave, she went off for a shower but didn't come back. They found her hanging from the cubicle rail. Her mother and sisters are hopping mad, talking about compensation, because they say the staff should have watched her better . . . but she was good at putting up a front.'

Dee nodded. 'She was very good at putting up a front. I'd no idea she thought about suicide. She never mentioned it and she always seemed to bounce back.'

'The ones who talk about it don't do it. It's the ones who keep their mouths shut that do,' said Mercy sagely.

A frequent sight in the street outside Dee's house was funeral cars on their way to the South London crematorium. The hearses were often heaped high with fantastic wreaths spelling out names or the words 'MUM' and 'DAD'. Sometimes the wreaths were in the shape of huge motorcycles, which signified that the deceased had died as the result of a motorbike accident. Others were made to look like big, scarlet, rose-encrusted pillow hearts – Dee wondered if they meant that a heart attack had carried the dead person off.

The cortège for Josie was much less showy. A few straggly bouquets were piled on top of her coffin, which looked pathetically small as it was carried into the crematorium chapel.

There were only eight mourners. They were led by a tired-looking old woman with dark purple bags like Josie's beneath her eyes. She was flanked by two angry-looking younger women, both with badly dyed blonde hair, a couple of shuffling men, a gangly teenage boy, Celia and Dee. There was no sign of Donnie or anyone from the middle-class family he now lived with in Beckenham.

The service was so perfunctory that it was over in a few minutes. The congregation filed out, looking as if they were anxious to be clear of the chapel as soon as possible. At the door Celia came up to Dee and clutched her arm.

'It's a tragedy, isn't it?' she said.

'Yes, it is. It's awful,' Dee agreed.

'I saw her the day before she did it. I went to visit her and she told me she was so looking forward to coming home again. We were going to drive to Brighton today. I think it must have been a mistake. I'm sure she didn't mean to do it,' said Celia in her high-pitched voice.

At that point, one of the women mourners overheard and turned towards them, saying, 'You're the neighbours, aren't you? I'm her sister Linda. It was no accident. She'd had a go at knocking herself off three times before. This time it worked. I bet she was surprised because she probably expected somebody to find her and make a big fuss, if you know what I mean. She was always showing off. Josie never thought about anybody except herself.' Linda's mouth was turned down at the corners and she looked as if she'd spent her whole life resenting her dead sister.

Dee's heart was sore. Losing her friend was more painful than she would have expected. It was hard enough to believe that prattling, hyperactive Josie had been consigned to the flames and it was even worse to listen to her sister bad-mouthing her.

'I think she must have been very unhappy,' she said.

Linda shrugged. 'Who isn't?'

'I'm going to miss her very much,' said Dee, and Celia agreed, saying, 'So will I.'

'Oh well, it's not so bad for you – you were only her friends. We're family,' said Linda dismissively.

It's not a question of *only*, thought Dee. I was her friend and she was mine. I hope Donnie will grieve for her when he's grown up and thinks about his mother, but it's possible that Celia and I are the only people here today who will really miss her. Why is the bond of friendship treated as something less important than blood links?

She turned and looked back into the shadowy chapel, remembering Josie's bravely hennaed hair, flashy jewellery, and fascination with women's magazines – especially the ones that emphasised the importance of sex. In her mind she heard the raucous laugh, and the voice crying out as she came through the door, 'What a joke. Wait till you hear this!'

Would Josie be shouting that out when she went through the Pearly Gates?

Chapter Twenty

Josie's death strengthened Dee's conviction that ill luck and malevolence hung over her house. *I've got to get away from here – as far away as possible,* she kept thinking, but, though the sale to the Greens looked like it was progressing satisfactorily, she still had no idea where she and the children were to go.

The sound of a newspaper thudding on to the doormat woke her on a sunny Sunday morning. She hated that day of the week because Ben had died on a Sunday and she always dreaded the end of the week, thinking, like Dorothy Parker, *What fresh hell is this?*

The clock by her bed told her it was only seven o'clock – too early to get up and start the day – but the lure of *The Sunday Times* forced her out of bed and she padded downstairs in bare feet to get it. Her bed was still warm but heartbreakingly empty when she climbed back into it and settled down to read.

It was nearly nine before she reached the classified section, which normally never detained her for long. As she quickly ran her eye down the 'Property for Sale' page, however, a small advertisement seemed to jump out at her. It was not highlighted or in a box and there was no reason why she should have been attracted to it.

For Sale. Near Jedburgh in the Scottish Borders, old farmhouse, 5 beds, 3 receps, 4 loose boxes, one acre paddock. Telephone . . .

The location was unspecific and it could have been anywhere within a thirty square mile radius, but for some uncanny reason, she thought she knew the house. It was as if some peculiar link had been forged between it and herself when she read the advertisement. It was calling to her.

Slightly scared by this conviction, she closed her eyes and visualised it. Though it was nearly thirty years since she'd last been there, she remembered ancient red sandstone walls and a rickety mill wheel over a little stream. Nearby there was a vast, green parkland grazed over by a herd of white deer that looked as if they should have been in an illustration for a fairy tale.

She had probably only passed that house three or four times in her life, hacking along the road to a meet of the neighbouring foxhounds, but it had made a deep impression on her, deep enough to come back vividly now.

More memories of it came flooding into her mind. She remembered Hughie pointing out the deer park and saying, 'That was where I had my first job. When I was twelve I went to work in the stables of the big house that used to stand there.' The house had burned down during the war but he reminisced admiringly about its Victorian grandeur and its privileged owner. 'Now he was a toff and a real thruster. He hunted three days a week, and jumped everything he could see,' he told Colin and Dee.

To Hughie, 'thrusters' were the equestrian elite. No matter if they ended up with broken backs, they showed their mettle and led the field. Dee and Colin were brainwashed into unthinking admiration for those daredevils, though Hughie took care to warn them not to be too impulsive. 'Your father'll kill me if you break your necks,' he said.

When they distinguished themselves by a bit of daring jumping, however, they received his full approval, which was rarely given. Any compliment from him on good riding made the long hacks home on bitter winter nights, when toes froze in the stirrup irons and icy water dripped down their backs, much more endurable.

As she lay in bed reading the advertisement she remembered Hughie pointing out the grassy mound where the thruster's mansion house once stood, shaking his head and saying, 'That's where I saw the ghost.'

Colin and she had groaned at that. 'Not another one!' Hughie had a fund of spooky stories and according to him there were ghosts all over the Borders. One of his favourite diversions was pointing out houses where there were apparitions, ghastly moanings or dragging chains. These were always mansions, never humble cottages.

'Dinna doubt it. That place had a real ghost. My hair stood up like the bristles on a porpentine when I met it in the stable yard,' he reproved the scoffers in a portentous tone.

'What did it look like?' Colin wanted to know. He always fell for Hughie's ghost stories.

'It was a tall, skinny man, in a long black cape.'

'But that could have been an innocent person out for a walk,' protested Dee, sceptical even then.

'No, it couldn't. Ordinary folk out for a walk hae a head between their shooders. This yin just had a bloody stump where his neck should be,' snapped Hughie, irritated by her lack of belief.

There was no argument against that.

Memories of the blissful past made Dee smile as she sat up and looked at the clock. It was nine fifteen – not too early to ring the number of the house for sale. She reached for the telephone and dialled. After a few rings, a woman answered.

'I've just seen the advert in *The Sunday Times*. Is the house still on the market?' asked Dee.

'Yes, it is.' The woman sounded bright and hopeful, as vendors always do when presented with a prospective purchaser.

'Before I go any further, please let me tell you which house I think it is,' said Dee.

'All right . . .' said the woman in a doubtful tone.

'It's a red sandstone house about two hundred yards off the road behind a beech wood. Beside it there's a farmyard with a wall round it and a wooden mill wheel above a little stream. On the other side of the road there's a big park where white deer graze. I don't remember its name,' Dee told her.

'Where white deer *used* to graze. They've all died out, unfortunately, or they've interbred with ordinary deer in the woods round about.'

'That's sad. They were lovely, like something from a legend,' said Dee.

'How do you know all that? We didn't put the location of the house in the advert,' said the woman.

'I just knew somehow,' said Dee. 'And if it's that house, I'm coming up to view it.'

Chapter Twenty-One

They first caught sight of Hayes House when their car rounded a sharp bend on the A68 from the south and, though none of them spoke, they were all thinking, *Oh, I hope that's it.*

A snaking stone wall ran along the left-hand side of the road. It had to be the wall of the white deer park. Dee remembered riding past it with her head barely coming over the parapet.

On the right-hand side of the road stood their objective – a comfortable-looking house with a porch built crossways between two gables, and a long shining window set above it. It looked as if it was watching for new arrivals coming up from the south, and was so pleased to see them that it was waving a welcome.

Over the centuries, bits and pieces had been added to what was originally a primitive, low-roofed cottage and stable. In ancient records it was recorded that the rent of Hayes Farm was the provision of two fighting men for the overlord. Both of the men, who had been sent to the battle of Flodden, died with the ill-fated King James IV of Scotland on that blood-soaked battlefield in 1513.

In the eighteenth century, at a time of agricultural prosperity, a first wing had been constructed on the east side of the house. A hundred years later, when farming was again doing well, another wing and gable had been added in a more imposing style. Four long, multi-paned windows faced out from it towards the main road. At that date, too, a front porch had been set in at an angle between the two wings. From the distance the porch looked like a smiling mouth.

'That's it!' cried Hugo when he spotted a fingerpost with the house name painted on it. Dee slowed down and indicated she was turning right. Everyone in the car held their breath as they jolted along a rutted lane, over a hump-backed bridge and up to a big wooden gate that marked the entrance to the garden.

A small lawn and a fringe of flower beds stood between the house and the lane. At the front stretched a paddock, bisected by a stream with mossy green banks. The paddock was screened off from the main road by a wood of mature trees – mostly beeches, but also a few oaks, two maples and a chestnut.

Hugo was the first to speak. 'Buy it, Mum. I like it.'

'I like it too,' said Katie.

Poppy said nothing, only sat and stared. She was a city child and the vast expanse of open country and fields round the house slightly appalled her.

For a moment after she switched off the ignition, Dee sat in the car and looked hard at the house. Half in love with it already because of the strange way it had manifested itself to her, she knew she had to keep telling herself, *Don't be hasty. Look for the snags. Keep your head.*

In spite of the hours she'd spent with the children debating where they should go, she'd always secretly known that she'd end up in her beloved Borderland, which was her idea of the perfect refuge. On sweltering Bombay nights, when sleep was impossible, she used to lie under the whirling fan and forget discomfort by remembering days spent on horseback, riding over undulating fields or down narrow lanes hedged by blackberry bushes and rowan trees. It had made her heart ache to remember such minute details as gateposts, gaps in stone walls, strips of woodland, or rocky outcrops where foxes always went to ground, thumbing their noses at the pursuing hounds. She was afraid that she would never see them again.

Now she was back, however. With an effort she pulled herself out of her reverie. The vendors of the house were standing on the porch, watching and smiling as the Carmichaels piled out of the car and trooped inside.

The front door opened into a long, narrow hall and staircase. At the end of the hall was a door covered with tattered green baize that led into the kitchen. The baize was a testimony to the pretensions of some previous owner because Hayes House had never been the sort of place that kept a large domestic staff, and certainly not a butler.

The front-facing drawing room had a black cast-iron Victorian fireplace in which a fire burned, but in spite of it the room was chilly and not particularly appealing. Everything was painted stark white – which added to the feeling of chill.

'We haven't put the heating on,' said the vendor's wife apologetically. 'But it warms the place up a lot. My husband installed it himself.'

Dee's heart sank when she heard that – on the two occasions that she and Ben had bought homes from do-it-yourself enthusiasts, the amateur handiwork had to be ripped out and redone.

Behind the drawing room was a gloomy dining room but, on the other side of the hall, there was a more cheerful morning room with a low ceiling and a multi-paned window looking into the side garden and the lane.

In the cavernous kitchen, little had changed since the eighteenth century. The floor was laid with large slabs of slate and there was a deep recess in one wall where the cooking had always been done. A Rayburn stove stood there now.

Beyond the main kitchen was a series of little rooms, comprising a scullery, two larders, a coalhouse, and a freezing cold bathroom, which was more than half filled by an enormous brass-tapped white bath on lion feet.

Above the kitchen, up a rickety ladder, was a charming

little servant's attic with a tiny window overlooking the garden. It had a tranquil, secretive air and Hugo's eyes lit up when they went to look at it. 'This'll be my room,' he said and sat down on a bed in the corner, laying his claim to the place.

While they were touring the kitchen again, Dee looked out of the window and saw a tramplike figure shambling down the lane from a wooded hill that rose behind the back of the garden. The woman who was selling the house saw where she was looking and said hurriedly, 'That's just Old Willie. He's a hermit who lives in a ruined cottage on the top of the hill behind us. The man who owns the land has been trying to evict him for years, but he's harmless really.'

The idea of having a resident hermit – something eighteenth-century landowners used to covet – appealed to Dee, but the use of the word 'really' put her on alert and made her doubtful about the wisdom of buying such an isolated place. There were no close neighbours. The next farm was about five hundred yards farther up the hill at the back of the house – just too far to be within earshot.

Why have I come all this way? There's nothing special here, Dee thought in disappointment. She was almost ready to call the whole thing off when they went back into the hall and climbed the main staircase. Then everything changed.

Her heart suddenly soared as she mounted the last step and found herself in a wide landing that stretched towards a tall window located directly above the front door. What made the hall magical and reassuring was the stream of golden light that flowed in through the bubbly, greenish glass of the window. It seemed to permeate the whole upper storey like a benison of bliss. Strangely, in time to come, Dee was to find that she was not alone in feeling the magic appeal of the upper hall, for several visitors to Hayes House commented on it.

She stood very still with her eyes closed for a second, warmed and reassured by the golden light. It was like being bathed in one of the streams of mystic light that used to be depicted in the religious paintings of the Middle Ages. It embraced and soothed her into happy contentment and filled her with feelings of love and confidence.

This is a kind house. This house will look after us, she thought. If, like her London home, Hayes House was haunted, this time the ghost was beneficent and meant no harm.

The decision was made. Fate had called her home. She was destined to live here.

'I'll buy your house,' she said to the surprised owner, who had barely launched into her sales spiel.

Chapter Twenty-Two

'That's very clever of you,' enthused Chris Mayne, the Carmichaels' army officer friend, when he heard that they were moving to the country. 'You're getting out of the city at the right time – civil insurrection could break out at any moment. The new crash barriers put up at Hyde Park Corner are not for cars, you know – they're to control the mobs – and the new High Court building is fortified for defence. When the cities erupt, people'll go flooding into the country for refuge,' he went on.

He was steadily gaining in seniority as the years went by and now adopted a mandarin-type air, as if he were in possession of information denied to ordinary members of the public.

Dee looked at him in horror as he calmly talked about civil insurrection and wondered if he was completely sane, but his earnestness was genuine and he seemed to want things to turn out well for her and her family.

'I hope there's a big vegetable garden in this new place of yours,' he said.

'Well, yes, there is a big garden, but—' She didn't have time to say that the vegetable garden was very overgrown by weeds and badly in need of cultivation.

'Has it a wall round it?' he asked anxiously.

'Well, in a way. At least it *had* a wall once, but it's nearly all fallen down now,' she said. In fact, it was totally collapsed in parts.

'Have it rebuilt straight away. You might have to defend

your produce. If the starving hordes rush in to the country from Edinburgh or Newcastle, you'll have to fight them off,' pronounced Chris in his best military voice.

'My God,' said Dee, half laughing at the idea of starving hordes from Newcastle pouring into her garden in search of Brussels sprouts. 'I hope it won't come to that.'

He looked hard at her, disapprovingly detecting the amusement she'd tried to hide. 'Don't be flippant and naïve, Dee. It could happen, and it's best to be prepared. The government has already made contingency plans for the breakdown of civil order, and you'd better expect it too. Buy a gun, because when the cities erupt, the mobs'll descend on the country. Law and order will break down . . .'

Dee was a sceptic, and her instinct was not to believe that sort of alarmist talk, but an irritating little voice inside her head said, *What if he's right? What am I letting myself in for by moving to the country?* She knew that Hayes House was very isolated and a woman and children defending it alone would not have a chance. Felicity Kendal and Richard Briers had a lot to answer for. Perhaps this idea was not such a good one after all. She couldn't remember John Seymour having anything to say about dealing with marauding vegetable thieves.

As the moving date grew near, these doubts almost overwhelmed Dee, who spent hours worrying in case she was making a terrible mistake. The children, however, were still enthusiastic.

Katie was especially enterprising – though under age for trading, she rented a stall at the antique market beside the Standard and sold off their surplus furniture and ornaments. Although Hayes House was big, their London home was bigger, and, after staggering sums were demanded by some of the more prestigious furniture removers to transport the Carmichael belongings from London to Scotland, they decided it was better to get rid of as much as they could rather than pay moving expenses for it.

163

After Katie and Dee pared their effects down to the bare essentials, Dee looked around for a cheaper removal firm. Eventually she found a small contractor in Woolwich who said on the telephone that he'd consider taking on the job.

She went to see him and found his shambolic yard in a back street near the Arsenal. When she walked into his cabin office, however, she warmed to him – he looked like the Irish horse traders her father used to do business with many years ago. She had fond memories of standing back and watching the interminable bargaining going on.

Like the horse traders, the contractor's skin was creased and yellow from smoking too many cigarettes, and he was totally indifferent to what he wore – his pants were baggy, his blue nylon windcheater was stained, and on his head he wore a misshapen brown felt hat that he'd probably acquired when he was demobbed. Yet in spite of the tramplike clothes, he was obviously not short of money, because one wrist was encircled by a large gold watch, the other by a chunky gold identity bracelet, and an enormous ring made out of a gold sovereign gleamed on his middle finger.

'I rang you up about taking a load of furniture to Scotland,' she said and he looked at her with his head cocked, as if he suspected she'd been sent to con a bargain out of him.

'Yeah, I remember. Where is it you're going exactly?' he asked.

'The Scottish Borders,' she said. 'I've brought a map to show you.' From her handbag she pulled a road map on which she'd traced the route to Hayes House in marker pen.

'There,' she said, laying it on his desktop.

'You on your own?' he asked. It was obvious that he was not used to doing deals with women.

She drew herself up. 'I'm moving to Scotland with my children. I'm a widow.'

He shot her another suspicious look and peered again at the map. 'That's no problem, though we don't usually take on such long trips. How much stuff have you got to transport?' he asked.

'Only one van load,' said Dee firmly. By this time she was hardened by discussions with Pickfords and Bishop's Move and knew the dialogue.

'I'll come along to your place and take a look before I give you a price,' said the contractor.

He turned up next day, and, after a bit of haggling, undertook to carry everything she wanted to go to Hayes House in one lorry and deliver it within twenty-four hours. The price he asked was less than half of that quoted by Pickfords. There was something about him – an almost fatherly surprise at what she was doing – that persuaded Dee he was worth trusting.

Before they finally settled their deal, he shoved his awful hat back on his head and said, 'Are you sure you know what you're doing, missus?'

'Not really,' she said honestly. 'But I'm going to try.'

He laughed. 'I'll get your stuff up there for you then.'

She could imagine him going home to regale his wife and family with an account of the crazy woman in the big house on the heath.

There were many things that had to be done before they left, but the first item on her list was to let Algy know where she was going. Because she had no telephone number for his office, she took the train to Charing Cross. She was disappointed to find Major Bullivant alone in the ground floor office. He looked up when she was shown in, raising his eyebrows as if querying her identity.

'I've come in to say I'm leaving London and want to tell Adam Byron where I'm going. Is he not at work today?' she said awkwardly. Bullivant made her ill at ease.

'Who?' he asked discourteously.

'Adam Byron. I came in here to see him not long ago. Don't you remember?' His blank scrutiny made her feel nervous, as if she'd become unrecognisable without realising it.

'Byron,' he repeated. 'I don't know anyone by that name.'

This was exactly how Ernest Nilsen had behaved when she'd gone looking for Algy after he disappeared in Bombay, she remembered. Maybe it was a technique they taught them in spy school. 'Well, whatever you call him, I want to leave him this,' she said pushing a card with her new address printed on it across the desk towards him.

'I've no idea who you're talking about,' he said.

She flashed him a look of disbelief and dislike, then left. There was obviously no point arguing with him. As the door closed after her, she wondered if the first thing he'd do when she left the building would be to tear up her card.

Once more Algy had done a runner. Where was he this time?

The last days in Blackheath were frantically busy. There was no time to feel ill or to worry about the future, but every now and again Dee would pause, seized by a feeling of panic, and wonder if she was doing the right thing by turning her back on London. In the city there were many outlets for a freelance writer; deep in the country the opportunities were far fewer.

Her doubts grew worse after she telephoned to tell her brother about the move and Colin asked in a concerned voice, 'What are you going to live on?'

'My writing, my articles. There's bound to be things to write about up there,' she said.

'You'll have exhausted all the possibilities in six months,' he warned her dolefully.

He's probably right, she thought and broke out in a cold sweat of worry. Not only was she taking a risk on finding work in Scotland, but she was leaving many good friends in London, people who knew her and had helped her through her troubles. It was too late to draw back now, though. She had to go. Why had it seemed such a good idea a few weeks ago?

In her heart she knew the answer. Like a sick animal going to ground, she was looking for a place to lie low till she felt better. She needed time to gather herself and lick her wounds. Her survival instinct told her that in the city she was running out of hand and would never pause long enough to get back under control. If she went on at the rate she was going, she would almost certainly break down – either physically or mentally – very soon. Her racing heart was little better in spite of the pills, and she was still obsessively grieving for Ben.

She was going back to the Borders because once before in her life she had found solace and relief from trouble there. Dee had been an anxious, worried child who lived in an atmosphere of constant tension. Then her family moved south from Dundee when she was eleven years old. Almost immediately her life changed for the better. Going to the Borders was like sailing out of a howling, manic gale into a peaceful haven.

They went there because her father bought a hotel in a little town near the junction of the rivers Tweed and Leader. It was a lovely place of wooded valleys and soft rolling hills that were a paradise of snowdrops, primroses and drifts of bluebells in the spring. Looming over all, in sombre majesty, was the mystic trio of hills called the Eildons that gathered the surrounding fields, farms and houses into their arms as if they were their protectors.

Not only did Dee find her new surroundings astonishingly beautiful – especially after the constant bustle of a crowded industrial city – but, what was more important, the move brought a cessation to the ongoing war between her parents.

Their marriage was a battlefield, but divorce was out of the question for people like them. Locked together for life, they vilified each other with words, quarrelling bitterly, loudly and frequently. Night after night, their children lay in bed with their hands over their ears trying not to hear the shouting.

Every now and again, when the dispute became really

vicious, they would be hauled out of bed by their mother and taken on long, complicated bus journeys back to the home of her parents. It always seemed that these journeys were undertaken in rain or snow, or late at night, waiting for buses that never arrived. When they arrived, they had to sleep in armchairs and listen to their mother and grandmother slandering their father.

Jean took the children with her as hostages because she knew their doting father would eventually come looking for them and be forced to make peace, always expensively. She tried to recruit Dee and Colin on to her side during these marital battles. At first Dee loyally backed her up – till she realised that her father, who she loved, was the real victim and she was being turned against him. Anything she said in response to her mother's complaints, no matter how innocent or mollifying, was later repeated back to him with added inferences so the original quarrel usually ended with her being out of favour with both parents.

Moving into the hotel – where life was lived on an open stage – put an end to the marital rowing, for Jean was acutely conscious of her image. 'What will the neighbours say?' was her constant watchword. If they still fought, they did so quietly in the privacy of their own room.

The relief this armistice brought to the children was palpable. No longer did they come home from school every afternoon worrying about what sort of drama was festering behind the front door. Their happiness was made complete because Archie had really only bought the hotel so that he could indulge his passion for horses. At the back of his new premises was a wonderful range of old coaching stables, and he set about filling them with a collection of hunters, hacks and ponies which he bought in Ireland and sold on to people in the district.

To look after this enterprise, Archie hired Hughie, a black-haired, bow-legged, alcoholic, chain-smoking womaniser, recently demobbed from the Veterinary Corps with which he'd served as a groom in Italy. Fortunately for Dee and Colin, Hughie took charge of them as well as the horses. He liked children and had time to waste with them.

In a short time Colin and Dee were recruited as eager assistants, riding the horses for sale and showing them off to purchasers. Dee, though small and skinny, was particularly useful in this regard because 'ridden by a lady' was the phrase used to describe tractable horses – often when they were anything but well mannered.

As he tutored and advised them, Hughie gave Colin and Dee their first experience of a protective, supportive relationship. Their father, though he loved them, was unreliable and unpredictable – he was over-emotional, irrational, erratic and hysterical, traumatised by his experiences in the trenches of the Somme, which haunted him till he died.

He loved to show off to his legion of friends and followers, and often demanded that his children risk their necks on flashy horses that were too much for them to handle. It was then that Hughie protested on their behalf, saying, 'Come on man, d'ye want to kill the bairns?' He probably saved their lives several times over. They trusted him and knew that he wouldn't let anything bad happen to them. If he said, 'Get on that horse,' they did as they were told.

It was to those remembered scenes of her childhood that Dee Carmichael was returning to lick her wounds. She was also hoping to recreate some of that old carefree life, both for herself and for her children.

PART THREE

SCOTLAND, 1979

Chapter Twenty-Three

The contractor from Woolwich and his young assistant whipped through the Blackheath house like a fire in a dry forest and left the place cavernous and empty. Katie, the two younger children and their dog Patch had that morning been put on the train to Edinburgh where Madeleine was to meet them and drive them to the Borders.

It was late afternoon by the time the furniture van left. Dee brushed out the empty floors before putting her two cats into baskets for their trip north. She was standing in the kitchen, leaning on the broom and thinking of the things that had happened to her there, when her neighbour Pat came in and stared into the empty rooms. 'Doesn't it look sad,' she said.

Dee shrugged. 'It'll cheer up when the new owners arrive.' In fact, now it was empty, the house seemed less sinister than it had done before. She hoped that its malevolence was sated and she had done the right thing by not warning the Greens against it. They were thrilled about moving in, so what good would a warning do now? Their die was cast, as was her own.

'Aren't you sorry to be leaving?' asked Pat, who was unaware of the terror Dee felt for the house and the malevolent spirits inside it.

'Frankly, no. I'm glad to go. It's like escaping.' Dee laughed when she said this but in truth she was afraid that the house might still try to reach out and grab her. She would not feel safe till she was miles away from it.

Pat put an arm round her shoulders and said, 'Come on.

I'll see you into your car. You've a long drive in front of you. Remember to stop and have a sleep when you feel tired.'

Immense relief was the only feeling that flooded Dee when she pulled the front door closed for the last time. She reversed out of the drive on to the A2 and as she drove away she looked back only once. The windows of the house seemed to be gleaming with malice as they watched her go.

After several hours of driving she stopped and slept for a few hours, stretched out in the back of her car beside a motorway service station halfway up the M1. She woke to one of those brilliant golden dawns that often glorify autumn. Having fed and comforted the traumatised cats, she then started to drive north again, past Scotch Corner towards the Carter Bar.

On its summit she stopped and stared down into the vast expanse of Border country. Below her the hills rolled away like vast, smooth green hassocks, kneeling pads for the gods. Sunlight was glittering over everything like fairy dust. It was so tranquil and beautiful that her heart lifted with joy. *I've come home. I'm safe*, she thought.

The rest of the journey was pure pleasure, for it was the most glorious period of autumn and the leaves of the beech trees that lined the roads were glowing in burnt orange and amber. Scarlet rosehips and purple elderberries hung in festoons over the hedgerow bushes. Gleaming, iridescent cock pheasants strolled disdainfully across the tarmac in front of her car. She took care to avoid them – it would have been sinful to kill something that looked so magnificent and was so supremely careless.

The children were comfortably installed in the house when she arrived. Hugo's face showed disappointment when he saw his mother, for they had made themselves a neat little camp in front of the Rayburn and were enjoying a picnic meal of sandwiches, potato crisps and Coca-Cola. They'd spread out beds on the floor, as if they planned to sleep there for another night.

Their dog Patch – a paranoid South London stray mongrel who obviously imagined the countryside to be full of dangers – was standing guard over them, every hair on her body bristling with suspicion.

'How's Patchy?' asked Dee, patting the dog's head.

'She doesn't like the field,' said Poppy. 'We tried to get her into it but she runs back inside all the time.' Patch obviously felt more at home with concrete under her feet.

'How are you?' asked Dee of the three children – Annie was still in Dundee and wouldn't arrive until the weekend.

'We're OK. We spoke to an old man who came into the garden and stared at us through the window,' said Hugo, who was assuming the role of chief male.

'What did he say to you?' Dee asked suspiciously.

'He just said it was a fine day, then he ran away,' they told her.

That's the hermit – I'll worry about him later, she thought.

Trailed by Patch and the children – who were already adopting proprietorial airs because they had reached the house first – she explored the new property, walking through the garden and opening the doors of the loose boxes, imagining how Hughie and her father would have enjoyed finding equine occupants for them.

It was not till three o'clock in the afternoon that she began to worry about her furniture. The twenty-four hour deadline was up at five o'clock. *What a fool you are,* she told herself. *You've put everything you own into that gypsy's van and sent him off with it. You'll probably never see any of it again.*

Rushing to the phone she rang his number in Woolwich. A woman answered, and when Dee asked for the boss she was told, 'He's out on an order.'

'Where's he gone?' she asked, hoping the answer would be Scotland.

'I dunno. Phone back tomorrow,' was the reply.

By five o'clock she was frantic. Everything they owned, including their clothes, was somewhere in limbo and she was alone in an empty house with her children, the cats and a neurotic dog.

'What'll I do?' she wailed on the phone to Madeleine.

There was a pause and her friend's voice said, 'Maybe you should have used Pickfords.'

'Oh God, don't say that. I bet he's not even insured. He didn't look like the sort who takes out insurance.'

Madeleine sighed. 'If he hasn't arrived by midnight, phone the police. I don't suppose you have his lorry registration, have you?'

'No.' Dee felt as if she'd taken leave of her senses and deserved everything that was coming to her.

In despair she drove a mile and a half to the village shop to buy some food and a bottle of whisky. *If he doesn't arrive soon, I'll drown my sorrows in drink*, she thought.

Returning to the house, she saw the old tramp lurking in her hedge, trying to hide but watching everything going on inside. *What have I done coming to this godforsaken place?* she asked herself in despair.

At half past six, as she was attempting to open a can of corned beef without a tin opener, she heard Hugo shouting from the front of the house, 'Here's the furniture van! It's coming up the lane.'

Top heavy and wavering like a mirage, it came jolting over the ruts and stopped outside the gate. The contractor jumped down from the driving seat and rubbed his hands. 'Let's get started!' he exclaimed.

Dee looked at him in consternation. 'Are you alone?' she asked. 'Have you no one to help you?'

'I had to leave the boy at home. We'll manage between us,' he said, ignoring the fact that most of the Carmichael furniture was old and solid.

She groaned. 'But the children can't carry heavy things and neither can I.'

At that moment, like a jack-in-the-box, the hermit hopped out of the hedge and came towards them rolling up his sleeves.

The contractor eyed his skeletal frame and said, 'Isn't there anybody else around to lend us a hand?'

The hermit nodded, put his fingers to his mouth and gave a piercing whistle. In a few seconds two young men appeared round the house as if they too had been waiting for the summons. There was no time for introductions. Soon it would be dark and the van had to be emptied as quickly as possible.

The three strangers handled the furniture as if it were made of cardboard, toting it up stairs and into various rooms as Dee issued directions. When everything was inside, she invited them all into the kitchen and poured glasses of whisky, which they downed while cheerfully toasting the new occupants of Hayes House.

The hermit introduced himself as William Wilson – or 'Old Willie' – and the two young men as Rob and Willie from the next-door farm. They were the nearest neighbours and, because the arrival of strangers is such a rare event in the country, they'd been eagerly anticipating getting a glimpse of the new people in the big house.

The farm boys and Old Willie had taken private wagers among themselves about how long this lot would stay. None of them guessed more than six months. Lots of people in search of the 'good life' arrived in the Borderland from distant towns with their heads full of dreams about country living – but these dreams swiftly became nightmares when the reality of hard winters, suspicious neighbours and isolation hit them.

Chapter Twenty-Four

U sed to living in London – where people went out of their way to avoid their neighbours – the Carmichaels found it strange to be the focus of intense local attention. No one came to call or was so impolite as to ask them direct questions in the local shops, but speculations about Dee's background, finances and prospects of success flew from house to house and farm to farm. Even people who had not yet set eyes on her were interested – the arrival of a woman with a clutch of children, but no man, was very unusual and suspect.

Dee remembered what it was like to live in a small community, so she simply volunteered information, believing it was better to tell the facts than to have people make things up. When meeting suppliers or tradesmen for the first time, she shook hands and told them her name, adding, 'I was brought up in the Borders. My father had a hotel here.'

When she named her father and the town where she'd lived, several people remembered Archie and his horses, and their attitude towards her softened. Even if they hadn't cared much for him – he'd had a great talent for getting into arguments – they were happy to be able to put her in context. Borderers like to be able to categorise people.

By the end of the first week, schools were found for the two youngest children and they happily went off every morning in a taxi that picked them up from the end of the lane. Hugo had the foresight to register himself in class as Hugh, which saved a lot of leg-pulling.

Katie, who'd just had her sixteenth birthday, bought a

moped and rode ten miles to the nearest big town to study for A-levels at a technical college. As the autumn days darkened into winter, she wore a fluorescent orange crash helmet and a long black astrakhan coat that she'd bought for £10 in the Standard antique market. People driving past her on the road stared at her batlike silhouette in astonishment.

Dee stayed at home and worried. It was impossible to write when the house was in chaos and, until it was set to rights, she could not expect to sell anything. She began to think that Colin was right. Nothing very newsworthy seemed to happen in the country.

The work she did for *Woman's Hour* could not continue – she discovered that there was a Scottish edition only four times a year, and all recording had to be done in Edinburgh, where she knew none of the producers. That outlet was closed to her and she had few others.

At the end of the first month, on a bleak November night after her children had gone to bed, Dee sat with Patch and the cats in the front drawing room, surrounded by the remnants of her elegant furniture that had looked so right in Blackheath but so totally out of place here. In the wardrobe upstairs lay an unworn pair of beautiful leather shoes that she'd bought in London believing them to be suitable country footwear. Her first look at the ankle-deep mud that filled the lane from November till March told her that she'd never wear them – and she never did. In the end they went to a local jumble sale with their soles unscratched.

Hayes House was basic but comfortable, though – as she'd suspected – the central heating didn't work. In spite of that, she'd made the drawing room warm by closing the old pine shutters on the two long windows. When closed and latched, they retained the heat from the fire of logs that blazed in the black cast-iron grate. A pot with a brightly flowering purple cyclamen stood on the planks in the middle of the carpetless floor, providing a splash of brave colour.

'I've blown it,' Dee said aloud to the dog, who thumped her big tail on the bare boards of the floor.

In some respects living in the country was wonderful. Her nervous spasms were lessened; she relished the loving reassurance that seemed to ooze from every part of her new house; the children were happy; and even Patch was settling down.

But she was earning nothing. Moving had been more expensive than she expected, and the small capital she'd amassed from the sale of the London house was steadily being eroded. In six to eight months, if nothing more came in, she'd be broke.

She tried to reassure herself. *Don't worry for now. Soon it'll be Christmas and we'll all be together.* Annie was coming home then and the house was perfect for old-fashioned celebrations. It gave off a feeling that it had enjoyed many happy parties before.

She decided to put off worrying till the festivities were over but, when New Year came, she'd have to launch into an all-out effort at finding gainful work. If she failed, they'd be forced to sell up and go back to London.

That prospect did not appeal and as she stared into the flames of the fire that leaped like dervishes, she remembered the tales Hughie used to tell when they sat around the tack room fireplace in wintertime. One of his favourites was about the brownies – the little fairy people – who he said lived in old Border farmhouses.

'Every old house had its own brownie,' he said, 'and if the people treated their brownie well, it'd look after them. Housewives used to put saucers of cream out on the hearth at night for the brownie to drink, and, in the morning, they'd wake up to find all their housework done.'

When she and Colin heard this story they laughed and said, 'Come on, you don't expect us to believe that, do you?'

'I tell you it's true,' he said solemnly. 'I've seen it happen.'

Amused by the memory, Dee went into the kitchen, found a saucer and poured some of the top of the milk into it. Laying it carefully by the dying fire in the sitting room, she said aloud to the dark shadows that lurked in the corners, 'All right. Don't bother about the housework. Just find me an outlet for my work and something to write about.' Then she went to bed.

Chapter Twenty-Five

After twenty-five years of living away from her native country, it was a surprise for Dee to remember that New Year's Eve was more of a significant festival than Christmas in Scotland. Christmas was not even a public holiday when she'd worked as a reporter in Edinburgh.

Not only was New Year the most important feast day, but it was always significant to the young Dee and Colin because Hogmanay – the last night of the old year – was the one occasion of the year that their father drank too much and invariably ended up weeping about the Somme. He never talked about it at any other time but, once started, he couldn't stop wallowing in horrible memories.

His tales of the trenches – of the brutality of sergeants who drove men over the side at bayonets' end, of executions for cowardice because nerves had snapped, and of his best friend who was killed by a bullet that ricocheted off his tin helmet – stayed vivid and horrific in his children's minds.

As a result, Hogmanay was always a dark time for Dee, and, particularly since Ben died, she approached the coming of every New Year with dread. For their first turn of the year in Hayes House she planned to fight off her demons by sleeping through the coming of midnight. She did not want to sit up waiting for it to strike, and be forced to review the past or to worry about the future.

However, at about seven o'clock on Hogmanay the telephone rang and a woman's voice said, 'This is Ellen, your

182

neighbour on the farm. We'd like to invite you to come up and see the New Year in with us.'

Ellen was the second wife of the farmer next door, who was the father of the boys who'd carried in the furniture. She was a smiling but cautiously reserved woman who'd spoken to Dee once or twice in the lane but had never shown any desire to develop their acquaintance further. To be invited to take part in the farm's New Year celebrations was a great compliment, however, and Dee accepted without hesitation. 'Are you sure you want us all, even the youngest ones?' she asked.

'Oh yes, bring everybody, including the bairns. This is the biggest night of the year and there's plenty of room up here,' was the reply.

Dee knew not to arrive at the party too early, because New Year celebrations never got going till midnight struck and were then expected to continue till dawn. As a compliment to her hosts, she dressed in her best green silk dress and spike-heeled Kurt Geiger shoes underneath a pale cream mink coat – the last remnant of her glory days with Ben.

At eleven o'clock the Carmichael family climbed the steep cobbled path from their garden to the farmyard's unprepossessing new bungalow. It was a sparkling night of deep, intense frost that caught at the throat. The stars glittered down on them as they walked past ancient stone byres from which they heard the peaceful sounds of animals gently settling down in straw. When they drew near to the house, a sheepdog bayed news of their arrival and the door was thrown open, casting a corridor of bright light on to the cobbled yard.

'Come in, come in. Welcome,' cried the father of the family, who everybody called the 'Old Man' without reference to any first or second names.

Inside the front room, dozens of people were sitting on rows of hard-backed chairs in front of a blazing fire. Because of the heat, everybody was sweating profusely, but every time the fire looked like it was dying down a little, someone would stand up and pile another shovelful of coals into its heart.

A display of photographs of prize rams lined the mantelpiece, and there was a glass display cabinet full of silver trophies and red rosettes won by the farm's animals at local agricultural shows.

Because the heat was so intense Dee gratefully divested herself of the mink, knowing that everybody present had noticed it. Thcy wouldn't think she was swanking, but would know she was paying her hosts a compliment by dressing in her best. Till then they'd only ever seen her in jeans, shapeless jerseys and Wellington boots.

An extended table, pushed back against the far wall, was loaded with plates of sandwiches, iced cakes, pancakes and fluffy scones liberally spread with butter and home-made jam. Hugo looked at the feast and rolled his eyes. 'Ellen's pancakes are wonderful, Mum,' he whispered.

'How do you know?' she whispered back.

'Because they invited me to tea last week,' he told her. He'd been the family's emissary and it was probably due to him that they'd earned their New Year invitation.

'Have a drink,' said the Old Man, pushing a tumbler half-full of golden-coloured liquid into Dee's hand.

She knew better than to refuse or to ask what was in it. It was whisky, of course. The only question he asked was, did she drink it with lemonade or water? Remembering Ben's scorn for people who drank lemonade with whisky, she said, 'Water,' and earned the Old Man's approval.

He poured a minuscule amount of it into the glass and watched as she downed her first sip. Almost undiluted malt whisky burned the back of her throat. She coughed, then sipped again. The moment she put her tumbler down the Old Man refilled it and went on doing so all night.

A young man with an abstracted air, who looked like a defrocked priest, responded to the urgings of the gathering to 'give us a wee song', and began singing *The Flower of*

Scotland in a fine baritone voice. The rest of the company, who had obviously been partying for some time, joined in. 'Oh Floo-er o' Scotland . . . When will we see . . . Your like again? . . .' they chanted in soulful tones. The trouble was no one knew more than three lines of the lyrics, so they sung the same words over and over again, adding more emotion and tremolo from time to time when they thought the repetition was boring.

Midnight came, announced by the booming of bells from a television set tucked away in a corner. They all stood up and everybody embraced everybody else, full of an excess of love for their fellow men and women. Joining hands and swaying in the crowded room, they started to sing *Should Auld Acquaintance Be Forgot*. Some members of the company were so moved that they wept and had to be consoled by being given more whisky.

Dee kept on sipping her drink and the host kept filling up her glass till she reached the stage when she was singing 'Oh Floo'er o' Scotland' with the best of them, though she didn't know any more of the words than they did.

By half past three Poppy was asleep like a puppy on the hearth rug. Dee's children hauled their mother to her feet, wrapped her in her coat and took her home.

During the party, the frost had taken an even deeper grip of the world. Every twig, every blade of grass glittered as if they were made of silver, and the path back down to Hayes House had frozen into a waterfall sheet of ice. Halfway down it, Dee's stiletto heels slipped from underneath her and she slid along on her mink-coated back, staring ecstatically up at a sky where the constellations glittered like diamonds.

'It's lovely. The whole world is lovely. We'll be all right here,' she cried in delight, filled with faith that her fears about the future were groundless and everything was going to turn out well.

Chapter Twenty-Six

T he New Year party broke the ice between Hayes House
and the farm. From then on the Carmichaels were taken
under their neighbours' wings and treated like wayward
relatives who must be looked after and prevented from doing
themselves too much harm.

The frost that had taken Dee's feet from under her on the
first morning of the year deepened, hardened and showed
no sign of thawing for three weeks. On several nights the
temperature dropped to fifteen degrees below freezing and
the water supply, which came from a hillside spring, froze
solid. Fortunately, Rob from next door thawed it out and got
it flowing again.

When snow drifted against the garage door so that the
car was blocked inside, he cleared it away with his tractor
and digger.

When the washing machine overflowed, he baled out the
stone-floored kitchen with a huge shovel.

When the car wouldn't start, he and his brother pushed it
down the lane till the engine fired.

Every member of the Carmichael family soon knew the
farm's phone number by heart and called them up every
time there was an emergency. If Dee needed a plumber or
an electrician, a carpenter or a supplier of dog and cat food,
all she had to do was ask the farm for a recommendation.
They knew every tradesman in the district and warned her
off the villains or the work-shy.

During the coldest, hardest days, when the sky looked like

beaten metal and the air was ominously showing that more snow was on the way, she watched Old Willie the hermit making his way down the lane early every morning carrying a metal bucket. He was on his way to fetch water from the smallholding on the other side of the main road.

This holding was owned and worked by a harassed-looking middle-aged woman who occasionally employed him as a farm hand and paid him in food and water. From time to time she could be heard berating Old Willie for some misdemeanour or other. In her youth she'd been a famous local singer and her voice was still loud enough to be heard clearly over the width of several fields.

On one of the worst mornings, when the temperature was ten degrees below freezing, Willie went down the lane wearing no overcoat, only an old sack draped over his shoulders and another tied round his waist with orange baling string. Through the kitchen window Dee watched and remembered that in a trunk in her bedroom she still had a tweed overcoat that had belonged to Ben. She'd kept it because it smelled of him and because he'd looked very dashing when wearing it.

She ran upstairs and fished it out, shaking the folds and stroking the silk lining. It was a beautiful coat. When Willie made his way back up the lane in the darkening afternoon, she was waiting for him at the gate. 'I found this in my cupboard,' she said holding out the coat, 'and I thought you might be able to wear it in the cold weather.'

He put down his bucket and took the coat graciously. His hands were deeply ingrained with dirt, as was his face, which had a few straggling grey whiskers hanging from his chin like the wispy beard of a Chinese mandarin.

'That's very kind of you, mistress,' he said and tucked the coat under his arm.

Next morning she waited eagerly, hoping to see him warm in the coat, but when he passed by on his regular trip, he was dressed in sacks as usual. Through all the winters that they knew each other, he never wore Ben's coat, and neither of them ever referred to it again. Dee learned that she must not patronise people like Willie.

He didn't hold it against her, however, and when spring came he often stopped in the lane to chat, making observations on the local wildlife. One day he told her that some ducks on a pond in the little valley beyond the farm were making their nests and would soon start raising their 'progeny'. His use of the word entranced her.

Their first winter in the country was an unusually hard one, as if it were a kind of initiation ceremony. When the snow finally melted, the paddock in front of the house burst forth in an unexpected benison of old-fashioned snowdrops with a thin line of green round their inner hearts. They covered the banks of the stream, spreading out like white satin sheets between the grey trunks of the beech trees. There were thousands of them and Dee wandered from drift to drift, gathering huge bunches that smelt divine and were never missed because there were so many. She filled jam jars with the delicate flowers and put them in every room of the house, thinking about Josie and her flower raid as she did so. Josie was one of the people from the past that she missed most.

Spring came, and the snowdrops in the paddock were followed by clusters of yellow primroses. Hazel catkins swung like tiny lamps from the branches of the bushes in the shrubbery, and birds began nesting in the pale pink clematis Montana that climbed up the front of the house.

One morning while walking Poppy to the school taxi, Dee realised that she'd not had an attack of palpitations for months. She felt fit and healthy and though Ben continued to come back to her in a series of vivid dreams, and she still missed him bitterly, she no longer brooded about him constantly.

When the lambing season began, Hugo started spending more time up at the farm than he spent at home. The men he met there called him Hugh and treated him like an equal. He thrived in their company.

'Mum,' he said one day, 'Rob says I can have two orphan lambs to raise. When I sell them I'll pay him for them and keep the profit. And he thinks we should get ourselves some hens, because we've got those four loose boxes and you're not getting a horse, are you?'

'Not at the moment,' said Dee. She had fantasised about keeping a horse but decided against it not only on grounds of expense, but also because she was scared of falling off or getting run away with – things that never worried her when she was young.

Because she'd brought only the basic furniture from London, she spent a lot of time tracking down local antique and junk shops looking for bargains. One afternoon, on a visit to one of the dealers, she saw some attractive little black hens with yellow beaks pecking around the cobbles of his yard.

'Where could I buy some hens like those?' she asked him.

His eyes lit up. 'You neednae go very far. I'll sell them to you.'

She should have known better, but had no knowledge of hens – and they were handsome little birds. 'They're grand layers. You'll get all the eggs you can eat from them, and I'll throw in a cock for good measure,' the dealer assured her.

She took her purchases home in delight and put them in one of the loose boxes. They quickly settled down in the straw, making lovely, contented clucking sounds. The children borrowed hen food from the farm and stood with their arms on the half-door watching the new acquisitions with fascination.

Soon the hens were allowed out into the garden, where they strolled about stirring up the earth with their claws, but unfortunately laying little. Occasionally an egg would be found nestling in the corner of the loose box straw, but these trophies were so rare that it somehow seemed wrong to eat them.

Sadly, after a few weeks the hens started to die. Poppy came in weeping one day and said that Bella – by this time all the hens had names – was lying dead by the back door. Grief reigned in the house – a grief that grew worse when another of the hens died.

The squeamish Carmichaels called Rob in to dispose of the corpses. He looked in on the hens every morning and, when he found another dead, went discreetly round the corner of the house carrying the latest casualty by its legs – hidden under his coat so the children didn't see it.

'What's wrong with our hens? Have they got some awful disease?' Dee asked him when the last bird turned up its toes.

'There's nothing wrong with them but old age. They're all ancient,' he said. 'Look at their legs. The skin's all crinkled and cracking. Young birds don't have skin like that. You were done when you bought them. They're too old to lay any more.'

She laughed and said, 'Well, that's a good lesson for me. I'll never buy any more hens from an antique dealer.'

The antique hens had a fortunate spin-off, however, because she sent an article about them to the *Scotsman* in Edinburgh. A couple of days later it appeared in that newspaper, illustrated with a comical little drawing. The story marked the beginning of a long and lucrative connection with the *Scotsman* for her.

The antique dealer who had sold her the hens phoned up and, instead of being angry at his castigation in print, was delighted. 'My word, that bit in the paper was really funny. Everybody's coming in here and asking me about it,' he said. Afterwards he always knocked ten per cent off his furniture prices for her.

More hens were bought – younger ones with lots of laying time before them. Hugo's lambs were fattened up by bottle-feeding and taken to market by Rob, who returned with a fold of banknotes in an envelope.

Hugo was carried away with delight at making a profit and invested some of his money in two brace of guinea fowl – beautiful-looking birds that immediately took refuge in the chestnut tree and rarely came down except to feed. All day and all night they gave voice to the most terrifying, blood-curdling screams, so nobody minded much when the foxes picked them off one by one.

The local newspaper appeared on Thursdays, and every week Hugo pored over it looking for more livestock to buy. He was dissuaded from investing in turkeys or piglets, but kept on pleading to be taken to see a goat and her kid that were advertised for two weeks running. 'Cheap to a good home,' said the ad.

'No goats,' said Dee. 'Definitely no goats. We're not the goat sort of people.'

By now she was beginning to recognise that there was a certain type of refugee from the city who arrived in the country and bought up all the animals that the wave of refugees before them were anxious to offload when the glamour of country living faded.

These were the sort of people that the farm family had obviously feared the Carmichaels were going to be. Indeed, they might well have been, if they were more efficient at self-sufficiency. As it was, they were so markedly inefficient that their neighbours took upon themselves to rescue them and thereby integrated them into local life by a sort of humorous sponsorship. The fact that Dee could claim a local connection saved them from isolation too.

Most new arrivals were not so lucky. They were usually couples with some source of unearned income or indulgent parents; they were vegetarians, teetotallers or home-brew makers, left-wing voters, idealists, conservationists, believers in flying saucers and astrology, into yoga, massage and healthy living. They rented redundant farm cottages without damp courses and painted their rooms peculiar colours. At night and on the weekends they drove in beat-up Land Rovers from isolated cottage to isolated cottage to visit each other, desperately seeking out kindred spirits. The local population shied away from them as if they had the plague.

When they first arrived, these settlers bought sheep so they could spin the wool and make primitive medieval-looking ponchos. They bought hens and geese for their eggs; goats for their milk; doves because they liked the cooing noise; cats to keep down the mice; and dogs to deter local villains who snooped round their cottages.

Burglars were attracted to them because they usually owned covetable things like record and tape players, guitars, electric mixers and bread makers, baby alarms, short-wave radios, walkie-talkies and big colour televisions.

Usually they only stayed a few years and then departed, disillusioned with country life when their money ran out. Once more their animals were up for sale.

'No goats,' repeated Dee when the ad appeared for the third week running, but she knew she was fighting a losing battle. Little by little her son wore her down and, against her better judgement, she found herself driving him to a remote cottage on top of a hill where the goat owners lived.

The wife was a friendly American girl from Chicago with a silent, long-haired, guitar-playing English husband who she'd met on the hippy trail. They wore alternative clothes and their house smelt of pot. It was decorated with flowing gauze curtains and peculiar pictures – one of which was a blown-up photograph of a human vulva surrounded by flowers. Dee hoped that Hugo wouldn't see it and ask what it was.

The couple took Dee and Hugo out to the barn to inspect the animals for sale. The mother goat was stately looking, very white, and had amber-coloured eyes with peculiar square lenses.

'She's called Ugly,' said the American owner.

'Why did you call her that?' asked Dee, who was quite taken by the goat's dowagerlike demeanour.

'Because she's ugly, that's why,' said the girl.

Ugly had a tiny female kid called Bopsie, who looked like an illustration from a child's story book – she was perky, bright-eyed and bouncy. The pair was irresistible and Hugo fell for them immediately.

'Please buy them, Mum,' he pleaded, for by this time he had spent his lamb money.

'I'm not sure. I don't know anything about goats. Will you be the one to milk the mother?' Dee asked him.

'She doesn't need milking. Bopsie's still suckling,' said the eager American girl. Seeing that Dee was still unconvinced, she added, 'If you buy them both we'll let you have them for fifteen pounds. That's what one goat normally costs round here.'

Knowing she was as bad as the most gullible 'good-lifer', Dee gave in and bought the goats.

'How will we get them home?' she asked Hugo.

'Let's put them in the back of the car,' he said. She had recently bought an old Volvo which was rapidly proving its worth as a carrier of anything and everything. After he loaded the goats into the back of the car, the hippy husband spoke for the first time.

'I say,' he pronounced in an impeccable high-class accent. 'You don't want to buy four geese, do you?'

Dee laughed. 'What the hell,' she said. 'How much do you want for them?'

'Four pounds will do,' he said. The geese went into some sacks and were put into the car too. The Hayes House mini-farm was expanding.

Chapter Twenty-Seven

'Old Willie's house is marvellous,' Hugo said one evening when he came home for tea after being absent all afternoon.

'What's marvellous about it?' asked Dee suspiciously, for Willie lived in a half-ruined cottage with ivy clambering over its walls and most of the roof collapsed.

'It's full of treasures that he finds in the dump,' said her son.

The dump was a water-filled, ancient quarry, out of which the stone for their farmhouse and Willie's cottage had originally been excavated. Local people often sneaked up there at night and threw their rubbish into it. The Carmichael children had been warned by Rob against playing on the edge of it because the water was very deep. It was a sinister place, ringed by spindly trees and avoided by everyone except those with something they were anxious to lose.

'What kind of treasures has he got?' asked Dee.

'Three hives of bees, lots of books, a violin, a baby's pram, machinery, old picture frames, sewing machines, bits of bikes – oh, and mummified rats.' Hugo had a boy's taste for the macabre.

'What?' asked his mother in horror.

'Mummified rats. He hangs the bodies from the rafters of his house and they dry out in the smoke from his fire – like kippers, he says.'

'My God, he doesn't eat them, does he?' she asked. As far as she knew Willie bought his provisions twice a week from the visiting baker's van and seemed to live entirely on sliced bread, potato crisps, Jaffa cakes and doughnuts – but she wouldn't put anything past him.

'Of course not,' said Hugo disdainfully.

'Then what does he keep them for?'

'To frighten away the other rats, of course.'

Worried by Hugo's fascination for Willie, Dee asked Ellen, 'Is it safe to let Hugo hang around Willie's place?'

'Oh yes. He wouldn't do a thing to hurt the bairns. He's a good person. It's only in the spring that he goes a bit funny, always about the time his bees start to come out and look for pollen.'

'In what way does he go funny?' Dee asked.

Ellen laughed. 'We never know, really. He surprises us every year. We wait to see what happens.'

One bright morning in March Dee opened her front door to find a little bouquet of flowers on the steps, tied round with the orange baling twine that Willie seemed to use for almost everything. Later the same day she saw him wandering in her paddock beneath the trees, with his eyes turned skywards. Surprised to see him on her property – he was usually very careful not to trespass – she went out of the front door and called, 'Are you looking for something, Willie?'

He came wandering towards her and asked, 'Have you seen Joe Bugner's monkey, mistress?'

Joe Bugner, the boxer, was much in the news, and Willie was fascinated by him – he claimed to have been a boxer himself in his youth, and to have taken part in fights in Madison Square Gardens, New York. Nobody round about believed a word of this, but nodded in pretend admiration when he told his stories.

Dee shook her head and said she hadn't seen any monkeys. 'How did it get here?' she asked.

'It came into my house this morning and stole a half-pound of butter and a bunch of grapes,' said Willie solemnly pointing at the big chestnut. 'I chased it down the hill and it's in your wood now, up that big tree. Joe's coming back for it.'

'That'll be interesting,' said Dee. 'Give me a shout when he turns up.'

'I'll do that,' said Willie. 'He'd suit you fine, for he's a fine-looking fellow.'

When Dee told the farm family about Joe Bugner's monkey, they laughed. 'That's this year's fancy,' said Ellen. 'I don't know how he thinks them up.'

'Anyway,' said young Willie cheerfully, 'it cannae be true because Old Willie's never had a bunch of grapes or half a pound of butter in that cottage of his for years.'

Dee was told that after his springtime breakout was over, Old Willie usually settled down for the rest of the year – but not always, as it turned out.

A few weeks after the Joe Bugner's monkey episode, the Carmichaels were invited, along with the rest of the district, to celebrate the twenty-first birthday of the local aristocrat's eldest son at a tea party in the community hall of a nearby village.

Hugo and Poppy were greatly excited at the idea of the party and Dee took them to the hall on the appointed afternoon. The farm family were not going because, as tenants of the lordly family, they had already been entertained to a large tenants' dinner.

The village hall was packed with non-tenants, however, all sitting round rickety card tables where tea was to be served. The din was deafening, and when the son of the peer rose to make an address he could barely make himself heard.

The Carmichaels were seated next to a table where Dee was surprised to see Old Willie making up a four with three embarrassed-looking elderly ladies who were doing their best to avoid addressing him or even looking at him. One very fat woman screwed up her face in distaste every time her eye rested on him.

He was in his usual working clothes, but had shaved

and was wearing a jacket instead of the sacks. Round the tops of his trousers he'd wound a rope – not baling twine this time.

After the speech and a delicious tea – for which all the local housewives vied with each other to produce the most feathery sponges and delectable cakes – the MC asked for volunteers to 'do a turn'.

One woman gave a comic recitation, another sang a sentimental song, and a man played the accordion. They were all politely applauded, and when there was a lull in the festivities, Old Willie jumped to his feet without introduction and announced, 'I'll do my rope trick. I used to be a cowboy in America and I learned to lasso when I was there.'

The hall fell silent as he unwound the rope from his waist, tied it into a loop, walked to the middle of the floor and spun the loop round his feet, skipping adroitly in and out of the spinning circle. He was actually very nimble for a man of his age.

Finally, with a magnificent flourish, he raised his arm and whipped the rope through the air in the direction of the most disapproving lady at his table. Over her head it went, down round her shoulders, pinning her arms to her sides. She gave a wild scream, lurched forward and knocked all the tea cups off on to the floor.

Amid the crashing of china and anguished cries from the pinioned lady, three men advanced on Willie and hustled him out of the door. 'Go home,' they hissed. 'Go away home and dinna come back.'

Dee followed them out – she did not want to see Willie get into trouble. 'I'll take him home,' she told the angry men, trying to hide her amusement.

He climbed into the back seat of the car beside the children, not showing the least bit of shame for his expulsion from the party, and chatted happily as they drove home.

'That was a grand do his lordship gave. I fair enjoyed it,' he said when he got out at Hayes House.

Is it my imagination, or does he have a mischievous glint in his eye? Dee wondered.

Chapter Twenty-Eight

A t the end of their first summer in Hayes House, when furniture collected from various antique stores was installed in the house and its rooms looked less bleak and empty, Dee invited her brother and his family – including their mother – to view the new home.

They arrived on a Sunday just before noon, and as soon as Jean was given a gin and tonic, she immediately became skittish. This could only mean that she had been drinking before she left home. She behaved as if she had seen Dee and the children only the other day, and there was no mention of Ben or enquiries about anyone in Blackheath. Dee was glad she did not have to tell her about Josie's suicide – she knew her mother would only say, 'Of course. I told you something like that would happen, didn't I?'

As they toured the house Jean was without enthusiasm, saying only, 'You'll get it looking nicer when you have more furniture.'

She had a genius for hitting where it hurt, but it was important not to rise to her bait. It had always been a matter of pride for the daughter not to show the mother when she'd scored a hit.

Before he left that evening, Colin asked, 'Have you been to see Hughie?' Like her, he treasured the memory of the man who had given them the happiest years of their childhood.

'No. He's not still alive, is he?' she said in surprise. The way Hughie smoked and drank would have killed a normal man years ago – and anyway, he must be over eighty by now.

'He's alive all right. I saw him about a year ago. He's retired and living in Galashiels. He goes to the pub on the bridge every day. Just go in there and ask for him,' said Colin with a laugh.

Hughie was easy to find. She went next day and spotted him at once, hardly changed, sitting at the end of the bar with his hands curled round a pint glass. He was pleased to see her, though it was obvious that for a few minutes he had trouble recognising who she was.

She bought him a whisky and he settled down to reminisce, talking about the adventures they'd had on the hunting field and their visits to horse shows all over southern Scotland and northern England. He remembered every place they'd won a red ticket, as well as the name of each horse they'd owned – and there had been many of them.

When she told him that she'd bought a house opposite the estate where he'd started his career, he was delighted. 'That's a grand part of the country. It's good hunting round there. Are the white deer still in the park?'

'No, they've all gone, but local people say that one big white stag might still be roaming in the woods. It was last seen a couple of years ago,' she told him.

He nodded his head approvingly. 'That's grand. I'd like to see the old place again. I saw a ghost there once, ye ken.'

She laughed. 'I'll come to fetch you on Sunday then. You can see my house, too, and meet my children,' she told him.

Before he visited, however, she decided to revive more memories by going to the Golden Lion – the hotel where she had grown up under his tutelage. It was still running in a little town fifteen miles north of Hayes House. She had been strangely reluctant to revisit it, but now she took the plunge, driving there with Poppy and Hugo.

From the outside it was unchanged – flat fronted, built of

slate-coloured stone, with ten windows facing on to the town square, which used to be cobbled but was now covered with tarmac. The hall and cocktail bar were more or less as she remembered them when she went in to introduce herself to the owner.

'I lived here thirty years ago,' she said.

He grinned – he had heard tales from the locals about the goings-on of Archie and Hughie. 'Were you one of the family that had all the horses?' he asked.

'Yes.'

'I've heard about your father and his racehorses that never won when he said they would,' he said.

'That's true,' she said ruefully.

'We've made a lot of changes to this place,' he said proudly. 'Would you like to look around?'

'Oh, yes please,' she replied.

On their tour, she was surprised to find that the hotel, which she remembered as vast and cavernous, was actually quite small. The bookcase where she'd kept her treasured library of books was still there on the top landing – but all the books had vanished.

When she went to university her parents moved out of the Golden Lion and her mother left Dee's books behind. 'A lot of old books only take up space and need dusting,' she'd said when asked about them. Dee had spent all her pocket money on books about horses and remembered the illustrated pony books, Siegfried Sassoons, a Somerville and Ross, and all her copies of Surtees' works. They had been particular favourites and 'Hellish dark and smells of cheese' was always what she and Colin replied if asked about the weather. It made people who did not recognise the Surtees reference suspect their sanity.

'Let me take you to see out the back. That's where it's most changed,' said the new owner eagerly. 'We've made a lot of improvements there.'

It was difficult to simulate enthusiasm for his new reception suite – complete with a dance floor and a plastic-veneered cocktail bar – that now stood where the old stables had been. The tack room – where they used to sit in front of the stove in the evening listening to Hughie spinning his yarns – had disappeared. So had the line of nine stalls and the four loose boxes that had housed horses ever since the days when stagecoaches used to come rattling into the big yard behind the hotel.

The round, egglike cobbles of that yard – which used to shine in iridescent colours, like pheasant necks during wet weather – were now also overlaid with smooth tarmac. The enormous stone drinking trough had gone too, as well as the tarnished brass bell with the dangling rope that used to hang above it. Long ago, travellers arriving in the middle of the night would have watered their horses at the trough and pulled the bell rope to summon an ostler. She asked if the bell was still around – she would gladly have bought it – but the hotel owner said they'd thrown it out.

As she mentally compared the modern improvements with how things used to be, Dee realised that she had lived a Victorian existence in the hotel. The life she'd known there seemed as out-of-time as a period film. It was depressing to realise that she had been cherishing memories of a long-vanished world. She never went back to the Golden Lion again.

On Sunday afternoon she cheered up when she saw Hughie waiting on the pavement outside his little house in a street of mill-workers' dwellings. He looked almost the same as she remembered him – just as in the old days, he was smartly dressed in a well-cut tweed suit that he must have owned for forty years. Old-fashioned grooms were always very dressy and had their clothes tailor-made out of the best materials.

As the old man was getting into her car, Dee complimented him on his get-up and noticed that he was wearing brown boots.

'I thought you said no gentleman ever wore brown boots,' she remarked.

He raised his eyebrows at her. 'No, they don't. It's not done. Real gentlemen never wear brown boots.'

'But you've got on brown boots,' she said.

'I'm a groom, and it's all right for the likes of me,' he said. He was always very conscious of social standing and the gradations of society.

Though they were brown, his boots shone like silk – he was expert at getting a high shine on leather and used to spend hours polishing her treasured black hunting boots with a bit of stag's horn. When he was finished she could see her face in them.

His headgear was, as usual, a cloth cap. When they were children she and Colin never saw him without a cap on his head except on hunting days, when he wore a black bowler. She wondered if he still combed his hair into a Sam Weller plastered-down kiss curl in the middle of his forehead. This curl was only revealed when he doffed his bowler to a 'toff' at the meet. Only people of title got the full salute. The bowler was raised on high to them and the curl was then shown in all its glory. The sight of it always reduced his charges to helpless giggles.

Hughie enthused about Hayes House, and especially about the four loose boxes. 'You'll have to find yourself a nice wee hunter,' he said, looking over the half-door of the biggest box.

'I can't afford to hunt any more,' she told him, not mentioning that fox-hunting was looked upon with disfavour by certain members of society nowadays. He looked at her sceptically, thinking she was telling lies.

'Ye've no' lost your nerve, have you?' he asked.

'Of course not!' she lied. In fact the thought of charging across country on a bolting horse terrified her, but it was impossible to admit that to him. His hold over her was still too strong.

'Then at least get a wee powney for the bairn,' he said, pointing at Poppy. He'd always pronounced 'pony' as 'powney'.

'I can't afford a powney either,' she said.

He made a humphing noise that she remembered signified disbelief. He wasn't going to let the subject lie.

As they walked round the garden, he paused at the broken-down garden wall, and said in a reproving way, 'That needs rebuilding.' He liked things to be tidy.

'Yes, I need a dyker but I don't know anybody who can do it,' she told him, forgetting that he'd always had a strong desire to sort out other people's lives.

'I'll find you a dyker who'll build it up for next to nothing,' he assured her. 'And I'll look for a powney for the bairn, too.'

Looking at Hughie, Dee wished she could turn back time and hire him to do for Hugo and Poppy what he'd done for Colin and herself. But she had to be realistic – he was old now and drink had ruined him. He asked her to give him a whisky instead of tea and as soon as it took effect he began to ramble incoherently. Filled with as much disappointment as she'd felt when looking round the hotel, she dropped him back at his favourite pub that evening. *When he sobers up, he'll have forgotten all about us,* she thought.

She should have known better. Hughie never forgot anything. A few days later she got a telephone call from him. 'There's a couple of animals for sale that we ought to look at. Come and fetch me tomorrow afternoon and we'll go to see them,' he said.

How he managed to hear about horse bargains all over the Borders she had never been able to fathom, but it was obvious he hadn't lost his touch.

She turned up with Poppy as ordered and, on their way to view the prospects, he cautioned her as if she were still a child, 'When we see those horses, keep quiet. You never know when to hold your tongue, so leave the talking to

me. Don't go saying how nice it is or they'll put up
the price.'

'I can't afford to buy a pony right now,' she told him again,
but he chose not to listen – he was in high spirits and chatted
merrily while they drove to a farm where a young woman
brought out a fifteen-hand mare to show them. Looking at
its rolling eyes and flaring nostrils, Dee said, 'It's far too
big and wild for Poppy. She's only seven.'

'But it'd do fine for you,' said Hughie, who was desperate
to buy a horse – any horse. Like her, he wanted to turn
back time.

'No, it won't,' said Dee firmly.

She prised Hughie away from the mare and they crossed
country again to a distant pub in the Cheviot Hills where
the landlord had a Shetland pony for sale. Dee had never
liked Shetlands – temperamental little brutes, she thought –
and was suspicious of this one because the owner said he'd
throw in the tackle if she bought the horse. He seemed a
little too eager to offload it.

'Let's put the bairn up on it and see how she gets on,'
said Hughie, who was waxing enthusiastic after having been
plied with beer by the vendor.

'But Poppy's never been on a pony before. She's only
ever ridden the donkeys at the gates of Greenwich Park,'
protested Dee.

'This pony's as quiet as a lamb,' intervened the vendor.

Hughie looked down at Poppy, who was standing beside
him looking awestruck. 'Should I give you a leg up on to
it? I'll lead you round,' he said.

Obviously his hypnotic power affected the child and she
nodded. The pony was saddled up and the little girl was
hoisted aboard. At that very moment, however, it threw
back its head, wrenching the rein out of Hughie's hand,
and headed off across the field like a bullet from a gun.

Dee screamed and watched with horror as her daughter clung frantically to the pommel of the saddle. Then

Poppy swayed, toppled and fell to the ground, where she lay still.

Terror seized Dee. 'You shouldn't have let go!' she yelled at Hughie, thinking as she ran towards her daughter that he must be drunk with all the beer he'd been given.

Please God, don't let her be hurt, she prayed as she bent over the little figure on the ground. Poppy looked up and groaned. She was winded and shaken but miraculously unharmed. In a fury, Dee picked her up and carried her back to the car, followed by a glum-looking Hughie.

I've been a fool, she thought. *I've been romanticising my past. It wasn't all wonderful. I've only been remembering the good times. In fact, I spent a lot of time being scared stiff and pretending I wasn't because I was ashamed to show cowardice. I'm not going to put Poppy through that.*

'I'm not going to buy that pony or any other pony till Poppy's been taught to ride properly, and only if she wants to,' she said firmly as they drove away.

Hughie said nothing. Even he realised that the carefree days were over.

Poppy got her mount eventually, though it was not the sort that Hughie would have chosen for her. A few weeks after the Shetland pony fiasco, the Hayes House collection of animals was increased by the arrival of Dillon the Donkey.

He was offered to the Carmichaels by a friend who hadn't enough grazing for him. 'Let him live in your paddock for the summer,' said Dee's friend, adding, 'He's very friendly and won't be any trouble, provided nobody tries to get on his back. He never lets anybody ride him – always bucks them off.'

'What is it with donkeys? They're always so contrary,' Dee sighed. In the Golden Lion, her father had owned a donkey called Patsy, who was extremely ill-tempered and terrorised their little town by biting and kicking everyone who got in its way. Archie had acquired Patsy as a luck penny from an Irish farmer when he was buying a horse from him, but he should have known there was a drawback to such an unexpected bonus. The farmer was keen to get rid of Patsy because she was too ill-tempered and old to work. She was crippled with arthritis, but still had a voracious appetite, consuming as much food as would have kept a pair of racehorses running.

As if she knew he'd saved her life, Patsy became devoted to Archie – but only to him. Just as witches have cats as familiars, Archie had his donkey who followed him into the public bar and stood with its hideous, mangy head leaning lovingly against his leg while he served pints to the customers.

Memories of Patsy made Dee reluctant to take on Dillon, but when they went to see him, he turned out to be a very handsome chap, grey and fluffy with a wide-eyed, ingenuous-looking face and perpetually forward-pricking ears. Poppy fell in love with him on sight, stroking the fur between his eyes with loving hands. To Dee's relief, Dillon did not try to bite – as Patsy would have done – and she allowed herself to be persuaded to give him the run of her paddock.

Though reluctant to demean himself by carrying anyone around, Dillon soon proved to be incorrigibly curious – he was fascinated by the other animals and the doings of his new family. If guests were gathered in the front drawing room for parties or drinks on Sundays, his furry face was always pressed up against the glass panes, watching what was going on inside. He was the animal equivalent of Old Willie, who still hid in the hedge and spied on visitors.

Poppy won Dillon round by pouring her love on him. She spent hours with him in the field, her face pressed into his neck while he endured these embraces with a soppy look on his face.

Bopsie, the young goat, also attached herself to Dillon. He yielded to her first by letting her jump up on to his back, where she stood for hours watching traffic passing by on the main road. The sight of a white kid standing on a donkey's back so enraptured busloads of tourists driving through the Borders that tour drivers started drawing up alongside the Hayes House wall so that their passengers could take photographs.

One day Poppy laid a square of cloth on Dillon's back and climbed on to it. He stood patiently and let her prod him around with her heels. There was no bucking, no kicking, no running away. Encouraged, Dee bought a felt saddle and a bridle and taught Poppy to ride him properly. The donkey and the little girl started going off on long treks through the woodlands that backed their house. Sometimes they were away for hours, with Poppy carrying a packed lunch in her pocket. Dee had total confidence that Dillon would look after her daughter and he always did. He loved Poppy and she loved him.

Dillon stayed with the Carmichaels for years, till Poppy went off to boarding school. When she left, he pined for her so much that eventually another home with children was found for him.

Though he now accepted that there would be no dashing thoroughbred hunters stabled at Hayes House, Hughie did not forgot his promise to do something about the collapsed garden wall. One day he arrived without warning, accompanied by a man who he introduced to Dee as a skilled dry-stone dyker.

Following her into the back kitchen, he whispered, 'He's a grand worker. He'll have that wall rebuilt for you in no time. All you need pay him is a fiver and a bottle of whisky.'

She looked over her shoulder at the friend who was sitting in an attitude of dejection at the kitchen table. He was quite young but extremely debauched-looking, with pouched eyes and mottled cheeks. 'Wouldn't it be better just to give him the money?' she asked.

'No, no, he'd rather have whisky. Do you have a bottle in the house?'

The first bitter winter had taught Dee that country dwellers always keep their store cupboards well stocked with everything from porridge oats to whisky – which was the traditional drink to offer visitors.

'Yes,' she replied doubtfully. Again she had the feeling that she shouldn't allow herself to be inveigled into this.

'Right then,' said Hughie, returning to the main kitchen. 'Let's get started.'

The two of them went out the back door into the vegetable garden and surveyed the tumbledown wall. It was a pleasant day so Hughie settled down on a wooden bench with a cigarette. 'OK, Alf, start on that wall,' he said and lit up.

Half-heartedly, Alf assembled the bigger stones and started piling them up. In an hour he'd rebuilt a fifth of the fallen wall, and then Hughie said to Dee, 'I think it's about time the laddie got a cup of tea.'

When she was pouring it out, he suggested, 'Maybe you could put a wee nip in it?' His power over her was so strong that she did as she was told and put whisky in his tea as well.

That was the end of the wall-building. The whisky bottle passed to and fro between them till they were incoherent and finally, in exasperation, she loaded them into her car to take them back to the town. The garden wall remained four-fifths collapsed forever.

If marauding gangs come after my potatoes, they can have them, she reflected bitterly. She was furious with Hughie but knew she had only herself to blame. Why had she not remembered the times she and Colin used to sit in parked horseboxes outside hostelries while Hughie caroused inside till closing time? Why did she not remember the anger he caused her father by his debauches? Every couple of months he would be dismissed for being drunk and given a fortnight's notice. Before the notice time was worked out, however, they'd always make it up and he'd be hired again. But she'd overlaid those memories with more palatable ones – again she'd romanticised the past.

What she had to do was get things into perspective and start living in the present. It had been a salutary lesson.

Chapter Twenty-Nine

On Hugo's fifteenth birthday, a fox terrier puppy called Towser was brought into the household. No sooner had it arrived when it began displaying symptoms of mental disturbance, attacking everyone indiscriminately – especially when the telephone rang.

Driven crazy by the ringing of the phone bell, Towser raced up and down the hall, snapping wildly. The children devised a routine of jumping into Wellington boots and grabbing a walking stick to fight off the dog before lifting the receiver.

One morning Dee answered a call from Colin. Over the frenzied barking of the dog, she heard her brother saying without preamble, 'You'd better come over at once. Mum's in hospital. She went in this morning. She's had a heart attack.'

'Is it bad?'

'Yes, I think so.'

'I'll come at once,' said Dee.

During the hour and a half drive to the other side of Scotland, she thought about her mother and was filled with guilt because she felt so little sorrow. *I must be unnatural. Surely everyone ought to love their mother?* she thought.

Jean had preached the doctrine of family love and had a selection of favourite phrases, including 'Blood's thicker than water' and 'Honour thy father and thy mother if thy days are to be long upon the earth'. She always said the last one in a portentous tone.

She never succeeded in convincing her daughter, however.

It was hard for Dee to admit, even to herself, that she didn't subscribe to her mother's doctrine. Love between people united by blood was not automatic, she thought. It had to be earned, and it was difficult to love someone who made it obvious that they did not love you back.

Dee loved her children deeply, and tried to go out of her way to praise them and not hang back from physical contact, but she knew that nobody is perfect. As a mother she had flaws too and her chief one was an obsession with work which took her away from her family for a lot of the time.

She felt guilty when she overheard Hugo saying to a friend, 'If you want to get my mother's attention, you have to go out and phone her up.' It didn't stop her working so hard, though.

The hospital in Dumfries was busy and impersonal. Jean was linked up to all sorts of monitors, but she was still beautiful and serene-looking and the only thing she wanted was the *Daily Mail* because she did its crossword every day. Dee went down to the shop to buy one and Jean smiled when it was handed over.

The nurses thought that she was out of danger and that nothing would happen during the night so, in the evening, Dee went home to the children. Before six o'clock next morning, however, Colin rang to say that their mother had died without complaint or fuss in the early hours. Neither of her children had been present.

The cremation in Carlisle was perfunctory and there were few mourners. As she surveyed the gathering in the chapel, Dee realised that she could not remember her mother ever having a single female friend or confidante. Even Colin – who had always been his mother's favourite – seemed unmoved by her death, and Dee could not force herself to weep. However, she was aware that there was an aching void in her life, and she wished she had loved her mother.

The village near Hayes House had an all-purpose shop that

sold everything from daily newspapers, firelighters and par-
affin to anchovy paste and smoked salmon. In the mornings
there was usually a queue of villagers patiently waiting for
the single male assistant to attend to their orders – which were
often extensive.

Soon after Jean's death, Dee was standing in the queue
behind a tall, erect, white-haired woman who had a cane
basket on one arm and, in defiance of a 'No Dogs' notice,
a shaggy Border terrier's lead on the other. She was dressed
in a tweed skirt and woollen twinset – the ubiquitous country
costume – and looked a typical upper-class lady.

When it came to her turn to be served, she addressed the
shopkeeper in a lofty, loud voice which showed that she
expected to be treated with deference – as indeed she was.
He bowed and scraped, saying, 'Yes, Miss . . . no, Miss . . .'
as he took her order.

The surname he gave her was unusual and caught Dee's
interest because it was the maiden name of her paternal
grandmother, who she had loved dearly and often thought
about with heart-aching affection. She had died when Dee
was eight.

When the woman turned to go, Dee heard herself saying without thinking, 'Excuse me. How do you spell your
name?'

'Sandell . . . with an 'e-l-l',' was the surprised reply.

'That's interesting. My grandmother spelled hers the same
way,' said Dee.

'Then we must be related, because there's not many people
with that name. Come to tea tomorrow afternoon.' And out
Miss Sandell stamped without another word.

The shopkeeper told Dee where the lady lived and next day,
at half past three, she turned up for tea with Poppy in tow.

Miss Sandell – whose first name, most fittingly, was
Victoria – lived in a little Georgian house tucked up at the end
of a narrow secluded lane. It looked as if it could have figured
in a novel by Jane Austen. The garden was full of burgeoning

rose bushes, and a magnificent herbaceous border surrounded a daisy-spangled lawn. Behind it there was an apple orchard where daffodils flowered under blossom-covered trees, and where Jacob sheep could be seen wandering around beside a gaggle of geese. It was a little corner of paradise.

Inside, the furnishings were slightly shabby, but comfortable and old-fashioned. Defying current prejudice, three mounted fox's brushes hung on the wall of the dining room – in her youth, Miss Sandell, like Dee, had been a keen follower of hounds.

Laid out on a large wooden tray, a repast consisting of elderflower-flavoured tea, home-made bread and honey, and a chocolate sponge with thick icing was waiting for the visitors.

The hostess quizzed Dee on her family connections and discovered that her grandmother and Miss Sandell's parents originally came from the same town.

'They must have been distant cousins,' she decided as she poured out the tea. When Dee and Poppy were leaving she said, 'Come back soon and I'll show you my family papers. Some of my ancestors – and probably yours as well – went to India with the East India Company. I've got letters from a poor fellow who died in Madras in 1801. They'll interest you as a writer.'

So my reputation has reached her, Dee noted.

Little by little, and very cautiously, their friendship grew. It became obvious that Miss Sandell's lofty manner was only a front. In fact, she was totally unsnobbish, uncritical and very kind, with an unexpectedly earthy sense of humour that made her laugh loudly at the dubious jokes Hugo saved up to tell her.

In the same way as the farm family had done, she took the Carmichaels under her wing. Through her Dee was introduced to interesting people, for Victoria had lived in the district all her life and knew everybody. She enjoyed phoning up with ideas for newspaper articles – and she had an acute instinct for what might make a good story – and infected Dee with a passion for the *Scotsman*'s crossword. Most of all, however, she undertook to educate her in good music.

She was shocked to find that Dee knew nothing of music except Gilbert and Sullivan and the jazz that she and Ben had played in the Gulmohurs. 'We must do something about that!' she exclaimed. 'I'm going to make you listen to opera.'

In 1920, Miss Sandell had been sent to be 'finished' in Florence, where she heard some of the finest singers of the time. In a cabinet in her sitting room she kept a magnificent collection of long-playing records of operas, which she played on a highly sophisticated turntable whenever Dee and the children were invited to supper. These nights were like islands of tranquillity for them all as they sprawled replete in front of a blazing fire, music flowing around them, with their dogs at their feet. Victoria Sandell was the only person who Towser was in awe of, and in her house he behaved impeccably.

When it was Edinburgh Festival time, she selected the best musical items from the programme and announced that she was taking Dee to hear a real opera. The first one they attended together was *Tosca*, which was a revelation to Dee and opened up a whole new area of enthusiasm for her.

After that, they went to the Festival together every year, taking turns to buy the programme because it would have been unthinkable for Miss Sandell to countenance buying two. Without being aware of it, they fell into a surrogate mother-and-daughter relationship – there was, after all, nearly twenty-five years' difference in their ages. Sometimes they were annoyed with each other, but that did not break their friendship. Victoria loved talking, Dee liked listening and they genuinely enjoyed each other's company.

Chapter Thirty

Five years after she left London, Dee realised that, in spite of Colin's reservations, there had been more than enough feature material in the Borders to keep her busy for years instead of months.

As one of very few freelances working a large area, she was able to sell stories to various programmes on BBC radio; to several newspapers, especially the *Scotsman*; to magazines like *Country Life*; and to many other publications – including some abroad. Whenever a good story turned up, she sold it to two or three customers, rewriting it for each outlet.

The work was tiring but exciting. Dee covered thousands of miles a year in her battered Volvo with Towser riding shotgun beside her. She drove herself on by thinking she had to keep up a flat-out pace so that she and her family could afford to live. The French had an expression for what she was doing – *le travail alimentaire*. Work in order to eat.

But now she was earning more than food money – in fact she was doing very well indeed, and she was the happiest she had been since Ben died. Her tranquillity was not even ruffled when Pat, her old London neighbour, telephoned to tell her, 'Your old house is up for sale. Guess how much they want for it?'

'I can't imagine,' said Dee.

'A quarter of a million!' said Pat. 'Don't you wish you'd waited a bit?'

'No, I don't,' said Dee truthfully. She knew that if she'd

stayed in the house, she'd have cracked up completely. Happily that danger was past now.

'Why are the Greens moving?' she asked Pat.

'Don't you know? He lost his job and they're getting a divorce!'

So the house wreaked its vengeance on them too, Dee thought, feeling guilty for not having persuaded the Greens against buying it. Her next thought was, thank God *I* got away.

She got up from her typing chair and walked across the room to look out into her garden, which had been transformed under the guidance of Victoria. There was now a deep herbaceous border packed with cuttings from her friend's garden; an elegant plum tree adorned the middle of the lawn.

In spite of the depredations of the goats – who had a strong liking for rose bushes and happily gobbled up their tender shoots – she had a pretty rose garden. Her favourite – a thorny bush covered by a mass of tightly furled pale pink rosebuds – was a Jacobite rose. It had been planted by the house wall two hundred years ago to tell passers-by that people of anti-Hanoverian sympathies would find a refuge and a welcome in Hayes House. The bush had burgeoned greatly over the last year, because the body of Towser had been interred at its roots after he'd gone dashing on to the main road and been killed by a passing car.

As she stared through the window, she saw Old Willie making his daily pilgrimage down the lane and noted that he was growing frail and thinner.

This hadn't prevented his yearly bout of madness, however, and this spring he'd been as wild as ever – in fact he had excelled himself by roping off a boxing ring at the side of the main road, stripping to the waist and performing workout exercises in full view of passing cars and buses. He chose Easter weekend for this – when the roads were busy with holiday traffic – and nearly caused several road accidents.

Hugo came home that night practically in tears because of Willie's exploit. 'I wish he'd stop carrying on like that,' he stormed. 'Everybody's talking about him and all the people on the school bus tease me. They say he's my grandfather and I can't get them to believe he isn't.'

Willie's madness only lasted a couple of days, as usual, and now he was back to his normal meek self. As she watched, he paused in the lane to exchange a few words with her gardener, who had just got off the bus.

When she realised she was earning enough money to employ help in the garden, she'd asked Rob to find someone who would be right for the job. It never ceased to amaze her how quickly the local network could operate, for Rob seemed to send out information and receive it back on the airwaves. Sometimes she saw him standing in his field, shouting gossip to a passing lorry driver, who would then carry it on to the next farm.

With his help, she found the perfect candidate for the job within a couple of days – a retired farm worker called Bobby Norris. He always arrived on the morning bus and came walking down the lane looking like a cardinal in mufti – when young, he must have been an astonishingly handsome man. Even now, in his late sixties, and though he'd spent his entire life working as a low-paid hand on Border farms, he was still incredibly impressive and dignified.

She went through to meet him at the back door. As usual, he shook her hand and said solemnly, 'Good morning, mistress.'

'Good morning, Mr Norris,' she replied – she would not have presumed to call him Bobby to his face. 'I saw you talking to Willie.'

'Oh aye, he was telling me about his time in America,' said Mr Norris.

Dee sighed. 'I'd like to go to America,' she said, and Mr Norris looked at her askance.

'No' me,' he said. 'I've never been to Edinburgh nor to Newcastle and I dinna want to go.'

218

'But Edinburgh's only an hour's journey to the north and Newcastle is an hour and a half to the south,' she exclaimed in surprise. 'They're not far. Wouldn't you like to see them?'

He shook his head. 'Aw no, mistress. I'm happy here. If I cannae see the Eildons, I'm no' easy in my mind.'

She was awed by this statement because, like him, she was very conscious of the mystical pull that the three Eildon hills exerted over all the eastern Borders. From every point of the compass, they drew eyes to them like a lodestone.

Local legend said that King Arthur lay in a cave in one of the hills, waiting for the call to sally forth and save his country. According to another legend, a mediaeval poet called Thomas the Rhymer was wandering on the Eildons one day when he was suddenly spirited away for seven years – which he thought was seven weeks – by the Queen of Faeryland.

The hills' triple summit could be seen just rising over the horizon to the north of Hayes House, and Mr Norris turned to stare in that direction as he spoke. 'If I wasnae able to see them from your garden, I wouldnae hae taken this job,' he said solemnly.

Mr Norris was one of the most contented men that Dee had ever met. He often told her with total sincerity, 'I'm a happy man, mistress. I don't think I've ever had a sad day in my life!'

How many people approaching seventy can say that? she wondered. He had achieved happiness by ignoring any bleakness that he'd ever encountered. He'd endured bitter days labouring in the fields, and a lifetime of pitiful wages and basic accommodation. In spite of that he was totally at ease with himself. His tie with his environment, and his acceptance of his life, was impressive.

Like everybody, Mr Norris had his less saintly side, too. He particularly loved gossip, and nearly always had a bit of juicy news to impart when he came to work. Because of the local network, he knew who was having an affair with who, which marriage was breaking up, and which child was not fathered by the man who thought he was its parent. He passed those tales on to Dee, though she often did not know the people involved.

'What's the latest news then?' she asked him. Immediately his ruddy face became solemn. 'Have ye heard about the man at the bowling club?' he asked.

She shook her head. 'What happened to him?'

'I was oot bowling last night, mistress,' he said, 'and Johnny Smart droppit deed on the green! He went just likc that. Doon without a word.'

'That's awful!' she exclaimed.

'And that's not all,' said Mr Norris solemnly and without any intention of being funny. 'Poor sowl. It was his turn tae bool.'

I did the right thing coming back here, though I did it for fanciful reasons, Dee thought when, laughing, she went back into the kitchen.

She had returned to the Borders hoping to recapture the happiness and security of her childhood, only to discover that her memories were romanticised. In spite of that realisation, Hayes House had become a different kind of safe world for herself and her children, though sometimes she suspected that she was hiding there, like Thomas the Rhymer in his Faeryland cave. For some unresolved reason, she was not yet ready to re-emerge and take on the outside world again.

Nevertheless, she was no hermit – she travelled a great deal for work. Annie or Katie came to look after the house when she was away, but she was always glad to return to her hiding place.

She made new friends and kept up with old ones. She met with Madeleine regularly, always in Edinburgh – Madeleine was an urbanite through and through, and hated tottering around the rough garden paths in her high heels.

Many times she thought about Algy and wondered where he had gone. She still remembered Major Bullivant's peculiar reaction when she had asked where he was, and she hoped her friend was safe. She would hate to think that Bullivant had a sinister hand in his disappearance.

When she asked Madeleine if she'd heard anything about him, the answer was always no.

'Ask any other press people you come across if they know where he is,' Dee said.

Madeleine said she would, though she added, 'I don't know why you're interested. He's the sort who just vanishes, you know.'

'He was very good to me,' said Dee, 'and I liked him. I found him amusing, though he never made jokes or anything like that. He just had an offbeat way of looking at life. His humour was very black, and mine is a bit like that too, I'm afraid.'

'I always thought he was a melancholic,' said Madeleine.

'I suppose he was at times, but aren't we all?' was Dee's reply.

In spite of her enquiries, however, none of Madeleine's contacts in Edinburgh or London knew anything about Algy – which was unusual in the small world of journalism. He'd completely vanished off the face of the earth and, since he didn't have any close friends that she knew of, and was an only child whose widowed mother was long dead, there was no chance of finding him through a family or contacts.

Though a long time passed without any word of him, Dee did not give up wondering – for some illogical reason, she felt sure that she'd see him again. After all, he'd cropped up so many times in her life before. Whenever she had to wait in crowded airports – especially during her trip to India – she found herself scrutinising the crowd, half expecting to see him go sauntering past.

Chapter Thirty-One

On her return from the Bombay trip, Dee was very unsettled. She went to Edinburgh to see Madeleine as soon as she could.

'I'm back,' she announced when she rang the doorbell of her friend's flat.

'How do you feel?' Madeleine knew how much Dee had dreaded dredging up old memories.

'It was cathartic. Revisiting the Gulmohurs was very painful, but it's made me think about everything that's happened since Ben died. It's all a bit confusing, but I'm working it out, I think.'

'I'm glad. I've thought for ages that you were still stuck in the past. In fact, I was thinking of suggesting you go to talk to someone about it,' said her friend.

'A shrink, you mean? I don't think that would help. I can work things out by myself. There's still stuff deep inside my head, but I'm getting closer to it now. I used to dream all the time that Ben came back. The other night, I dreamt it again, but this time, instead of being glad to see him, I told him to go away because everybody thinks I'm a widow! Isn't that strange?'

Madeleine laughed. 'It shows you've accepted your official status, at least. It sounds quite healthy. Have you tried wearing your ring again?' She knew about the rash that had plagued Dee's wedding-ring finger after Ben's death.

Dee spread out a bare left hand and looked at it as she spoke. 'No. I don't want to. Maybe that's the next thing I've got to work out. There's one thing I've accepted, though. I'm not looking for another husband. The last thing I want to do is get married again. I like being in charge of my own destiny. The last few years, doing my own thing, has been good for me.'

Celibacy, she realised, had not been a burden for her during the crowded years at Hayes House, probably because she was always so busy and her life was full with work and her children. From time to time she received a romantic poem from her burglar friend but the memory of her time with Calum was still making her very cautious about starting any other close relationships.

'Yes, I know what you mean. Independence is very heady for a woman,' agreed Madeleine.

'Yet there are times when I feel terribly lonely. Especially on Saturday nights. Isn't that silly! It's always then that I feel sorry for myself and think that everyone else is out enjoying themselves. Hopefully I'll get over my Saturday-night syndrome in time,' said Dee.

'Maybe you should wait till all the children have left home and then look around for a man to enhance your life,' said Madeleine.

Dee laughed. 'You make it sound like buying a new car. At my age and with my track record I guess I'll have to go for a used model.'

The persistent idea that there was something she must do now she'd confronted her fear of going back to Bombay niggled away at Dee. She thought that as soon as she sat down at her typewriter, the unacknowledged ideas would start to emerge. Very often she did not know what she thought about a subject till she put her hands on the keyboard. Then the words and ideas flowed out on their own, like automatic writing.

On a day when the house was empty and silent, she rolled a sheet of paper into her typewriter and began. Four hours later she had the first draft of a long article about coping with bereavement. It charted the various phases experienced by the bereaved, describing the stages of grief leading towards the acceptance of loss.

In the article she said that part of the healing process was to get a realistic grip on what the marriage had been – the bad bits as well as the good. When she wrote that, she was thinking not of herself but of Nellie Hallam, whose cloud-cuckoo-land version of her marriage was a way of denying her relief that her husband had died.

The article ended on a positive note, emphasising that no matter how bad everything seemed at the beginning of bereavement, a new life could be built out of the ruins of the old one. Though it did not explicitly say so, it insinuated that in some cases, widowhood should be looked on as an opportunity to start a new and better life.

She worked on it for two days and, when she was satisfied, she sent it to an upmarket woman's magazine. It was accepted by return.

However, she was still uneasy about it for reasons which she could not pinpoint. Something had been unsaid in the article, perhaps only to herself. She was dodging an important issue, but either could not or did not want to pin it down.

The weather in February took a bitter turn and, in a spasm of remorse, she remembered that she had not paid her usual Christmas visit to Hughie. As a present she always took him a dozen cans of beer and a calendar with a picture of a horse on it.

To her surprise she found his house closed up. A neighbour, peering out when she heard the knocker rattling, said, 'Looking for Hugh? He's gone, dear. He was taken to hospital last month, and now he's in the old folks' home in the Park.'

The receptionist at the home responded enthusiastically when asked for details of Mr Fairweather. 'Yes, he's here. Last room on the left,' she said. When her eyes fell on the carton of beer cans, she added, 'You're not meant to give him alcohol, but I'll pretend I didn't see it.' Even in his eighties, roguish Hughie could still win women on to his side.

In a pleasant room on the ground floor, looking out on to parkland, he lay on his bed fully dressed, reading the racing section of the *Daily Mail*. For once his cloth cap was not on his head and his hair was revealed as pure white.

At first he looked the same as usual, but then she noticed, propped up on the floor by his bed, a knee-high, hideously pink, artificial leg wearing a black sock and a brightly polished boot. It was shockingly stark, just standing there as if waiting for an order to march into action.

Seeing her horrified stare, he said, 'They took my leg off in the hospital and I was glad to be rid of it.'

From as far back as she could remember, he'd had a limp. When the pain was especially bad he smelt strongly of what he called 'antiphlegistene', a medicine he applied to the legs of injured horses. When she had asked what was wrong with him, he explained that his ailment was caused by the rowelled spurs he'd had to wear in the army. 'They grew into my heels,' he had joked.

He was pleased to see her and, as always, eager to talk over the old days. 'Look under the bed,' he said pointing downwards, 'and get out that suitcase of mine. I've some grand photeys in it.'

Beneath his bed he kept the same small leather suit-case that he had toted around with him nearly fifty years ago. It contained everything he owned. Dee remembered it being ceremoniously packed every time her father gave Hughie notice.

She laid it on the bed beside him and he asked her to take out some creased and folded black-and-white photographs. Nearly all of them were of Colin and herself mounted on various horses. He remembered all their names and charac-teristics. 'That's Bovril. Mind how he'd only go over bridges backwards . . . and here's wee Dorinda – my word, could she jump . . .' he said, happily going back to the past.

225

A cardboard-backed photograph was lying face down at the bottom of the case. Dee turned it over and saw that it was a wedding picture. The groom, with black plastered-down hair and a broad grin, was Hughie. The bride, a sparky-looking girl in a flower-decorated hat and a skimpy dress, clung to his arm glowing in triumph. As soon as she lifted it up, he recoiled and snapped, 'Put that away.'

She did as she was told, but a memory of the drama about Hughie's marriage came back into her mind. She remembered that, while he was in the army during the war, his wife, a local mill girl, had gone around with men from a battalion of Polish soldiers based in the Borders. Whether it really went further than mere flirtation, no one really knew, but some malicious 'friend' wrote to tell Hughie that his wife was carrying on with the Poles.

He was furious. On his return he refused to meet her and every attempt she made to see him was cruelly rebuffed – as far as he was concerned, their marriage was over. She was sure she could win him round if she could only speak to him, so from time to time she turned up at the hotel and asked Dee's father to intercede with her husband.

Archie would then go out into the stable yard and engage the groom in earnest colloquy, but Hughie would only shake his head violently until his boss gave up and returned to the bar. Being a man who was always courteous to women, he gave Hughie's weeping wife a large gin and orange and escorted her to the next bus back to town, slipping a ten-shilling note into her hand to pay the fare.

Dee remembered that the rejected wife looked like the cartoon character 'Jane' from the *Daily Express* – short, bottle-blonde and busty. For her visits to the hotel she always dressed in tarty clothes and impossibly high-heeled red shoes with ankle straps. She obviously intended to attract his eye, but to no avail – he'd never let her near him.

Strangely, though everybody knew that he had a series of ongoing affairs with women working in the hotel, no one blamed him for the way he treated his wife. *It's so unfair!* thought young Dee, who was on the side of the eager and pathetic wife.

One day she waited for her father in front of the hotel after he'd put Hughie's wife on to a bus. 'Why won't he speak to her?' she asked.

Her father looked mournful. 'Because she's a high-stepper,' he told her.

'But he's not innocent himself,' she said indignantly.

'There's different rules for men and for women,' said Archie.

As she closed up Hughie's old suitcase, Dee longed to ask what had happened to the girl in the photograph, but knew better than to try. That night, however, when she phoned Colin to tell him about Hughie's leg, she asked him, 'Do you remember his wife, the high-stepper? What happened to her?'

Her brother sighed. 'Don't you know? That was a sad business. After we left the hotel, he got a job as head groom at the stables of a big house on the river Tweed, and she kept trying to see him there too. One day he threw her out of the stable yard and that night she came back after dark, walked into the river, and drowned herself.'

Dee wished she hadn't asked. It seemed that every time she turned over the stone of an old memory, something unpleasant or disappointing was lurking underneath it.

Chapter Thirty-Two

T he bitter weather continued. Steel-grey skies showed that more snow was on the way, and the air was suspiciously still, as if the world was holding its breath in anticipation of an onslaught.

On a cruel night of driving sleet, a figure went staggering up the yard and hammered at the farmhouse door. Ellen answered it to find what she first thought was a bundle of rags on the step. In fact, it was Old Willie bleeding from a gastric haemorrhage. 'I think I'm sick,' he muttered when she bent over him.

An ambulance was called and he was taken off to hospital.

'They don't think he'll live,' Rob told the Carmichaels next morning.

But Old Willie was not to be written off so easily. A week later, news came through that he was on the way to recovery, at least temporarily. It had been discovered that he was suffering from stomach cancer.

Dee went to visit the old man, carrying a bunch of snowdrops gathered from the drifts of flowers that surrounded his cottage. As always, he accepted the gift graciously.

'This is a grand place,' he told her, looking round the ward. 'They give you the best food I've ever tasted.'

He was a model patient during his stay in hospital. On discharge, he was sent to a local old people's home, where he quickly took over the care of patients less fortunate than himself. A blind man especially relied on Willie to take him outside, something the overworked staff had not been able to do very often. The two old men were seen every day going arm in arm up and down the main street of Jedburgh.

One day, Willie was brought back to his cottage by a social worker to salvage some of his possessions. The landowner was demolishing the ruins and selling the land for building.

Willie's neighbours were apprehensive that revisiting his old home would make him nostalgic, but that was not the case. 'I wouldna want to be back here,' he told them when he called in at the farm for a cup of tea. 'There's central heating where I am now and it's like heaven.'

Three months later he died. For years he'd kept his age a secret but his death certificate now revealed he was eighty-seven. His spartan life had obviously done him little harm.

Dee went with the farm family to his funeral. After a short ceremony in the old people's home, the coffin was taken to a remote and tranquil burying ground, deep in the hills above Hawick. There, beneath a tall cypress tree, William Wilson was laid to rest beside his parents. His father, he'd told Dee, had been a farm shepherd whose greatest achievement, in the eyes of his son, was his ability to walk on his hands – a feat he once performed going up the Waverley Steps in Edinburgh.

There was a fair number of people at the ceremony, among them a smart-looking American woman who was Willie's niece from Washington. She said that Willie and her father – Willie's brother – had emigrated to America together as young men. The brother started a carpenter's business and thrived, ending up a rich man. Willie, always a romantic wanderer, went off to be a cowboy and eventually took up boxing, fighting as a bantam weight for a while in Madison Square Gardens.

During the drive home, the mourners talked about Willie and regretted that they had never believed his stories about being a boxer. 'He wasn't telling lies after all. So maybe Joe Bugner's monkey really was running wild in my wood,' said Dee.

*   *   *

At the end of the summer it was time for another Edinburgh Festival. Months ago, Victoria had selected the best items from the programme and, in continuance of Dee's musical education, persuaded her to buy tickets for the opera.

'What one is it this year?' Dee asked. Under Victoria's guidance, she was becoming an enthusiast.

'It's *The Pearl Fishers*. You must hear it,' was the reply.

They had a routine for their opera outings by this time. Because Victoria was growing too old to drive to Edinburgh, Dee was the chauffeur and Victoria provided a picnic tea, which they ate in the parked car before the performance began. It would have been unthinkable to spend money going to a restaurant or café.

The food was always the same – sandwiches made from home-made bread and filled with pâté, freshly baked cake, tea in a flask for Dee and coffee for Victoria. In the interval, they treated themselves to chocolate ice creams, taking turns to pay. The feeling of continuity was comforting and Dee would have been concerned if the routine ever changed.

The opera was magnificent, but during the walk back to the car, Victoria suddenly said, 'My legs hurt a bit. Take my arm please, my dear.'

When Dee took her friend's arm, she was overwhelmed by an uprush of affection for the old woman. Victoria, though she did not know it, was filling a void in her heart. Now Dee realised that, if she could have chosen a mother, or had one made to her own special design, it would have been Victoria.

On their drive home that night, while crossing the summit of Soutra Hill, Victoria gazed up at an azure-coloured night sky spangled with stars and said, 'When I'm out on a night like this I'm always astonished at my good luck to be alive. We're so lucky to be living in this beautiful part of the world.'

'That's true,' agreed Dee. 'I feel the same. I'm only just beginning to realise that it's possible to be happy again.'

'You have to work at it,' said Victoria. 'Every night I go to bed and say my prayers and think about the things that make me happy – my garden, the animals, having enough money to live on and my health. I lie and think "I'm happy", and it makes me so grateful.'

She awed Dee. At her age and with her disabilities – arthritis was rapidly crippling her – many people would have descended into crabbiness, but not Victoria.

I'll always remember her, and if I'm lucky enough to be as old as she is, I'll try to model myself on her, Dee thought.

Chapter Thirty-Three

Lines of rowan trees heavy with fruit edged the narrow road that climbed into the heart of the Cheviot Hills. Bunches of glowing berries – yellow, orange, deep tangerine and scarlet – weighed the branches down, an autumn bounty for the birds. Dee, driving to interview a farmer who still worked his land with horses and refused to use tractors, was filled with happiness.

The sky was pale blue and cloudless as it arched above her. Birds cruised lazily over heather-covered hills. A long double row of stone walls stretched towards the horizon, marking the line of the road to York laid out nearly two thousand years ago by the Romans. There was not a soul to be seen, not a sound to be heard.

In a moment of transcendental awareness she heard herself saying aloud, 'Victoria's right. I'm happy.' She'd broken through.

It was like recovering sight after being blind, and she thought that people who experienced religious revelations must feel as she did at that moment. The feeling of happiness danced in front of her tantalisingly, but still, somewhere at the back of her mind, there was a shadow, an unresolved conflict. Before the secret music could come back into her mind, she must bring it into the open.

A short time later, while browsing in her bookshelves, she came upon a dog-eared copy of Thomas Mann's *The Magic Mountain*.

She remembered starting to read it when she was pregnant with Poppy. Every time she had a baby, she associated the pregnancy with a particular book. Annie's was *Son of Oscar Wilde*, which had been given to her by her friend Shadiv; Katie's was Virginia Woolf's *Orlando*, Hugo's was Anthony Powell's *Books Do Furnish a Room* and Poppy's had been the Thomas Mann. The baby was delivered before *The Magic Mountain* was finished, however.

Leafing through its pages to find where she'd left off, she was surprised to see that the book's endpaper was covered with her own scrawled handwriting. The words she had written transfixed her, forcing her to sit down suddenly because, for the first time in ages, her heart started to beat uncontrollably.

'What am I going to do? I can't see any way out,' it began. As she read, the misery of the woman who had written these words came back and engulfed her.

Lonely, unhappy, with no one to talk to, she'd sat in a large and beautiful house outside Manchester and written a letter to herself. Exiled from friends, with her marriage on the rocks, she had three small children and another on the way. She had no money of her own and no confidence that she would ever be able to earn any. Her life-force and enthusiasm were badly eroded and she was on the verge of melancholia.

Looking back on that terrible time of disillusion, she was stabbed by a painful memory of bitter unhappiness.

The miserable missive, scrawled inside the book like a message in a bottle from a desert island, went on, 'I am so unhappy. I can't see any way out. I'm trapped. If I left, I'd have four children to support and we wouldn't be able to survive because he'd give us nothing.'

She remembered how desperate she was then, at the worst time of their marriage. Ben had a mortgage on the house, but had paid little or nothing of it back. He had no life insurance and no savings – he lived on a perpetual overdraft. Though he was a very high earner, he was improvident and his money seemed to disappear. If she sued for divorce, she would probably be awarded alimony and child support, but if he had no funds, how could he pay any of it?

Shocked by this unexpected glimpse of her deliberately forgotten past, Dee stopped reading, got up and went to pour herself a drink – she knew she was going to need it. Long-suppressed and unwanted memories started crowding into her mind, jostling for her attention.

How could I have been so blinkered for so long? How did I manage to completely shut all this misery out of my mind? she asked herself.

As someone who was suspicious of shrinks and psychiatry, it was difficult for her to accept that her memory could play such tricks on her. Yet, now that her awareness had been triggered, she knew that the memories had been there all the time, waiting for her to look at them. She was every bit as bad as Nellie Hallam, every bit as self-deceiving.

Her re-examination of the past began by remembering Ben's last phone call. It had never really been forgotten, of course. The trouble was that she must have censored that memory too.

Time after time she told people that she found it difficult to accept he was dead because he'd telephoned her the night before he died and was perfectly all right then. What she did not say, and did not accept till now, was that though *he*'d been all right, *she* was not. With her new clear-sightedness she knew that Ben's last phone call had deeply antagonised and worried her. It set up a conflict in her mind that had to be resolved. Only his unexpected death prevented that resolution from happening.

With the memory muffler stripped away, she was now able to recreate the phone call almost word for word. Ben had been drunk and his speech was slurred. 'It's all over,' he told her. 'I've lost the contract. The Japanese got it. I've only just heard. It's not official yet but they'll announce it to the press on Monday.'

She knew how much that contract meant to him. He'd been working on it for over a year, making trip after trip to Singapore, and, when at home, telephoning contacts in the middle of the night. He'd been smoking heavily and drinking too much, living on his nerves. He knew that his career depended on pulling off this big job. At one time she would have been as distraught as he was about the loss of the contract, but as she listened to him she felt completely calm, almost detached.

'You'll be all right. You'll get another job,' she told him. 'You should go back to India.' She had unconsciously said 'you' instead of 'we'.

Going back was his only hope really, and perhaps the only hope for their marriage as well, because India was where they had been happy and in his career, he'd been far more effective there than he had ever been since he came back to Europe. In India he was surrounded by able men who supported him fully, who believed in him, and she'd been involved in his business life there too, helping to keep his feet on the ground. Left to himself he tended to take his eye off the main concern and be diverted by trivialities.

When he was offered his big chance of a senior job in Manchester by Lord Affleck, he'd been determined to keep her out of his business life, for he wanted to prove – if only to himself – that he could go it alone. He'd blown it, however.

The engineering company he'd been brought in to pull together was never put back on its feet because Ben, the new managing director, went off touring the world looking for orders that never materialised.

Instead of concentrating on serious things, he spent money redecorating his office, modelling it on a tycoon's with a desk in the middle of the floor so that people had to walk towards him like acolytes towards an altar.

When the news spread that Ben Carmichael had landed a big job at home, letters of application from old ex-India friends and acquaintances began to arrive. One was delivered to the Carmichaels' home and Ben read it to Dee over the breakfast table.

'It's from Alex Allan,' he told her, 'He's looking for a job in PR.'

'I thought he went to Australia after he left Bombay,' she said. Alex, an old rugby friend of Ben's, was idle and subversive, amusing in conversation but unreliable as far as work went and always highly critical of his employers.

'He doesn't like it. He wants to come back home,' said Ben, re-reading the letter.

'Don't hire him,' she said.

He looked hard at her. 'He's my friend. I owe him.'

'Don't hire him,' she repeated.

He didn't listen and she could see that he thought she was hard. Alex was eventually fired, but not before he undermined Ben's authority and judgement with the rest of his employees and, more importantly, with the men who had brought him in to sort out the ailing company.

Lord Affleck would never have let Ben go when the company was sold after three years if he'd come up to expectations. Ben knew that, and she did too, though they had never talked about it.

In his last telephone call, when she said he should go back to India, he wailed brokenly, 'I can't.' She could tell from his voice, however, that going back was what he really wanted to do – turn back the clock and start again. He had many contacts in India and still wasn't too old – only forty-three, after all.

It was at this stage of the phone call that he became maudlin, saying over and over again how much he loved her. 'I love you, you know that, don't you? I've been telling everybody in the bar here what a wonderful woman you are,' he said.

Her hackles rose. It embarrassed her when he began saying how much he loved her in public – something he'd taken to doing a lot lately, especially when drunk. She particularly loathed the idea of him sitting in a hotel bar boring strangers with his maudlin outpourings. She felt herself to be demeaned by them. But perhaps he knew that she was drifting away and wanted to hold on to her.

Unaware of her resentment, however, he went on. 'I want us to start again. I want you to buy me a wedding ring for Christmas. When I come home I want to tell you everything. I've not been a good husband, you see. You know that, don't you?'

Acutely conscious of her mother hovering in the hall listening to the conversation, Dee said stiffly, 'Yes. I know that.'

'I want to tell you everything. I want to get it off my chest.'

Her resentment increased as she realised that he wanted to clear his conscience about the mess their marriage had become. He was casting her as a confessor and, presumably, he fully expected that, when he poured out his story, she would forgive him.

It never occurred to him that she might not. In the past, even at the worst times, she'd not left him, but now she had moved so far away that it was impossible to return. If he opened up his secrets and confirmed her worst fears, their marriage would be over.

'Will you buy me a wedding ring?' he repeated.

She stiffened and her hand on the telephone went white with the effort of holding it to her ear. She had never asked him to wear a wedding ring. It was not important to her, but he'd frequently scoffed at men who did sport rings, so it obviously mattered to him. Presumably he found it easier to lie about his marital status without one.

Looking back, she knew without a shadow of a doubt that Calum had been right when he said that Ben had been a serial adulterer. She'd known all along really. That must be why her body had rejected the ring that represented their marriage.

She did not reply to his wedding ring request, but her mind

was saying, *No way am I going to buy you a wedding ring. It just doesn't matter any longer.*

'I want us to talk about it. I want to tell you everything,' he repeated.

'You should go and lie down – you've been drinking too much,' she said sternly.

'I know I'm drunk but I want to tell you how much I love you. I've lost the contract and I don't know what's going to happen now . . .'

When his career went on the slide so did their marriage. She knew very well that he chased easy sex as an ego boost. Several times he'd taunted her with hints about the 'mile high club', where travellers had sex with strangers on planes – usually in the lavatories. She never rose to his bait, but watched coldly and dispassionately while he flirted with other women at parties. He was not above making assignations with those who were prepared to take him up on his offer, and little by little his behaviour became more blatant, as if he were trying to force her into challenging him.

The memory still rankled of the last New Year's Eve party they had attended together at the house of friends in Chelsea. Ben got very drunk and started pestering a pretty woman whose husband grabbed him by the lapels and told him to leave her alone. Though it was not yet midnight, the host and hostess persuaded him to leave and loaded him into the car, where he immediately passed out. Dee left with him and drove to Trafalgar Square, suddenly taken by a desire to watch other people being happy. Creeping slowly along the road while young revellers blew paper trumpets at the windows of the car, she thought, *What am I doing here with this man? I want out of this.*

Over three miserable years she'd gone through a gamut of emotions from desperate hurt and self-criticism to cold distrust and despair – but, as she had written in the back of *The Magic Mountain*, she was trapped and could see no way out. So she built a protective carapace around herself, hiding her feelings. That shell was still there, shutting her off from forming another relationship, making it impossible to trust another man.

She had to accept that his death had solved her problem. As a widow, she received a state pension, and the company, in spite of themselves, for they were probably planning to fire him, were stuck with paying for his funeral and establishing a trust fund for his wife and children.

The fund they set up had its capital halved in the stock market collapse but by that time Dee was on her own feet and it did not matter to her so much. She had never honestly felt she was entitled to that money anyway and dissolved what was left of the trust by distributing the remaining fund among her children.

Now she could look dispassionately at what had happened, she realised that Ben's death was not the tragedy she had once thought it was. With her illusions stripped away, she could hardly believe how fortunate she had been.

But at what a cost – his life. And her mental stability – paradoxically, she had loved him, and truly mourned him.

What she'd gone through, what confused her for so long, were the combined emotions arising from disillusion and bereavement at the same time. Part of her grieved; the other part felt tremendous relief. Because of that conflict, it had taken ten years to recover from his death. She'd needed a lot of cruel self-examination to bring the two parts of her reactions together.

In tears she lowered her head into her hands, remembering how Madeleine thought that Ben had been murdered. Perhaps Madeleine was right. Perhaps the person who killed him, by wishing him gone, was his wife. They'd been engaged in a duel to the death and she had won.

It made her feel as guilty as if she'd stabbed him in the heart.

Chapter Thirty-Four

H ugo was the first to really leave home.
Uninterested in school, he'd found a job as a trainee shepherd on a nearby farm. After a year of working there, however, he came home one evening and announced, 'I've bought a ticket for Australia, Mum.'

Dee was standing at the cooker, stirring soup, and felt a weird stabbing pain in her heart as she listened to him. 'When are you going?' she asked, without turning round.

'Next week,' he replied. There was a pause and he said, 'I'm using my trust money. You don't mind, do you?'

'I think it's a good idea. You've got to see the world. But we don't know anyone out there,' she said. Inside she was thinking, *You're the first of my children to leave me. The tight little cocoon I've built around myself is breaking apart.*

She had to let him go, though. It would be selfish to try to hold on, and in a way she knew she was herself responsible for encouraging his desire for adventure – she'd told him stories about her father, who'd run away to Canada when he was only fifteen.

The family was shrinking. Katie had gone to university in Durham where she was studying English and Annie was working for a magazine in Edinburgh, but, though they were no longer living in the house full time, they came back frequently – it was almost as if they had never really gone away.

A week later she drove Hugo to London. When she dropped him off at Heathrow, he did not want her to go into the Departures entrance with him.

'I'll just get off here. Don't hang around, Mum,' he said when she drove up the concrete ramp. She had to fight against breaking down in tears – she knew it would agonise him if he saw her weeping. They hugged each other desperately and then he left.

Dee's heart was breaking as she watched her skinny son, with his thatch of unruly yellow hair, trudging into the thronged departure hall, weighed down by a huge backpack. To her he still looked as if he were only fourteen years old.

Will I ever see him again? How will he manage out in the big, cruel world? Oh God, I can't bear it, she was thinking as she drove away with tears pouring down her cheeks.

Back at Hayes House, she and Poppy attempted to clear out Hugo's eyrie above the kitchen. It took them days – he had lived in happy squalor for years, refusing to let anyone up the rickety stairs to clean his room. They brushed down festoons of cobwebs from the eaves and pushed Polyfilla into the holes he'd made in the wainscoting by shooting at mice from his bed.

As she put his treasures into cardboard boxes, Dee wept some more and wondered how her little boy was coping so far away. The way she felt made her sympathise with her father, who could not disguise his anguish when she announced she was going to live in Bombay.

The loss of Hugo was still hurting when Poppy came home in tears from school one evening. At first she would not tell Dee what was the matter, but eventually it was coaxed out of her. 'I hate that school,' she said. She'd been supremely happy in the little village school, where there were only two classes and rarely more than twenty pupils, but a year ago, she'd been transferred to a large primary school in the town seven miles away.

'Why do you hate it?' Dee asked.

'Some of the girls bully me because they say I'm a snob and talk funny. I've spoken to the teacher but she never does anything about it.'

Poppy was a resilient child who rarely complained, so Dee knew that her distress was genuine. She went to the school herself, but the headmaster proved to be both ineffectual and indifferent. Poppy's sufferings at the hands of her classmates did not improve.

Eventually she told her mother, 'My friend Marion's going to boarding school because she's being bullied too. Her parents are sending her to a place in St Andrews. I wish I could go to boarding school.'

Dee phoned Madeleine. 'You went to a boarding school, didn't you?' she asked.

'Yes, I did. Why?'

'Was it in St Andrews?'

'Yes . . .' The tone was guarded.

'What was it like?'

'Sheer hell. When I left I swore that if I ever had a daughter, I'd never send her there. Why do you ask?' said Madeleine.

'Poppy wants to go to boarding school. Her only friend is going to St Andrews, you see, and she's miserable where she is. I think living here on her own with me is not right for her anyway, because it's going to be difficult to have a social life when she gets bigger. She'll have to be taken to and fro by her mother all the time. There's no fun in that.'

Dee, who had also lived seven miles from her school, remembered going to dances and having to leave before the last waltz because Hughie was waiting outside in her father's car to drive her home. The last waltz was always important because it was then that the boys swooped on the girl of their choice. No one ever got the chance to swoop on her.

'Don't send her to an all-girls school then. Try to find her a co-ed one,' advised Madeleine, who had bad memories of growing up in an all-female establishment.

They researched the market and found a suitable school. Dee did her sums to see if she could afford the fees. The answer was 'yes, just about', so Poppy was enrolled for September.

A school trunk was bought and packed with clothes from the prescribed list. Even Poppy's nail brush had to be inscribed with her name. As more and more things were laid in the trunk, Dee's spirits sank and her daughter's rose.

The school was about sixty miles from home, in a pleasant and prosperous-looking mid-Scotland town. They drove there in a state of high excitement and when Dee drew up at the front door of the Victorian villa which was to be Poppy's home for the next five years, she had to restrain herself from saying, 'Don't leave me, Poppy. I don't want to live on my own.'

They had been close companions for so long that it was hard to imagine living without her daughter who, from childhood, had always said, 'When I grow up I'm going to buy a little cottage so you and I can live together, Mummy.'

That was not the life that Dee wanted for her child, however, and she had to face reality. She had raised her children to be independent, so it was her own fault if they wanted to move on.

The trunk was not heavy and they carried it into the house together. Poppy's bed was in a long room on the first floor and she immediately set about putting her new duvet cover on the quilt and setting her teddy bear against the pillows. Dee watched this in hidden distress, very aware that Poppy wanted her to leave. She was anxious to move into the next phase of her life, to become independent.

'I'd better go then,' said Dee lamely.

'Yes,' agreed Poppy. 'Goodbye, Mum. I'll be all right. Don't worry. It's only six weeks till half-term.' She was saying the sort of things that mothers were meant to say to weepy children, not the other way around.

Back home Hayes House seemed sad and empty, as if it too was feeling abandoned. Dee opened the front door and walked into the silent hall feeling the brooding sense of an empty house gather in around her. She slumped down heavily on the bottom step of the stairs with her handbag still hanging from her shoulder.

As she sat there she was aware, for the very first time since she'd moved in, that she could hear all the clocks ticking. There had never been such a profound silence in the house before.

Tick, tock, tick, tock, they went in unison – led by the big grandfather clock in the hall, followed by her grandmother's Westminster chimes clock on the drawing room mantelpiece; and the carriage clock that stood beside the telephone. They were playing the background music to what was to be a solitary life from now on.

PART FOUR

TARIFA, 1989

Chapter Thirty-Five

The telephone rang early on a bright March morning and Dee reached out from bed to grab it. Always frightened by unexpected or early calls – especially now that all her children were scattered – she was barely able to speak when she held it to her ear.

'Is that you, Dee? This is Robert Crawford.'

Relief filled her. He was Victoria's next-door neighbour – a fussy, retired academic with a passion for gardening.

'Yes?' she managed to say. The clock by her bed told her it was five minutes to eight. *Why is he calling so early?* she wondered.

'I'm sorry to have to tell you, but Victoria was found collapsed in her kitchen this morning by her daily woman. We think she had a stroke. I've sent for the ambulance but I'm afraid she's dead,' he said dolefully.

'I'm coming,' she said, and jumped on to the floor.

Victoria's house was only five minutes away. As Dee's car tyres crunched over the gravel of the drive, she saw how orderly the garden looked with the beds all dug over and the rose bushes neatly pruned. The old lady had obviously spent a vigorous few days in it preparing for the coming summer. A grave-faced Robert was standing in the open kitchen doorway with Victoria's daily help hovering behind him.

'The ambulance has taken her to hospital. She wasn't dead after all, only unconscious,' he said. He was even older than Victoria and his lined face looked grey and drawn.

'Thank heavens she's alive. I'll go there now,' said Dee,

and ran back to her car. Her mind was a complete blank, as if she was not capable of coherent thought. She drove ten miles to the general hospital, where she tracked Victoria down in a busy, crowded ward on the first floor.

Her mentor, who had always appeared so tall and imposing before, now seemed tiny – almost childlike – as she lay there with her thinning grey hair spread out on a pillow. Her body was swathed in aluminium foil – it made her look like a female knight in armour, a kind of aged Joan of Arc.

'She's suffering from hypothermia. We think she'd been lying on her kitchen floor since yesterday and it was very cold last night,' said the nurse by Victoria's bed.

'Is she conscious?' Dee asked.

'No. She doesn't know what's happening. There's not much hope for her, I'm afraid,' said the nurse dolefully.

Dee sat down by the bed and took Victoria's wrinkled, work-chapped hand in hers. There were still some grains of earth from the garden in her fingernails.

'It's Dee, Victoria,' she said, stroking the hand gently. A gentle mew, like the sound of a hungry kitten, came from the old woman, and Dee knew that though Victoria was not able to open her eyes or say anything, she was aware that her friend was with her.

Eight hours later, like a flickering fire going out, she died painlessly with her hand still in Dee's. She never made another sound.

There was nothing to do then but get up and leave.

Victoria's family all lived in England and would have to be informed of the death by a lawyer. Trustees and lawyers would take over the formalities, arrange the funeral, sell the pretty little house with its cherished garden, get rid of the beloved sheep and the geese. The shaggy little Border terrier had died six months ago, and, looking back, Dee realised that Victoria had gone into a gentle decline since then.

Dee could not bear to think of her old friend's special world disappearing. With an indescribable pain in her heart, she drove home to an empty house and sat in the kitchen drinking whisky till it was time to go to bed. As she leaned her elbows on the kitchen table she remembered everything Victoria had done for her.

She had given her a lesson in living, she had nurtured her love of flowers and gardening, and she had educated her in music. But above all, she had taken the place of the mother Dee had always yearned for – a woman to admire and to emulate.

'My only aim in life is to be happy,' Victoria had once said, but her pursuit of happiness did not entail taking things from other people. Her happiness came from within. Dee laid her head down on the table among the used supper dishes and wept. *I don't believe in life after death, but I know Victoria did. I hope, if it does exist, that she's very happy now*, she thought.

Victoria was buried in a peaceful little graveyard beside a meandering river, in a plot beneath an ancient, low-branched yew tree. Dee and her girls stood at the back of the group of official family members, many of whom rarely saw the dead woman. When the coffin slid into its fold in the ground, it struck Dee as appropriate that Victoria's body should be returning to the earth, to nourish more growing things. Dee resolved that, before the little house was sold, she'd dig up some of her friend's favourite plants – especially the dog-tooth violets of which she had been so fond – and spangle them in the grass that covered her.

It was hard to remember that Victoria was not just a short distance down the road. It was hard not to lift the phone every morning to make sure she was all right. It was hard to drive past the lane that led to her house without turning in.

The grieving she did for her friend was more therapeutic than the tears she had shed for Ben. The way she missed Victoria was more philosophical, and she became more accepting of her own mortality as she went through it. It concentrated her mind and made her more accepting, as Victoria had always been.

About a month after the funeral service, a letter arrived from an Edinburgh lawyer who informed her that, among her bequests, the late Miss Sandell had left Mrs Carmichael a legacy of seven thousand pounds – as well as the same amount for each of the Carmichael children.

'It's amazing,' Dee told her daughters on the telephone. 'I'm so pleased because it means that she thought of us as family, just as we did about her.'

It also meant that Victoria had never been as hard up as Dee imagined, and the memory of their surreptitious tea parties outside opera houses to avoid paying for meals in restaurants and cafés made her laugh. Victoria had never believed in unnecessary spending.

When Dee's cheque finally arrived she was ill in bed with bronchitis, racked by coughing fits. The cheque and its accompanying letter lay under a glass of barley water on her bedside table, and was splashed with drops by the time she felt well enough to pay it into the bank.

As she signed the counterfoil she asked herself, *What would Victoria want me to do with this money? Why did she leave it to me?*

She knew her old friend well enough to realise that it would be a disappointment if it were frittered away on new clothes or another car. It should be spent on something really worthwhile, something genuinely life-enhancing.

She folded the counterfoil and put it into her pocket. 'I'll only spend it on something that would please you,' she said to Victoria's memory.

Chapter Thirty-Six

Weakness and a hacking cough – a legacy of her bronchitis – dragged on through the spring and summer. Depression, something which had not bothered her since she returned to the Borders, took hold of her. It deepened when she heard that Hughie had died in his retirement home at the age of eighty-nine.

No one had let her know about him – he had few relatives and they would not have known about Dee and Colin's affection for the old man. He'd been dead for three months by the time she found out.

Dee felt that all the people who were important in her life were disappearing. She was very lonely and began to regret her solitary state. She was so lonely that she even started reading the 'Contacts' columns in newspapers and magazines – but could not summon up the courage to answer any of the entries.

With all three older children away from home most of the time, and Poppy on the verge of going to art college in London, Hayes House reflected its owner's solitude. It missed the children's hustle and bustle – the hot water always running, the constant telephoning, the revving of car engines, the smell of midnight cooking – things that had at one time been annoyances to Dee but were now remembered with longing.

Surrounded by empty rooms, she was conscious that the house too longed for company. It wanted to be hospitable, to have voices ringing through the passages and people banging doors. In a way she felt she was letting it down by living in it alone. Whenever people visited, or when any of her family came home, the house perked up like an old person who had been sleeping and woke eager for entertainment.

For the sake of it, if for nothing else, she began to think about moving again, but the effort it would require appalled her. She simply did not have the strength to change her situation.

When she went to her doctor to ask for a tonic that would give her more energy, he looked at her levelly and said, 'Isn't it time you had a holiday?'

'A holiday?' she asked in surprise. 'But I was in Paris on a story in March and I've been down to London twice since then to see some editors—'

'I mean a real holiday. Not meeting people or interviewing people, but doing nothing except lying in the sun and sleeping all afternoon. That's the sort of holiday you need,' he said.

She sighed. She'd not had a holiday like that since her time in India. A group of friends used to repair to a hill station called Mahabaleshwar during the hot weather. In those days she'd taken leisurely walks through the little bazaar in the mornings, slept away silent afternoons, read lots of books and played bridge under a hissing tilley lamp at night. It all seemed so idyllic and long ago.

'I can't afford that kind of time off,' she told the doctor. For years she'd only taken holidays that she could write about afterwards so that she could earn back the expense.

He frowned. 'You can't afford *not* to have that kind of holiday,' he said sternly. 'Think about it.'

She thought about it for several days, until, impressed by the doctor's solemnity, she decided that the best use for Victoria's legacy was to spend it on a holiday in the hope that it would help her to recuperate from her current malaise. She could imagine Victoria approving of that idea.

Where will I go? she asked herself. It was as difficult a question as deciding where to take the family when the London house was sold.

It would be fun to go to New York at last, but perhaps Manhattan was not exactly the sort of holiday resort her doctor had in mind when he told her she needed a break for rest and recuperation.

She loved France, but driving along French roads on one's own was not much fun. Perhaps it would be more interesting to seek out a different destination.

For years she had disdained Spain as the resort of the masses in search of beer and beaches, but it kept popping into her mind as a possible destination. Why?

Because you've never been there, she told herself.

But you've never been to Sweden or South Africa and you don't want to go there, do you? was her silent reply.

So why did she suddenly think she ought to go to Spain?

Somewhere else kept popping into her mind as well – Cyprus. She'd never been there either and, till now, had never felt any great desire to go.

So why Cyprus? Why Spain? she wondered.

Eventually she had to accept that the *raison d'être* of this holiday was a search for Algy. These were the two places he claimed to love best in the world and, in particular, she remembered his glowing enthusiasm when he talked about the little town in Spain where he'd hidden out during the CIA crisis.

Maybe she'd go on a sort of pilgrimage in his steps. If, when he disappeared the last time, he'd gone on the run again, it seemed likely he'd return to the places he enjoyed, where life was familiar. Even if he was no longer alive, perhaps she'd be able to pick up some trace of him, and reconcile herself to the idea of never seeing him again.

Why did he matter? Perhaps because he'd been a background figure in her life for so long – even before she met Ben. She remembered how much she owed him, though they often went for long periods without meeting. It had always been reassuring to think he was somewhere around.

She missed him and it was important to be able to put an end to his story.

Don't be stupid, said the sensible section of her mind. *Wandering across Europe looking for him would be like looking for the clichéd needle in a haystack. Besides, how do you know he's still alive? He's probably dead, or you'd have heard from him by now.*

Something told her he was still alive, however. The certainty was purely irrational, but she clung to the idea. *One day, I might turn a corner and bump right into him.*

That was why she still scanned the faces of people in airports.

You're being daft, scoffed her logical side again. *Pick a pleasant holiday resort, just to be in the sun. Don't expect anything unusual to happen or you'll be disappointed.*

The local travel agent's office displayed brightly coloured brochures advertising various Spanish resorts where there was 'all-night entertainment'. She read a few and discarded them before turning to brochures on Cyprus which, more discreetly, tried to attract a different kind of custom.

After leafing through a few of them, she asked a man at the counter, 'Are there any brochures for Kyrenia? These ones are all for the Greek parts of Cyprus.' Kyrenia was the place that Algy had talked about with such enthusiasm.

He looked scornful. 'Nobody goes to Kyrenia any more. It was taken over by the Turks. All the Greek-owned hotels were ransacked and the tourist trade's ruined.'

A ruined tourist trade appealed to Dee more than a thriving one, so she asked, 'But can't tourists still go there?'

'It's difficult. You have to sail from some little port in Turkey. We don't do the bookings from here, I'm afraid. If it's sunshine you're after, what about going to Portugal?'

'No thanks. If I can't go to Kyrenia, it'll have to be Spain,' she said.

He brightened. 'I've some good deals for Barcelona. Or Marbella. It's very nice in Marbella. Sean Connery lives near there.'

She shook her head. It was not an inducement to go. 'Actually, I'm trying to remember the name of the place I'd like to visit. I think it's the most southerly town in Europe. Do you know the one I mean?'

'Gibraltar!' he said in triumph. 'Now that would be very nice for you. There's lots of British people, lots of shops and they even have a branch of Marks and Spencer there.'

She backed away from the desk wondering if she looked like the sort of person who'd want to go abroad so she could shop at Marks and Sparks. She didn't even like it in Edinburgh.

'That's not the place,' she told him. 'I'll find out what it's called and let you know.'

'You do that,' he said indifferently. Dee could tell he'd given her up as an unprofitable case.

That night, using Hugo's world atlas, she found the little Spanish town of Tarifa – a mere spot on the map a few inches along the page from Gibraltar but indubitably further south when she measured it with a ruler. That was the place Algy said he'd lived near when he bolted from London after the CIA débâcle.

She'd go and have a look at it, keeping back enough of Victoria's money to take a trip to Kyrenia if Tarifa was a disappointment. Surely it had something special to offer if he liked it so much, though.

She didn't return to the travel agent, and instead spent two days packing up her car with a bag of casual clothes, books, binoculars, camera and film, suntan oil, tapes for listening to while driving, a road map of Spain, boiled sweets for sucking, bottles of mineral water, and chocolate bars, dried bananas and digestive biscuits to stave off hunger pangs.

Deliberately, she did not pack a tape recorder or a reporter's notebook – things which always used to be the first items into her suitcase when she travelled.

She parked old Patch the dog with Annie in Edinburgh and gave the house keys to the people at the farm, who promised to feed her other animals.

On September sixth, at six o'clock in the morning, as the sun beamed down through the trees of her wood, Dee jumped into the car, turned the ignition key and headed off down the road to England. She was exhilarated and already feeling healthier.

That night she reached Plymouth, and the next day she was on the ferry to Santander.

The day after that her car rolled off the boat on to Spanish soil.

Chapter Thirty-Seven

It was almost as if Victoria was sitting beside her and approving of everything as she went bowling along with the roof of her little Citroën – a relatively recent purchase – open and the sun beaming down on her.

She could feel radiance filling her lungs, clearing up the bronchitis and banishing her cough. As the days went by she began to feel better, younger, more optimistic. It was wonderful to be loose and carefree, not always worrying that she wouldn't find a subject to write about.

From the cassette player came the voice of an actor reading Thomas Hardy's *Far From the Madding Crowd*. She spoke along with the tape, voicing her thoughts aloud, unafraid that she would be overheard and thought peculiar.

For once she was not in a hurry. She planned to be away for a month and was determined that, though her final destination was the deep south, she would see as much of Spain as she could.

Poppy was safely in school – she'd gone back for her last year the day before Dee left home. Annie was making a name for herself as a news reporter in Edinburgh. Katie had graduated with a first-class degree and found a job in the office of a London literary agent. Hugo was still wandering through Australia.

They were all perfectly capable of looking after themselves, and the anxiety about them that used to haunt her when they were younger had dissipated. She certainly did not want to become a hanger-on to her children, as her mother had been to her.

The time had come to make arrangements for her own future. Most of all, she wanted to stop being lonely. 'When I get back from Spain, I'll enrol with one of those dating agencies,' she promised herself. It was not matrimony she was seeking but, in spite of her brave words to Madeleine, and her genuine enjoyment of calling her own tune, she did not want to spend the rest of her life alone. She craved male companionship. She wanted a lover.

Her rage against Ben had dissipated and she could look back on her life with him dispassionately, realising that there had been faults on her side as well as his. When they argued, especially in the last years, she had never drawn back from telling him that it was her who pulled his strings. No wonder he rebelled!

In the glove compartment of the car was a road map and a Baedeker travel guide for Spain. On the ship going over, she'd marked on the map places she wanted to visit – Santiago de Compostela, Coruña, Avila, Mérida, Seville, Jerez, Cádiz, Cape Trafalgar and, finally Tarifa.

The last town on her personal odyssey was not listed in Baedeker. Perhaps that meant it would be tourist free. She hoped so. Once she'd seen it and made enquiries about Algy – the outcome of which she really had little hope – she planned to head back to Santander again by autoroute.

Santiago de Compostela, which she reached by secondary roads after three days, was a disappointment because it was so sinister. The walls of the buildings were hung with drifting grey moss that was reminiscent of Miss Haversham's house in *Great Expectations*. Every street smelt of incense.

The huge cathedral, a centre for pilgrimage for centuries, was blood-chilling. She stood beneath a giant eye painted in the centre of its dome, and looking up at it, felt sure that she was being watched by a god, but not a merciful one. The god up there was the god of the Inquisition and the bloodiest crusades, a cruel, merciless deity. Before gloom could overwhelm her, she drove away from the horrible place and headed for somewhere more cheerful.

At the end of the first week, she found herself in Mérida. 'This is a wonderful place, a Roman town with so many ancient buildings that it's like going back to when it was founded. If a legionary in a toga comes striding down the street I won't be a bit surprised,' she wrote to Madeleine on a postcard.

As if she was putting off reaching her final destination because she was afraid of disappointment, she retraced her route to Avila. Stunned by the sight, she stopped the car as she approached the town and gazed in astonishment at the vast range of city walls that made it look like a place from a mediaeval romance. It delayed her for two days because there was so much to see.

When she left she was heading for Seville. And after that? With her finger she traced a route – Seville to Jerez, Jerez to Cádiz, Cádiz to Tarifa. As she grew nearer to her objective, she thought more and more that her search for Algy was nonsensical. What she was really doing was making a whistle-stop tour of Spain, and she had to content herself with that.

Driving along, she realised that one of the reasons she spoke aloud all the time was because she hardly ever heard a human voice. She knew no Spanish and communicated with people in hotels by smiling and pointing at phrases in her phrase book. In one town, unable to find a place to stay, she was given an escort to a suitable hotel by two friendly policemen in a squad car. Everyone was friendly and courteous, although they often seemed surprised at seeing an older woman driving through the back roads of Spain on her own.

'I don't want to spend the rest of my life alone like this,' she heard herself saying aloud one day.

But not just any company would do. The company of her

children had cocooned her from loneliness for a long time but now that they were leading their own lives, she badly needed someone she could talk to, someone to amuse and accompany her, someone with whom she shared enthusiasms and, ideally, with whom she could share a bed at night.

Algy certainly didn't fill the bill of the ideal companion. True, he'd always amused her with his dry cynicism, but he'd been married three times and there must have been a reason why each of these marriages had ended in trouble. Besides, he'd never given any sign of wanting to form a relationship with her. She was just another one of his protégés, one of the people he helped because he liked doing it.

And yet, and yet . . . she wanted to find him again if possible – or at least she wanted to put a tidy end to his story and stop wondering if he was still alive. That was why she was driving all the way across Spain, after all.

'What a joke! You're crazy,' she said to herself and laughed aloud, knowing that Algy would find it amusing too. She laughed a lot as she drove along, amused by thoughts that kept popping into her head. This trip to Spain seemed to be clearing away the last of her demons.

In Jerez, on a bright sunny morning, she sat in a street café pretending to read her guidebook, but actually watching through her sunglasses as a smartly dressed couple about her own age sat bickering at the next table. The conversation between them was strained and the man was barely able to conceal his irritability. The woman was querulous, and her voice had a shrill note to it as she harangued him. 'You never listen to me, do you?' she said at one stage.

'Why should I?' was his reply.

Would Ben and I have ended up like that? Dee thought, but mentally shook her head. They would almost certainly not still be married if he were alive today. It would have been impossible for her to go on living with him if he'd come home and unburdened himself of his infidelities. She had a pretty good idea that more than one of them would have proved to be a very unpleasant surprise for her. It didn't matter any longer, though.

After Jerez, her last major stop was Cádiz, a city that attracted her more than any of the other places she'd visited. She spent a night there and the next day wandered through the old town under vast white sunshades that stretched over the streets to keep the sun off shoppers, till she found herself in a flower market full of colour and heady scents. There she bought a bunch of roses, a pair of smart leather shoes with high heels, and a blue cotton hat because the white one she'd been wearing for the past two and a half weeks was coming apart at the seams.

She found a stall selling two-day-old English newspapers, and lunched on an omelette and a glass of wine in a café beside the enormous domed cathedral, alternately reading and dozing, before wandering back to her car.

If she was a real tourist she would have searched out the church where the guidebook told her there was an altarpiece by El Greco, but something inside was driving her forward. She must get back on the road. She wanted to reach Tarifa that night. Now that she was so near it, it seemed to be pulling her on.

The heat inside the car was suffocating, so she took out her road map and spread it on to the bonnet, tracing the next part of her journey with her finger. In about two and a half hours, she reckoned, she'd arrive at her final destination.

Chapter Thirty-Eight

The most southerly town in Europe did not advertise itself well. The road from Cádiz was lacking in any spectacular sights or landmarks and the approach to Tarifa was a long straight stretch, past a line of beachside hotels and a deserted-looking petrol station. Everything seemed to be overlaid with a thin sprinkling of sand. On the headland leading down to the sea were ranged lines and lines of modern electricity-generating windmills, like tall grey spectres, their blades whirling in the breeze.

A street, lined on both sides by unappealing shops, led to the centre of the town. At the end of it, facing the oncoming traffic, was a stone arch inscribed with a dedication to a thirteenth-century hero called Guzmán the Good, who had defended the town against Arab attackers.

The oldest part of the town lay behind the arch and a line of ancient battlements. Dee turned into it down a steep cobbled hill and found herself staring across a narrow stretch of water at Africa, which looked so near in the pellucid light that it seemed almost possible to stretch out and touch it. *No wonder Algy chose this place as a hideaway*, she thought. *It looks secretive somehow, and it would be so easy to slip across to another continent – and another life.*

She backed her car into a parking space at the side of a church that towered up – as bleak and unadorned as a beached battleship – at the end of the main street. As she switched off the engine the little car gave a sigh, as if relieved at having arrived at its destination. 'You've done well,' she told it, for

262

by this time it had acquired a personality for her. They were co-voyagers, like Don Quixote and Sancho Panza.

She got out of the car and stretched, easing her cramped limbs. The church bell began to chime with a peculiar cracked note, like a voice breaking with emotion. It was six o'clock on a Tuesday evening, and there didn't seem to be another living soul around.

Carrying her guidebook, she made her way to a café on the other side of the narrow street. All the way along the sidewalk stood tall orange trees, globed with fruit, and the air smelt citrus-sharp from the scent of their leaves. A young man in a long white apron came out to take her order when she sat down at a rickety iron table on the pavement under one of the trees.

'A beer, please,' she said, making a drinking gesture with her hand. By this time she was used to communicating by mime.

'Certainly. A beer. What kind?' he said in good English.

'Any kind, so long as it's cold,' she replied, surprised to come across an English speaker in this unlikely place.

She drank the beer, ate some tapas – egg mayonnaise and a plate of potato salad with anchovies – and finished with a cup of black coffee. By this time the café was filling up and she asked the waiter, 'Is there a hotel or *pension* in town?'

He nodded. 'There's a big hotel where tourists and windsurfers go, called the Hurricane. It's on the road to Cádiz, about three kilometres outside the town.'

'That's not the sort of hotel I want. I'd like to stay in the centre, really,' she said. There had to be some reason why Algy liked this out-of-the-way place, but so far she had not noticed anything particularly appealing or unusual about it – except that it was gratifyingly tourist free, as far as she could see.

'There are some *pensions*, but most of them are full for the *feria*,' said the waiter.

'You're having a *feria*?' she asked.

He leaned a hand on her table and nodded at the church. 'It's in there. The feast of our lady, the Virgin of the Light. It's very important for the people round about. I thought you'd come to see it – many people do.'

She shook her head. 'No, I don't know anything about it, but I'd be interested to watch if I'm still here. When is it?'

'On Saturday night – in four days' time. It's a magnificent procession. The men of the town take the Virgin out of the church and carry her around the streets. Then they take her to her shrine on the hill five kilometres away and she stays there till Easter, when they bring her back again. It is a very holy occasion.'

Dee was interested, because there was nothing in any of the guidebooks she'd read about the feast of the Virgin of the Light. It was probably a well-kept secret. Perhaps she should stay to see it, but when she looked around the narrow main street there did not seem to be much in Tarifa to detain her for four days. Her journey to reach the place was beginning to seem like a pointless caprice.

'I'll probably be gone by Saturday,' she said, 'but I need to find somewhere to stay for a couple of days at least. I'm tired of driving.'

Darkness had begun to dim the sky and the streetlights flickered fitfully, making her head swim. She felt tiredness sweep over her. It was as if the exhilaration, which had buoyed her up and kept her going for nearly three weeks, was evaporating all at once. The thought of starting back immediately for Santander appalled her.

The waiter looked at her with sympathy, sensing her exhaustion.

'We have a little apartment on the floor above this café that we rent out. The couple who take it every year for the *feria* cancelled this morning. Would you like to see it?' he said.

'Oh yes, please,' she told him.

The apartment had two rooms – a sitting room and a bedroom with a tiny bathroom opening off it. The furnishings were basic but clean. Taped music from the café downstairs filtered up through the uncarpeted floor, interrupted every now and again by the church bell – which tolled quarter- and half-hours as well as hours. There was a long window with an iron balustrade overlooking the main street. The tops of the orange trees brushed against Dee's legs when she opened the window and looked out.

She sat on the bed, which was so deep and soft that she was filled with a sudden longing to lie down and go to sleep. 'I'll take it,' she said.

'It's to rent by the week,' said the waiter, who was part owner of the café.

'How much?' she asked.

The rent he named was less for a week than she had paid for one night at some of the *paradors* she'd stayed in so far. 'That's all right,' she told him.

A boy from the café carried up her bags, her books and other belongings – it was not a good idea to leave things in the car overnight, she was told. When everything was installed in her apartment, Dee began to feel at home. She had a shower, put on a towelling robe, and sat in a cane chair at the open window watching the world go by till she fell asleep with a book open on her lap. The church clock was striking midnight when she woke and crawled sleepily into bed.

She was surprised to discover that it was eleven o'clock in the morning when she was wakened by a tap on the door. A girl with flowing black hair handed her a cup of coffee. Unlike the waiter – who was probably her brother, judging by the physical resemblance – this girl spoke no English, so Dee could only smile and say *gracias* as she took the cup.

She walked over to the window to survey the outside world. The streets had been swept and washed down, all the household chores were done long ago, and women were coming back from the market with carrier bags of provisions. By craning her neck, she could see her car tucked safely in at the side of the church like a child hiding under the skirts of its mother. Satisfied that it was still there, she went down to the café for breakfast.

'What should I go to see in the town?' she asked the same waiter when he brought her bread and coffee.

He smiled. 'There is a lot to see here.'

'You speak good English,' she told him.

'I worked for ten years on a cruise ship with many American passengers. That's how I saved up enough money to come back and buy this café with my brother and sister,' he said.

'Is this your home town?' she wanted to know.

'Yes, we were fishermen. Our father and his father were fishermen too.'

She smiled at him and said, 'All right, tell me about your town's attractions.'

'We have a castle. A boat goes across to Tangier every day – you can book a ticket from here. In the old town there is a good museum. But you should also drive to a village called Bolonia. It's only twelve kilometres,' he told her.

She had the map open in front of her and he put his finger on a spot. 'There's Bolonia,' he said. It looked minute. She asked, 'Why should I go there? What's special about it?'

He smiled again. 'It has a magnificent beach with the best rollers in Europe, and there's also the ruins of a Roman town called Claudia Baelo. And there are some fine fish restaurants – the best one belongs to my aunt Rosa. You mustn't leave Tarifa without visiting Bolonia and tasting Rosa's paella,' he said.

She remembered Algy talking about a ruined Roman town and thought, *At least I've found a place that has a link with him!* To the waiter she said, 'You're good at drumming up business for your aunt.'

'You'll thank me. Her paella is famous and the Roman town is very interesting,' he said.

'You obviously think I should see it. You've convinced

me. A Roman town and a good paella! I'll go,' she replied, folding the map.

The road to Bolonia branched off up a steep, winding hill from the main route to Cádiz. As she drove along she saw people gathering snails from the fields and putting them into buckets, presumably to cook, and she wondered what they tasted like. When the car breasted the top of the last hill and began coasting down to the shore, she could see far below her a cluster of little buildings following the line of an immense golden beach. White-edged waves were breaking on the sand, and a few figures could be seen bathing in the water. She wished she'd brought a bathing costume – the sun was beaming down and the water looked deliciously inviting.

'Claudia Baelo', said a signpost at a fork in the road, and she followed the way it pointed. On her right, she passed a tumble of broken pillars, huge monumental stones, capitals and carvings. The ruins stretched up the hill as far as she could see – it looked as if a giant had reached down from heaven, grabbed a fine town and scattered its bits like a capricious child playing in a toy box.

Astonished at the scale of the place, she stopped the car and climbed out. The gate to the site was open and a young man was standing there looking expectant.

'Are you the guide?' she asked.

'Yes. You want to see the town?' he asked in halting English.

She nodded, staring round and wondering how it was possible to negotiate a route through the chaos of tumbled stones that had once been buildings. The guide looked at her feet. She was wearing rubber-soled plimsolls, and he nodded as if the shoes were all right. 'It is very hot. You have a hat?' he asked.

She nodded. 'I've one in the car.'

'Get it,' he advised.

For over an hour she followed him up long slopes of what

had been magnificent stairways, through a formerly grand forum, past the ruins of a theatre, temples and municipal baths, and round a huge black basalt stone basin that had held the water for a fountain. Enthusiastically he recreated the life of the people who had lived in the town, and she listened entranced.

'Why is it so ruined? What happened to it? Where did the people go?' she asked him.

'An earthquake hit it – about the third century AD, we think, but no one knows when exactly. The people who survived just moved out, and their descendants are probably still living around here,' he said, waving his hand in the direction of the straggling village.

His guided tour ended up at the beach, where there had been a berthing place for boats. He stopped beside two large stone tanks that were set in the ground a few yards back from the shore. Following his pointing finger, she walked over and peered down into one. 'What were they used for? Bathing?' she asked.

'No, for fermenting fish sauce – *gurum*, it was called. The people of this town were famous for making it and they exported it all over the Roman Empire. Kneel down and sniff – you can still smell it,' said her guide.

She did as she was told. She thought she could still detect the salty, astringent smell of rotting fish. This tiny detail was more evocative of the people that had once lived there than anything else she'd seen that day.

'What a wonderful tour. I'd no idea this place existed. There's nothing about it in any of my guidebooks,' she told the guide.

He shrugged sadly and said, 'Not many people come. We're still excavating, but every year only a small part of it gets done and then we stop because there's no more money. There's far more to be found than I've shown you today. One day perhaps it will all be discovered – but not in my lifetime, I'm afraid.'

He refused a tip and an offer of a drink or something to eat. They shook hands in a friendly way and before they parted she asked him, 'I was told to go to a restaurant owned by a lady called Rosa. Do you know where it is?'

He smiled. 'That was good advice. You'll find her behind the place where you've parked your car.' He indicated a collection of huts with straw roofs and walls made out of woven wicker panels. 'That's Rosa's,' he said.

Dee sat down at an umbrella-shaded table outside the main dining room. After a while a young boy came out to offer her a menu and she chose *calamares*, prawns and tiny clams in their shells. A carafe of wine appeared and as she sipped it she realised she was ravenously hungry.

When she finished eating, she sat back and sighed, blissfully contented. The sun, the simple food, and the deceptively light wine worked magic on her, soothing her and turning her into a lotus-eater who gave not a thought to the morrow.

Pulling the brim of her hat down over her eyes, she stared over at the site of the ruined town and thought that, by concentrating really hard, she could call it back into existence. It was easy to understand the young guide's enthusiasm for the tumbledown town that had once been so magnificent.

A feeling of drowsiness crept over her and she felt her head nodding. A female voice brought her back to consciousness.

'You are American?' The accent was rough and grating, like the voice of a singer with laryngitis.

Blinking, Dee sat up. 'No,' she said.

'German? *Allemande?*'

'No, I'm British. Scots, actually,' she replied, looking up towards the voice.

A short, stout woman with a formidable bust was standing on the step staring at her. She had long, very dark hair – so uniformly black that it was obviously dyed. Her corseted body was encased in a tight, sleeveless yellow dress with a plunging neckline, and round her neck hung a crucifix on a heavy gold chain.

Dee's claim to be Scottish did not seem to impress her much. 'We get not many British,' she said. 'How old are you?'

Taken by surprise by this unexpected tack, Dee told her the truth. 'I'm fifty-six.'

'I am fifty-six also,' said the woman. Lifting a lock of her hair, she added proudly, 'And not a grey hair.' In fact, she looked closer to seventy than to sixty – and the hair was definitely dyed.

Dee laughed and took off her cotton hat. 'You're better off than me then – I have some grey hairs, I'm afraid.'

The woman walked closer and peered at Dee's hair. 'Not too much. You should dye it. And wear make-up. Have you a man?'

'No, I'm afraid not. I'm a widow.'

'I too am a widow, but I have a man,' was the proud reply.

'Lucky you,' said Dee with feeling. Then she asked, 'Is your name Rosa?'

The affirmative noise was like a deep breath of suspicion. 'Aaaye.'

'Your nephew told me to come to your restaurant. He said you make a very good paella,' Dee said.

'Which nephew?'

'I don't know. He has the café opposite the church in Tarifa.'

'Oh, that one. A good man. But you did not eat my paella, did you? You will have to come back – perhaps tomorrow,' said Rosa.

Dee looked around. She was now the only customer on the terrace – the other diners must have left while she was dozing. It was obvious that Rosa was intent on getting rid of her – it was time to shut down for the afternoon.

She got up, feeling almost too languorous to move. All

she wanted to do was go back to her room above the café and sleep.

'I will come back,' she told Rosa as she gathered her possessions together. Then, on an impulse, she suddenly turned and asked, 'You don't know a man called Adam Byron, do you?'

She had deliberately not asked anyone in Tarifa about him yet – perhaps because she did not want to find out that he was unknown there.

Rosa's plucked eyebrows rose. 'Who?' she asked.

'Adam Byron,' said Dee slowly, pronouncing his name clearly.

'What does he look like?'

Dee frowned. There was nothing very unusual about Algy. 'He's about five foot ten or eleven. His hair is sort of brown and his eyes are blue.'

'No. I do not know him,' said the jet-haired woman, waving her hand to usher Dee off the premises.

Chapter Thirty-Nine

A ll next day the lotus-eater feeling stayed with Dee. Minutes slipped into hours, hours into days. She drifted around, not going anywhere in particular, happy to be idle and unworried by responsibilities. She felt as if she was living in another dimension.

Like a woman with all the time in the world, she wandered round Tarifa's castle and watched the ship setting out for Tangier. She idled away hours in the town museum – which was full of Roman relics – and ate in the café by the church, sitting at a table on the pavement with a mystery novel in front of her. She didn't really read anything, however – even making the effort to follow a plot was almost too much trouble.

On the third day she went back to Bolonia and ate Rosa's paella. Though the formidable proprietress hovered over packed tables in the main dining room, she did not come out to speak to Dee, who was sitting outside. She'd obviously found out as much as she wanted about the stranger.

On that visit Dee swam, though tentatively because she was afraid of the pounding waves. She sat in the surf with the water breaking round her sun-baked body, eddying over her thighs and sweeping across her breasts. *This is bliss*, she thought. Without even realising it, her thoughts drifted to Algy.

She was now thinking about him in the past tense – as if he was no longer alive and there was no longer any question of looking for him in Kyrenia. She knew he was not there.

Her pilgrimage in search of him had merely been an effort to release another side of her own character.

In a strange way, she had now completely caught up with herself, and it was bringing her immense peace of mind. The past was behind her; the agonies and angers about Ben were gone. She would now be able to make the best of life on her own.With Victoria's help, she was learning to be kind to herself.

That night when she returned, tanned and tasting salt on her lips, her waiter friend in the café asked, 'Will you be here for the *feria* tomorrow?'

She nodded as she made a sudden decision. 'Yes, I'll stay to see it. It would be a pity to miss such a special occasion.'

He was pleased and said eagerly, 'In that case, I'll keep you a seat near the front of the pavement. All the best chairs are booked well in advance.'

'Can't I watch the *feria* from my room?' she asked, nodding up at her window.

'Oh no! You must be down on the street, so you can see all the people and especially the Virgin. If you look down from above you'll only see the top of her head,' was his reply.

On Saturday morning she was surprised at the change in the atmosphere of the town. Gone was its laid-back sleepiness – it seemed to be imbued with an almost electric excitement as people came thronging in to watch the Virgin's trip round the streets. 'Don't move your car,' cautioned the waiter. 'You won't find another parking place if you do.'

Darkness began to fall at about seven o'clock. The discordant music of a band burst out a few minutes later and she looked out of her window to see a group of about twenty people in gold-braided uniforms parading along the main street towards the church. They were quickly followed by another band, playing a different tune in equally resplendent uniforms. The two bands took up position in the open area before the church door and waited while the cracked bell rang seven times.

Elisabeth McNeill

Crowds of people were jostling along the pavements, chattering and laughing, all very excited. A cavalcade of caballeros in sombreros and spurs with lovely girls in frilled dresses riding pillion at their backs came cantering along the street on beautiful, mettlesome horses.

Dee recognised a couple of the cavaliers as local boys she'd seen in Tarifa. One was a motorbike pest who roared along the main street late at night. The other was the traffic warden who blew a fearsome whistle if any driver tried to park in the wrong place. On their horses they seemed uncharacteristically dignified – transformed into heroes from a more glamorous past.

As Dee was dressing, the waiter's sister came up and rapped on the door, beckoning with one hand to tell her to go downstairs. Her urgency was unmistakable – if Dee did not claim her reserved chair soon someone else would take it.

Wearing pink trousers and a white shirt, with her hair tied back under a bandanna, she went downstairs and was installed in her seat by the smiling waiter. As she sat down, both bands began to play and all the spectators turned expectantly to face the church.

Then the action started. Stern-looking middle-aged ladies in magnificent gowns, accompanied by solemn husbands buttoned into tight business suits, began filing into the church. Yet another band appeared, and, after about an hour – when darkness had engulfed the town and the crowd was growing restless – the church door opened a crack. The sound of voices singing hymns swelled out. Everyone outside stiffened in anticipation. Moments later, the huge door was thrown wide open and the procession began.

Local male dignitaries led the way, followed by a phalanx of women – young and old – in modern couture gowns but with mantillas draped over their heads. Many of the mantillas looked as if they were family treasures.

After them came a couple of bands, and then troops of riders on prancing horses with curving necks and rolling

274

eyes, their carefully combed tails sweeping to the ground. Yet another band followed them, the members blowing away on silver instruments.

Finally the life-size Virgin herself appeared. Preceded by priests and acolytes swinging incense burners, she was carried shoulder-high on a wooden platform by a group of brawny men whose strained faces were eloquent testimony to the weight they bore. The Virgin was richly dressed in silver gauze with a diamond tiara glittering on her head. She stood on a table on top of the platform, surrounded by immense ewers, tall silver vases full of white lilies, and branched candelabras in which dozens of white wax candles burned. Her right hand was raised in blessing and her skilfully painted face bore a sweet smile.

When she emerged into the lamplight of the main street, a gasp of reverence swept through the crowd. Even Dee felt her breath escape in a hiss of admiration. The music from the band was low and reverent as the statue passed along before the people crowding the sidewalk. The most pious knelt and crossed themselves. Many were in tears.

Sweating and groaning, the men bearing the holy effigy went down the street to the first stopping point, where another group waited to take over their burden. The solemnity of the occasion and the reverent demeanour of all the people raised goose pimples on Dee's skin.

She was reaching behind her to find a sweater to draw over her shoulders when a man suddenly detached himself from a crowd of watchers standing along the café wall. He threaded his way between the closely packed chairs and walked towards her.

'Hi,' he said softly, leaning down beside her.

She looked up and her heart jumped into her throat. 'So you *are* here after all,' she said. In a peculiar way she was not surprised to see him.

'Yeah. I've been hoping that you'd track me down eventually. It was always me who had to find you in the past. But you're not very speedy, are you? I'd almost given up,' he said, turning to grab a chair that some devout worshipper had vacated in order to follow the Virgin's parade.

He had changed very little, though the unruly quiff of hair was sprinkled with grey now. His long, lugubrious face was lined and tanned, but he still had the boyish air that she remembered.

'Rosa told me you were at Bolonia asking after me,' he said, leaning his elbows on the table.

'She said she didn't know you. How did you guess it was me, anyway?' she asked.

'Rosa said it was a woman with very bright blue eyes, who smelt of Mitsouko perfume. You've always worn Mitsouko, haven't you?'

Now she was surprised. 'Yes, I have, for years and years – but how did you remember?'

He laughed. His teeth were still white and strong-looking. 'You told me once. I know a lot about you, Mrs Carmichael. I was a spy, after all – we're trained to notice and remember things, especially if they're important.'

'I remembered things too. You said you liked Tarifa. I happened to be driving through Spain and decided to stop here to ask if anyone knew you. You disappeared from London so quickly, I didn't have a chance to tell you I was moving back to Scotland.'

He nodded. 'But I'd planted the hints for you. I wondered if you'd take them up. The trouble about my business is that we think everyone's going to follow the trails we lay . . . and I thought you had the instinct. I tried to get in contact with you again, but you'd moved. The letter came back with "Not Known At This Address" printed on it,' he told her.

'I left my forwarding address with that Bullivant man in London, but I had a good idea he wouldn't pass it on to you,' she told him.

'The only thing he wanted to pass on to me was a bullet. I was lucky to get out, I reckon. He'd have set me up.

Those guys were the biggest villains I ever came across – pure psychopaths, worse than anybody in the CIA. When I found out what they were doing in Ireland, I wanted out as quickly as possible.' His voice was solemn.

'What were they doing?' she asked.

'Setting up ambushes and planting bombs that killed innocent people. Then they blamed it on the IRA,' he said bitterly.

'So you did a runner,' she said.

He nodded. 'A "sprint" is a better way of putting it. They thought I informed on them. I've never gone back.'

'You've quit entirely?' she queried.

'Long ago,' he replied. 'Now I write books for a living. I've got a villa on top of the hill behind Bolonia. I live here under a different name, but there's one or two people who know who I really am, people I can trust. Rosa's one of them – I've known her for years. I used to come here in the sixties and seventies.'

'I really thought she'd never heard of you,' said Dee.

He laughed. 'She's great. The minute you left her place she was on the phone and it was fixed up with her nephew not to allow you to leave before the *feria*, so I could give you a surprise.'

They looked at each other across the table and said in unison, 'I always knew I'd see you again.'

He stood up. 'Do you want to come and see my villa? It's lovely. I've my own pool and I look right across the strait to Morocco.'

Suddenly Dee was filled with the same sort of wild excitement that she used to feel on the hunting field when faced with a difficult jump. The adrenalin rush of gathering the horse and preparing to take off filled her again – she hadn't felt that sort of thrill for years. *Throw your heart over first*, she thought, reaching down for her handbag. 'OK. I'll come. What sort of books do you write?' she asked.

'Spy stories and thrillers. My most popular series is about

a woman detective who is knee high to a mouse, has bright blue eyes and always smells of Mitsouko . . .' he replied.

'I hope she's made you rich,' she said.

He laughed. 'Not really. But now she's making me very happy.'